GHOST TEAM

A TOM ROLLINS THRILLER

PAUL HEATLEY

INKUBATOR
BOOKS

Published by Inkubator Books
www.inkubatorbooks.com

Copyright © 2023 by Paul Heatley

Paul Heatley has asserted his right to be identified as the author of this work.

ISBN (eBook): 978-1-83756-290-9
ISBN (Paperback): 978-1-83756-291-6

For Aidan

PROLOGUE

Lorne Henkel is injured. He's trapped. He's pinned down in a ditch, bullets flying overhead, pinging off the framework and shattering what remains of the glass in the long-bombed-out car upended on the ridge opposite.

Lorne's ears are ringing. His left leg is broken. Blood is soaking into his fatigues, clinging to his skin. He can't pull his trouser leg up to see how bad it is, but he thinks the bone has burst through the skin. He grits his teeth, grinding down, suppressing a scream that chokes in the back of his throat.

Afghanistan. Helmand Province. When he first arrived here, despite it being a warzone, he thought it was a beautiful country. Beautiful people. He had never seen a place that looked so desolate, and yet he found it peaceful. The air was hot, but he didn't mind and he'd breathe it deep. The sun would burn his skin, so he'd stick to the shade as much as possible.

Now, he hates it here. He's seen nothing but pain and

death. Too much blood. He wants to go home. As much as his leg hurts, he knows it could be his ticket out of here. The only problem is, he needs to survive first. Right now, that isn't looking likely.

It's not looking likely for the man beside him, either. Adam Lineker. Adam is not injured. Adam could get out of here if he wanted, but he won't go. He won't leave Lorne behind.

"We're pinned, man," Lorne says. Adam isn't listening. He holds his M4 close and tries to peer over the top of the ridge, but their attackers are watching closely and he has to duck back into cover before they take his head off. "You can get yourself out of here. Just leave me here – I'm deadweight. I can't even stand." Lorne doesn't want to die, but he doesn't want Adam to die because of him, either.

Adam doesn't answer. He lies back, holding tight to the M4, trying to find a direction from which they're not coming under fire.

They were on patrol when the attack occurred. There had been reports of the Taliban moving closer to their camp, sneaking into nearby settlements and lying low like they were gradually massing for an attack.

It was late evening when they set out on the patrol, and getting dark when the ambush came. Soon, it will be full dark. Lorne knows that when the night comes in, they're as good as dead. Unless they can hold out long enough for reinforcements to rescue them, but it's not looking likely. The area has been blocked off. The Taliban were ready for their coming. Anyone trying to get to them will have a severe firefight on their hand.

Lorne was riding shotgun in the Spartan armoured vehicle as they rolled through a settlement sixteen klicks out from their camp. Adam was one of the half a dozen men on foot, inspecting the area and the buildings. Then came the ambush. The Spartan was struck on the driver's side with an RPG. The driver was killed instantly. The Spartan rolled. Lorne isn't sure, because everything happened so fast, in a blur, but he thinks this is when he broke his leg. He crawled from the wreckage to find himself in the middle of a pitched battle. He saw men from his platoon gunned down, their bodies mutilated by fire from the Taliban's automatic rifles, their skulls blown apart, their faceless bodies falling limp, never to get back up. He saw their blood sinking into the cooling ground. Lorne was dazed, blood running down his face from a gash on his forehead and a wound on his temple.

Then, a hand was upon him, dragging him toward the ditch, dropping him into cover. It was Adam. It feels like long ago, but it could only have been five minutes, max. They've been stuck here since, but there was nowhere else for them to go. It seems likely that the rest of their platoon is lying dead not far from where they cower. All Lorne knows for sure is that with every minute that passes, it is getting darker and darker. He dreads the night. The night brings their death. His head is swimming. He wipes blood from his eyes.

"I think they're all dead," he says.

"Don't say that," Adam says, glancing at him. "Don't talk like that."

"They're only shooting at us," Lorne says. "I can't hear them shooting at anyone else. They're gonna be creeping in closer."

"Let them creep," Adam says, sliding down as low as he can into the ditch and raising the M4. "I'll take as many of them with us as I can."

Time passes. Lorne does not know how long. It can only

be minutes, but it feels like hours. He can hear shooting. It's never really stopped. Except now it sounds like it's coming from further away. Like it's not aimed toward them. Sand and dirt does not shower them from bullets that land close by.

Adam cocks his head. "Do you hear that?" he says.

Lorne isn't sure what exactly he's talking about. "Do I hear what?"

Adam doesn't respond. Lorne listens, same as him. He hears a scream. He doesn't think it's American. He doesn't think there's any other Americans left alive here. He hears a gargled cry. Lorne props himself up on his elbows, turning an ear toward the sounds. When he moves, the pain in his leg pulses. "Back-up?" he says, not daring to be hopeful.

"I don't – I don't know," Adam says, and it's clear he's trying not to get his hopes up, too.

The Taliban aren't firing as often as they were. When they do, their shooting is more erratic. It's unclear what they're aiming at. Nothing is coming Lorne and Adam's way anymore.

In the fading light, a dark shape reaches the burned-out car, pressing its back to its bumper and crouching low for cover. Adam wheels toward the shape, M4 raised. The figure speaks. American, accent flat and western, not so pronounced as to be Texan. New Mexico, maybe. There are – were – a couple of New Mexicans in their platoon. Lorne is from Colorado. He's familiar with the accent.

"I'm trusting that the two of you realise I'm on your side," he says, "and you're not gonna shoot me."

Adam instantly lowers his M4. "Who is that?" he says. "We thought everyone else was dead."

"No time," the man says. His face is in shadow. "Get up out of that ditch and let's get out of here."

"He's busted his leg," Adam says, tilting his head toward Lorne.

"Just go," Lorne says. "Don't lose your lives on account of mine, damn it."

"I didn't work my way over here just to leave one of you behind," the man says, and he scans the area with his own M4 before he slides down into the ditch. Closer, Lorne can see his face, make out who he is. Tom Rollins.

On the patrol, Tom was on foot, outside of the Spartan, when it was struck. Lorne had assumed he'd been picked off like all the rest. "Rollins," he says. They've never spoken much in the past. Nothing more than was necessary. Rollins has always kept to himself. When he's not on duty, he's usually working out or reading a book. Lorne isn't sure if there's anyone in the platoon that Rollins is particularly friendly with. Before now, Lorne has never spared him much of a thought. "You made it. Did anyone else survive?"

"Just us," Rollins says. He inspects Lorne's leg, then hands him a bullet. "Bite on this. What I'm about to do is going to hurt."

Lorne's eyes are wide, but he doesn't question. He takes the bullet and bites down in preparation.

Rollins has another M4 on his back, likely taken from one of their fallen brothers. His hands moving fast, he disassembles it. He passes the magazine to Adam, who stores it away. Adam does not watch what is happening. He monitors the area beyond the ditch. No one is shooting at them. It's grown very quiet.

Lorne watches as Rollins pulls out a roll of tape. He places the barrel of the rifle on the inside of Lorne's leg, opposite to the break, and places the stock directly next to the break. Lorne understands what is about to happen. Rollins is splinting his leg. Lorne breathes hard. He's sweating. Rollins looks at him, nods, and then gets to work. He presses the barrel against the jutting bone, sliding it under the skin and pushing it back into place. With his other hand, he pins Lorne's leg down by the ankle. Lorne bites down hard enough on the bullet that he cracks a couple of back teeth. He blacks out with the pain.

When he comes back around, the splint is complete. Rollins is finishing wrapping tape around his lower leg, holding the barrel and the stock in place on either side of his break. His movements fluid, Rollins puts the tape away, scoops up the still operational M4, and then throws Lorne over his shoulder. He carries him out of the ditch and Adam follows, covering their six.

Through the night and the next morning, Rollins carries Lorne and guides Adam. He keeps them alive. He gets them back to camp. Without him, they would both be death.

Lorne never forgets Tom Rollins. He owes his life to him.

Soon after this, Tom Rollins disappears. The rumour is that he has been recruited – some say he has gone into a specialist unit, others mention the CIA. No one knows for sure.

Lorne will not see him again for nearly ten years.

1

It's late, and the diner is quiet.

Tom Rollins sits in a booth at the rear, his back to the wall. An elderly man sits at the counter, making small talk with one of the waitresses when he's not reading the newspaper he has spread out before him. The old man sips from his coffee and accepts another refill. In another booth a few down from Tom, a middle-aged couple are just finishing up. The husband motions for the check. They'll be back on the road soon. At a table close to the door, a single father and his young daughter smile at each other over the top of their milkshakes. There is no one else here. The dinner rush has long ended.

It was after half-eight when Tom first came in, his shift finished. He's had a burger. He's finished now. He picks at what remains of the salad he ordered with it. For the last six months, he's been working as a delivery driver. It was an easy job to get, but it's not the healthiest lifestyle. He gets to choose his own hours. He chooses to work long days. It keeps him busy. Before he sets off in the morning, he makes sure to work out. When he takes his meals, he makes sure to have vegetables or fruit with them, or a smoothie. While a sedentary and unhealthy occupation, the job makes him quick, easy money while he decides where to go next. For now, he's in Colorado. Out the diner window, he admires the Rocky Mountains in the distance, cast in shadows. The twinkling lights of townships at their base look so small in comparison. Like bugs. So insignificant.

The middle-aged couple leave, and soon after them follows the father and his daughter. It's after half-nine, now. It's a late night for the little girl. It's a Friday, though. No school tomorrow. The diner is open twenty-four hours, but Tom and the older man are the only two remaining. Tom has nowhere else to be, and he doubts the old man does, either. He's happy enough sitting at the counter and reading his paper. He's getting close to finishing it.

Tom's place is not far from here. Just another fifteen-minute drive and he's home – a small apartment in a small block. He's yet to have met any of his neighbours. He's barely there. He leaves before they rise, and returns long after they've settled in for the night.

His eyes return to the mountains. They go back to them, again and again. While he drives around during the day, he admires them from afar, and all that they represent. The wild. Freedom. He's hiked their trails a few times while he's been in Colorado. He's enjoyed going up there alone. He's enjoyed the time alone.

He needs to be alone. For a while, at least. A sense of guilt gnaws at him, thinking of what he has left behind in New Mexico. Of Hayley, and their home, and the life they were building together. The guilt tells him he wasn't entirely honest with her. He meant it when he said that he couldn't keep putting her in danger – he truly believes that as long as he was in town, she wasn't safe. There'd been too many close calls already. But the guilt knows that there may have been another reason for his leaving, too. His guilt knows that he might have feelings for someone else.

Tom doesn't think about this. He never does. He works and he exercises and he keeps himself busy. Keeps his mind busy. But perhaps he needs a distraction, too. Something or someone to distract himself completely from his guilt.

He turns away from the dark mountains and sees the older man paying for his cups of coffee, and then shambling out of the diner. He leaves his newspaper behind. Still open on the counter, next to the till. Tom is the only person left. The two waitresses behind the counter make whispered conversation between themselves, and with the chef who leans in over the pass. It's a quiet night for them. Tom knows it can get busy. He's come here at two in the morning before, and was surprised to see how full it was.

He takes a deep breath and gets to his feet. He goes to the counter to pay. To the till. One of the waitresses catches his eye and they smile at each other as she makes her way over to run up his check. They recognise Tom's face. He comes in here often and they're familiar with him. He always leaves a good tip.

The waitress is pretty. They both are. The one serving him has red hair cut short, and pale skin with a smattering of freckles across her nose and cheeks. Green eyes. She's still smiling at him, but Tom has looked away. He's glancing down at the newspaper, to the page it has been left open at. The obituaries.

A name catches his eye.

Tom feels a chill run through him.

The waitress and his check are forgotten. He leans closer to the newspaper. The obituary is brief, but it tells of the man's Army service. It gives his age. It gives the date of his funeral. The day after tomorrow. It gives the address for his service, in the town of Samson, Colorado. It does not say how he has died. He was the same age as Tom – thirty-three.

Adam Lineker.

"Where is Samson?"

The waitress blinks. The question has taken her off guard. "Who's Samson?"

Tom turns the newspaper toward her and points at the address.

"Oh, the town? It's north of here – about five hours, maybe? I've only ever been once before. There's a skiing resort close by it."

Tom nods. He can work out a route when he gets back to his apartment. He can set off tomorrow morning. He hasn't seen Adam in many years. The last time he saw him, Tom was saving his life. Shortly after, Tom's time in the Army came to an end. Tom saved his life, and now Adam is dead. Tom grits his teeth until his jaw cramps. He thinks about the funeral. He should go. He knew this man. He *saved* this man. He has to go.

"Are you all right?"

Tom looks up. The waitress is concerned. Tom realises he hasn't paid yet. He hands over notes without checking what they are. It's a big tip – too big – but he doesn't care. He has other things on his mind. He tears the obituary from the newspaper so he has the address, and then leaves the diner and stands outside in the cool night air, breathing deep. He stands for a long time and looks toward the mountains. He thinks about Adam.

He will go to the funeral.

Tonight, he will return to his apartment and he'll try to sleep. Tomorrow morning, he will go to Samson.

2

When Tom reaches Samson he takes a drive around the town to get an idea of its layout. He didn't sleep well last night. Found himself pacing the apartment. He plotted his route. That didn't take long to do. He flicked through the television, but there wasn't much that interested him. In the end, he got about three hours.

Samson is not a big town. It's about five miles from east to west, and four miles from north to south. Tom finds a motel to spend the night. It's down the road from the station that powers the town, but he can barely see it. It's concealed behind trees and bushes, likely so as not to be an eyesore for the tourists. He checks in and drops off his bag, then puts on the local news to see if there's any mention of Adam. There is not. He feels antsy in the room so he heads back out in his car. He drives to the funeral home, just to see where it is and what it looks like. He passes by the graveyard, too.

Tom finds the nearest bar. It's opposite a trailer park. Tom goes into the bar. It's late afternoon and the place is quiet. It's dark inside. Tom takes a seat at the counter. The television is on. It plays a rerun of a football game. Tom doesn't pay it much attention. He catches the bartender's eye. The bartender comes over. He's tall, broad across. His cheeks are hollowed out, but his gut hangs over his belt, age clearly catching up to him. "Get you something?"

"Just a soda," Tom says. As the bartender gets his drink, Tom looks into the mirror above the bar, eyeing the rest of the patrons. There are only three other men present, and none of them sit together. Each of them is alone, nursing their beers.

The bartender places the soda in front of Tom and starts to turn away.

"Ask you something?" Tom says.

The bartender pauses, stays where he is. "Guess that depends on the question."

"Did you know Adam Lineker?"

The bartender raises an eyebrow. "I was aware of him, yeah. He came in here sometimes. Not often, but a buddy of his is one of my bartenders. He'd come in to see him. Was Adam a friend of yours?"

"I haven't seen him in a long time."

"Army?"

Tom cocks his head. "How'd you figure?"

"Lorne was hoping to see more of y'all. He wasn't sure how to get hold of folks so he put an obituary out and hoped for the best. Frankly, he's been a little disappointed by the turnout – Army-wise, that is."

"No one's turned up?"

"Not that he's seen.

"Did you say *Lorne*? Lorne Henkel?"

The bartender grins. "The one and only. You know him too?"

"We all served together."

"Yeah? What's your name?"

"Rollins."

The bartender's eyes widen. Suddenly, his hand shoots out, wanting to shake. "I've heard about you, Mr. Rollins," he says. Tom takes his hand, surprised, and they shake. "I'm Colin Bellamy, and this here's my bar. Lorne works for me, and he's told me what you did, how you saved him and Adam." The bartender takes his hand back, beaming. "Thank you for your service, by the way."

Tom nods at this. "Lorne works here? Is he working today?"

"No – truth be told, he's been real distraught over what happened to Adam. I've had to give him a few days off. He'll be pleased to see you, though. You *will* be at the funeral, won't you?"

"Yeah," Tom says, glancing around the bar, at the establishment that Lorne has found himself working in. He wonders what Adam was doing for a living. He asks.

"Overseas work," Colin says. "Oil."

It sounds more lucrative than where Lorne has ended up. "What *did* happen to Adam? Thirty-three is no kind of age. It must have been sudden."

"It *was* sudden," Colin says. "A real surprise to us all. He killed himself. Hanging."

Tom feels something tighten inside, but he mostly takes this news in stride. Tries to, at least. He knows it's not uncommon for vets to commit suicide, but this knowledge makes it no less distressing. As he drove here, wondering what could have happened, suicide was one of the possibilities he'd considered, along with an overdose, alcoholism, or – distantly – natural causes. "I'm very sorry to hear that," Tom says.

"We all were," Colin says. "All of us who knew him. Say, you want me to give Lorne a call, get him over here? He shouldn't be too far away."

Tom considers this. The funeral is tomorrow, in the morning. It's not long. And the news of how Adam died has shaken something in Tom. The prospect of the darkness that must have been engulfing him to the point that he took his own life. The thought of him feeling so alone, and so isolated, that he only saw one way out.

"No," Tom says. "Thank you. I'll see him tomorrow."

Colin nods, understanding. "Of course. You'll have plenty of time to catch up. I only hope a few more of y'all turn up before then."

Tom starts to stand. He leaves his soda, untouched, on the counter. "I hope so, too."

3

Jason Bell and Harry Smart have been in the town of Samson for two days. There is not much here to excite them. It's the tail end of ski season. The snows are melting on the nearby mountains, and the town's tourist trade is drying up. Neither man, however, skis. That is not why they have come here. They're glad that things are getting quieter. It better suits their needs.

They're staying in a hotel in the centre of town. They have separate rooms, though they spend most of their time in one of them. They were able to get both rooms cheap, on account of it being off-season. Right now, they're in Harry's room. Jason sits at the open window, smoking a cigarette. He looks down at the road below. There's not much to see. The sun is shining but it looks cold. The few people that are walking along the sidewalks are wrapped up in thick coats, and some wear woolen hats. He sees them go into the super-market just over the road from the hotel. He watches the cars that go by. A red one. A green one. Another red, and then a truck. No one seems to be in any kind of a hurry.

Behind him, Harry sits at the small round table tucked into the corner of the room, next to the television stand and opposite the door.

"I'm getting hungry," Jason says without turning. "We should eat soon."

"Where you thinking?" Harry says. "Chinese?"

"No, I don't want Chinese again."

"There's a couple of places we haven't tried yet."

"Let's just go to the diner. The diner was okay."

Harry chuckles. "That waitress you were eyeing was more than okay."

Jason grins to himself, remembering her. Remembering when she bent over to clear the table right next to their booth. Her uniform was short. Shorter than it needed to be. Short enough to get her plenty of fat tips to go with her fat ass. "You gonna get jealous if I bring her back?"

"No," Harry says. "I'm sure I could find someone of my own to pass the time with."

Jason flicks the butt of his cigarette out the window, and blows out the last of the smoke that fills his lungs. "Gunnar wouldn't like it," he says, smirking.

"Gunnar ain't here. It can be our little secret. There's gotta be some perks to being sent to some shithole little town at the ass-end of nowhere."

Jason looks toward the mountains. He can see ski lifts running, but it's impossible to see if anyone is riding in them. Sunlight pours down over everything, making the town and the mountains golden. "I'm not sure it's fair to describe this place as a *shithole*."

Harry grunts. "You know what I mean."

Jason turns away from the window, but remains seated on the sill. "So, we're decided? The diner?"

Harry leans back, lacing his fingers over his taut stomach. "Of course," he says. "I look forward to watching you try your luck with that pretty little waitress."

"How old you reckon she is?"

"Old enough."

"Wearing her uniform like that."

"She knew what she was doing."

"Exactly."

A noise sounds from Harry's laptop before he can say anything else. He looks down at it, unlacing his fingers and leaning forward.

Jason recognises the sound. It's an alert. Potentially important. "What's it for?"

"Person of interest," Harry says, tapping keys and clicking the mouse pad while he intently studies the screen.

Jason slips down off the windowsill and steps behind him so he can see the laptop screen, too. As soon as they arrived in town, they hacked into the security cameras and implemented facial recognition software, and they got into the sheriff's database and set up more alarms for names. All potential persons of interest. Mostly people that Adam Lineker served with in the US Army.

"Expected more of them to have shown up by now," Jason says. "Was starting to think none of them were going to turn up."

"It's just the one guy," Harry says. "And most of the men he served with were killed, don't forget. There can't be that many left to come along."

Jason leans closer, studying the face on the screen. The same man, in different locations. Driving the main road into town, his features picked up through the windshield.

Checking into a motel, and leaving the motel a couple of hours later. Entering a bar, and leaving the same bar shortly after. "So who is it?"

Harry clicks a few keys, pulling up a file and checking details. "Tom Rollins," he says. "Heard of him?"

"Can't say I have."

"He's got an interesting file. Ex-Army, and then for a few years his details are redacted."

"Government work?"

"More than likely. Resurfaced and he's been living a nomadic lifestyle ever since. A *busy* nomadic lifestyle, according to this. Stopping a terrorist attack in Texas. Broke up a heroin ring in California while he was working as a forest ranger. A few other things that he could be involved in, but no clear proof – most recently some noise down in Honduras."

"*Busy*," Jason agrees.

Harry leans back again. "The waitress might have to wait."

Jason bites his lip. "Yeah," he says, disappointed. Business comes first. Always does. A slight indiscretion, Gunnar never needs to know. Fucking up and missing something important because they're out chasing tail – that's the kind of thing Gunnar would cut them loose for if they're lucky. More likely he'd put them in the ground.

"We know where he is," Harry says, pointing at the image showing Rollins outside the motel. "There's a clear shot of his room. I'll get into the live feed and keep it up. We can monitor him that way. You can take first shift. I've been staring at this screen for long enough. My eyes are starting to feel like fucking sandpaper."

"Sure," Jason says, taking Harry's place at the table while Harry gets up and walks around the room, stretching his back and legs. Jason watches on the live feed as Rollins returns to the motel, and silently curses him. He's thinking about the waitress still. Thinking about what could now potentially never be.

4

Tom hasn't brought a suit. He didn't spot a suit store while he was driving around yesterday. Early morning, he goes to the supermarket and checks their clothes section. He's able to find some black trousers and a black shirt. He puts them on in the changing room, handing over the ripped-off tags and paying, wearing the new clothes out. He drops his jeans and shirt into the back-seat of his car. He drives to the funeral home.

It's quiet in the parking lot. Tom doesn't go straight inside. He's early. He waits to see how many more people turn up.

Lorne is the first to appear. He comes on foot. He limps, favouring his left leg. The leg that Tom had to crudely splint with a dismantled M4. Tom isn't surprised if it hasn't healed straight – the jagged bone was through the skin. He's sure the medics did the best they could to set it straight. Down in the ditch, Tom's first priority was keeping him alive.

Lorne looks older than he is. Pale and thin. His hair is

shaggy, and he flicks it out of his eyes. His beard is patchy, but thick where it grows. His suit hangs baggy off his frame. It looks like he's had a hard time since he left the Army. It looks like he's maybe had problems, the same problems that Tom worries Adam had – drugs, alcoholism. The list goes on. It pains Tom to see him like this – but at least he's still alive.

Lorne heads straight inside. A few minutes later, a blue BMW pulls into the lot and parks a few spaces down from Tom. An Indian woman, her black hair tied back in a plait, gets out. She's wearing a black pantsuit. Everyone coming here will be wearing black. Tom is glad he was able to find the trousers and shirt. She's very attractive, but her striking features are overcast, her brow furrowed. Tom wonders what her connection to Adam is as she heads inside.

The next vehicle is a Ford, which parks next to the Indian woman's BMW. A man with dark hair gets out of the driver's side and opens the passenger door for a blonde woman. She takes his proffered hand and gets out of the car. They speak to each other, their heads close. The man nods at what the woman says. The man is tall and broad. The woman is about a foot shorter than him. As they head toward the building, the woman dabs at her eyes with a crumpled tissue, but Tom did not notice she was crying. Perhaps getting closer to the building, and the reality of where they are going and why, has set in for her. Again, Tom wonders who these people are, and what they meant to Adam, and he to them.

A few more vehicles arrive and people enter the building, and ten minutes after that Tom realises no one else is coming. Just over a dozen people altogether. Tom didn't see anyone who he thinks could have been Adam's parents. He wonders if they live nearby, or if they're still alive at all.

Tom gets out of his car and goes inside. He sits at the back of the room, and listens to the funeral director deliver the service. Adam's coffin is at the front. It's not open casket. Tom finds himself staring at the coffin. He doesn't hear much of what is said. He thinks about his own inevitable death. He thinks about how few people will be at his own service. Less than are here, perhaps. He doesn't keep many people close, and even those he does do not know where he might be at any given time.

No one else gets up to speak. The service does not last very long. Tom slips out of the building and goes to his car, not ready to talk to Lorne or anyone else yet. He makes the short drive to the graveyard and stands to one side, leaning against a tree and watching as a few more words are shared over the burial site. Tom is too far away to hear what they are. He can see the blonde woman from the parking lot. Her tears are more visible now. Her cheeks are flushed and her eyes are red. The man with her has an arm around her shoulders, holding her up, supporting her. The Indian woman stands to the side, alone. She appears plagued, still, her mind racing. She looks from the director to the coffin and back again. She glances at the crying blonde woman and winces, like she can feel her pain.

Lorne looks numb. He stares down into the hole. After a moment, he raises his head. He can feel Tom's gaze upon him. He looks to where Tom stands, under the tree, and he stands up a little straighter. A slight smile plays at the corner of his lip, realising that Tom is there, that he's come. That he's come when so many have not.

After the coffin is lowered and the group has dispersed, Lorne makes his way to Tom. Tom steps forward to greet him. He offers a hand. Lorne ignores it and steps in closer for an embrace.

"Thank you for coming," he says as they part. He holds Tom by the shoulders and looks him over. "Damn, you're looking well, man. How long has it been? Shit, it's been too long – ten years, right?"

"Nearly," Tom says.

Lorne steps back, shaking his head. "Hell, I was starting to think I'd never see you again. How did you find out?"

"By chance," Tom says. "I was in a diner and I saw an obituary."

Lorne nods. "I didn't know what else to do. I sent out some emails and some messages on Facebook, but I was trying to cover all bases. Not everyone is online, y'know? Of course you know – you're one of the people I couldn't find on there! But I just wanted to make sure that people knew, and that they had a chance to come." He gestures into the space behind him. "Not many did. No one from the Army, anyway – only you."

"I'm sorry to hear that," Tom says.

Lorne purses his lips. "I'm not going to dwell on it. People have busy lives, and it's a long way to travel. It's just disappointing, is all. Adam deserved more than this."

"Were his parents here? His family?"

"No family. Adam was fostered, but even when he was young they were old. They're both long dead. Say, are you coming to the wake?"

"Sure," Tom says. "Where's it at?"

"It's at the bar where I work. I can give you directions."

"Oh, Colin's place?" Tom gives a wry smile.

Lorne blinks. "You've been by already?"

"Just by coincidence."

"How long have you been in town?"

"I got here yesterday. Do you need a ride to the wake?"

"I'd appreciate that. I'm really glad you turned up, Rollins. I think out of everyone from back when we served, I hoped you would get here the most. Y'know, it's funny – this right here, I think this is the most I've ever heard you speak. Even when you were carrying me back to camp, you barely spoke."

"It was hot, and we needed to preserve moisture," Tom says, but he laughs. "I'm just glad I spotted that obituary. You and Adam stayed in touch?" Tom turns and starts walking and Lorne joins him, heading toward the car. Lorne's limp is obvious, but it's not too pronounced. It does not seem to slow him down. He does not wince with every step.

"We did, yeah. And it turned out we didn't live far from each other in the first place. Adam was from here, Samson, and I was only fifteen miles away. After I was discharged, I kind of just floated around my hometown for a while, but once Adam was out of the Army he told me I should move closer. Let me crash on his couch for a few weeks while I found somewhere to stay."

"Sounds like the two of you really looked out for each other," Tom says, pausing when they reach the car.

"Well," Lorne says, "it was more he looked out for *me*." There's a grimness to his face when he says this, and a sadness, and Tom thinks about how thin and pale he looks. How bedraggled he is, despite having clearly made an effort for the funeral.

Tom nods and then gets into the car. Lorne slips into the passenger side.

"You get a good look at the others who came?" Lorne says. "I'll introduce you at the wake. Provided they all come along."

Tom starts the engine. "It's a real shame what has happened," Tom says, starting to drive.

Lorne is silent. Tom imagines he's thinking about how things could have been different. Blaming himself for any signs or indicators that he might have missed. Tom gives him a moment with his grief. He knows that words of comfort will be nothing more than just words right now. Lorne needs to get through the worst of blaming himself before he'll be willing to hear that it's not his fault.

However, when he speaks, he does not sound grief-stricken. His voice sounds harder. "Do you mean how he killed himself?"

"Yes," Tom says, surprised at the sudden change in Lorne.

And then Lorne says something that Tom is not prepared for. "He didn't kill himself."

Tom glances at him, sees how Lorne stares straight ahead and his face is set. His brows are knit and it looks like he's grinding his jaw.

"I'm sorry, I think I've maybe misunderstood," Tom says. "Colin told me Adam hanged himself. That's not right?"

"Oh, that's what it looked like," Lorne says, turning to Tom now. "But that's not what happened. Adam did *not* kill himself."

Tom frowns. "Then what happened?"

Lorne nods up ahead. They're nearly at the bar. "I don't wanna talk about it in there, okay, but the top and bottom of it is I don't believe for a goddamn second that Adam killed himself. I don't know what happened, but I don't believe it was suicide. Listen, we can talk more about it after, but I don't really have much more to say other than that my gut feeling is that this is wrong. This isn't how it looks."

Tom parks in front of the bar. "Okay," he says. "Let's talk more later."

5

Inside the bar, at the wake, Tom thinks about what Lorne said. About Adam. About the hanging. About things perhaps not being as they appear. He wonders, too, if maybe this is the grief talking. If Lorne's bereavement is making him concoct wild theories that could have no basis in reality.

Of course, Tom knows all too well how possible it is to make someone look as if they've killed themselves.

Lorne guides him around the room. An older man comes up to Lorne, nodding his head briefly at Tom. Tom recognises him from outside the funeral home. One of the people he saw arrive. "Lorne, I can't stay," the man says. "I just wanted to stop by to show my respects, but I need to go." The older man looks agitated. His eyes are shifty, cutting from side to side.

"Sure thing, John," Lorne says, shaking his hand. "We all appreciate you coming out."

John nods, lips pursed, and then hurries from the bar.

Lorne watches him go. He leans closer to Tom and

lowers his voice before saying, "I didn't realise he and Adam knew each other well enough for him to come to the funeral. I can't say I ever saw them talking before. But I guess that was Adam. He could have that effect on people. He was good to them, and they appreciated it."

Tom says hello to Colin behind the bar as Lorne orders a drink.

"Good turnout?" Colin says to both of them, handing Lorne a bottle. "Sorry I couldn't make it, but I got everything set up here."

"It was okay," Lorne says. "It could have been better. But I understand you already met Tom Rollins here? This is the guy I've told you about."

"The one who carried you across the desert," Colin says. "Yes, you've told me the story. And yes, we're already acquainted. It's good to see you again, Mr. Rollins."

From the bar, Lorne leans close to Tom and points out who the other people are. Most of them are loose acquaintances of Adam's, and by extension, Lorne's. Very few of them are anyone either Adam or Lorne considered friends – mostly drinking buddies, and people they know from around town. Some of the people present, however, are of interest. Tom perks up when Lorne reaches the teary-eyed blonde. "And that is Adam's ex-wife," he says. "Olivia. She still goes by his last name – Olivia Lineker. She used to be Olivia Jackson. They got divorced a few years back now, but they were estranged for a couple before that."

"They stay friendly?" Tom says.

"Yeah, they did, actually. Adam never really spoke about Olivia with me much, but I got the impression he blamed himself for their marriage falling apart. It's the Army, y'know? It does that to people. Even after you've left it, it's still got a hold on you. It's still messing you up."

The blonde – Olivia – sits at a table off to the side, nursing a beer. The man she arrived at the funeral home with is with her. He strokes her arm, comforting her. Olivia looks like she's still teary. She takes deep breaths and tries not to break into a full sobbing fit.

"Who's she with?" Tom says.

"Stan Seeger," Lorne says. "Her boyfriend."

"Did *he* and Adam get along?"

Lorne shrugs. "Far as I know. They never had any problems that I saw. Reckon Adam was happy so long as Olivia was happy."

Tom spots the Indian woman. She sits alone, nursing a glass of white wine. She's deep in thought, and judging by the expression on her face they are not pleasant thoughts.

Tom turns to ask Lorne who she is, but Lorne is in conversation with Colin. Tom takes it upon himself to find out. He crosses the room to her. "Hello," he says, when she senses his approach and looks up. By that point, Tom is already next to her table.

"Hello," she says.

"Do you mind if I sit?"

She motions toward the seat opposite. "Suit yourself."

Tom takes a seat.

"You don't have a drink," she says.

"It's a little early in the day," Tom says.

"Yeah, well," she says, and takes a sip of her wine. "I think I need it."

Tom watches her while she drinks. From across the parking lot at the funeral home, where he first spotted her, he found her to be striking. High cheekbones, a thin, regal nose. It's clear through her pantsuit that she keeps herself in shape. Up close, however, she's positively beautiful. Tom wonders if she and Adam were involved. He can easily see how Adam could fall for her. "Did you know Adam well?"

"Quite well," she says, putting down her glass. "He was my patient."

Tom is intrigued. "Your patient?"

"I am – I *was* – his therapist."

"Therapist? Like a psychologist?"

"Exactly like a psychologist," she says. She offers her hand. "Malani Sandhu."

Tom shakes her hand. "That's a very nice name. Indian?"

"What gave me away?"

Tom grins. "Tom Rollins."

"Oh," she says, raising her eyebrows. She recognises his name. Adam has clearly mentioned him in their meetings. Tom wonders how many other people in Samson are aware of him.

"I hope he said good things."

Malani recovers herself. "Did you travel far to come here today?"

"Not too far. I was already in Colorado. A lucky coincidence, I guess, otherwise I would have missed the news. Speaking of, is there much call for therapists in a town as small as Samson?"

"I do online consultations, too," Malani says. "And some people are willing to travel."

"How far away is the closest town? On my way here, last one I saw was around twenty miles out."

"Did you come from the south? There's another town fifteen to the north."

"A whole five miles closer."

"Makes all the difference."

"So Samson's pretty isolated."

"Pretty much, but we get busy during the skiing season. Sometimes in the summer, too, but not for as long. It's very beautiful here in the summer. We're heading into quiet season right now, though. Usually lasts a few months."

"I don't suppose there's much of a tourist trade for therapy?"

"You'd be surprised."

"I'm sure I would. How long were you having meetings with Adam for?"

"That was a very abrupt topic change," Malani says. "And I'm not going to discuss our meetings."

"I don't expect you to go into too much detail," Tom says. "But telling me how long the two of you were seeing each other for isn't exactly divulging personal information."

Malani looks at him. "A few years," she says. "That's as much as I'm willing to share. And don't try to lull me into revealing anything else like you just did. Did you think I didn't notice that? You think I haven't done that myself?"

"As a therapist?"

"No – I used to be a deputy."

"That so? That's impressive. Here in Samson?"

She nods.

"Why'd you give it up? The money?"

"That's also something I'm not going to discuss, especially not with a man I've only just met."

"Fair enough." Tom glances around the bar. He sees Lorne still talking to Colin at the counter. Lorne runs his hands back through his hair. Tom turns back to Malani. "Let me ask you something," he says. "I'm not asking for details. This is a broad question, and you can give a simple answer."

Malani sits back. "We'll see."

"Did you think Adam was suicidal?"

Malani doesn't answer straight away. Tom sees how her eyebrows twitch, as if the question has touched a nerve. She bites the inside of her cheek, then takes a deep breath. "I don't think I can give a simple answer to that."

"Then give a detailed one."

She shoots him a look. "It's not as straightforward as that. She looks around the room, looks over toward where Olivia and Stan sit, and then leans in closer and keeps her voice low. "Do I think he was suicidal? I never saw any sign that he was. When I found out what had happened, it shocked me." She takes another deep breath. "And it makes me wonder if I missed something. If I...if I failed him..."

Tom considers this. "What if you didn't see any signs because there *were* no signs," he says. "Do you believe it could be possible that he *didn't* kill himself?"

"I don't see how it could have been an accident," Malani says.

"That's not what I mean. Could someone else have killed him and made it look like a hanging?"

Malani stares at him. "What makes you think that?"

"Lorne doesn't believe he killed himself."

"Did he give a reason?"

"Just a gut feeling. But I'd rather have facts and reasons. Did Adam mention anyone to you that could have put him at risk? Was there anyone he was afraid of? Any sense that he was in danger? Any kind, no matter how trivial it may have seemed."

"If I thought that was a possibility, I'd pass that information on to the law," she says. "Not you."

"It's interesting that you say 'the law'," Tom says. "As an

ex-deputy, I'd have thought you would refer it to the sheriff's department. Aren't they the ones that would be investigating his death?"

Malani is silent for a moment. She looks back at him, their eyes locked together. "First of all, there is no investigation," she says. "Not when it's all so cut and dry. And second of all–"

Before she can continue, there is movement off to Tom's right. Olivia and Stan are getting to their feet. Olivia is choking back a sob, her emotions finally overwhelming her. They make their way toward the counter, to say goodbye to Lorne. On the way, Olivia's legs begin to buckle. Stan has to catch her. Lorne comes to them. They speak briefly, and then Olivia and Stan leave the bar. Lorne comes over to Tom and Malani's table.

"She's taking it bad," he says, meaning Olivia. "She says they wish they could stay longer, but she doesn't think she can manage it. I told her not to worry."

"If you'll excuse me," Malani says, "I need to go too. It was nice to meet you, Tom Rollins." She stands and shakes both of their hands, and then leaves. Tom turns to watch her go.

"You were talking to Adam's therapist for a while," Lorne says when Tom turns back.

Tom nods. "I didn't realise that's who she was when I came over."

"Did she say anything interesting?"

Tom doesn't answer straight away. He thinks on what she said. He thinks on what Lorne has said, too. About not believing Adam killed himself. About Malani not seeing any signs that he was suicidal. It could be nothing. It could be everything.

It could be that Adam has killed himself. It could be that something more sinister has occurred. Either way, Tom needs to know for sure. He can't leave until he does.

"I think I'm going to hang around for a while, Lorne," he says. "Find out whether you're right about Adam's death."

Lorne's face brightens. He leans closer. "Did she say something? Does she think it was faked, too?"

"No, she didn't say that," Tom says. "But she was shocked he'd killed himself. That was plain for anyone to see. It's rocked her. It's got her doubting whether she's good at her job. And that makes me curious – was it carelessness on her behalf, or was there nothing *to* miss? I'm going to find out."

6

Lorne invites Tom to stay in his trailer while he's in town. Tom says he can extend his stay at the motel but Lorne won't hear it.

"Do you need to go pick your stuff up?" Lorne says.

"It's already in the car," Tom says. "I checked out when I left the room this morning. I wasn't planning on sticking around."

They hang around at the wake until everyone else has gone, and then they stay a while longer. Lorne is drinking, but he doesn't seem to be getting drunk. He nurses each bottle that Colin hands him. Tom does not drink anything alcoholic. He alternates between water and soda. It gets late. Tom is eager to leave, and to talk more of Adam, but the bar has filled up and he'd rather speak in private.

Tom watches Lorne as he drinks. Again, he wonders about potential alcoholism. He hasn't noticed Lorne's hands shaking, or any other tell-tale signs, but that doesn't mean anything. There could be other signs, and some that don't show. He looks very sickly.

Colin makes them each a burger, and refuses payment when Tom holds out cash. "On the house," he says.

Tom nods appreciatively and pockets the money.

When Lorne goes to the bathroom, and Colin has a lull in serving patrons, Tom motions for him to come over so they can talk. "How's Lorne holding up?" Tom says. "And I don't just mean with Adam's death – I mean before that, too. He looks ill."

Colin gives a sad nod, like he understands exactly what Tom means. "He looks it, but he's not. Not physically, at least. Up here, though." He taps the side of his head. "Lorne's got some problems."

"What kind of problems?"

"Probably best he tells you himself," Colin says. "I don't want it to seem like I'm talking about him behind his back. I like Lorne. I like him a lot. He's a good kid. Good worker, too, when he's able to come in."

Tom notes this last phrase. "I appreciate you don't wanna talk about him when he's not here, but tell me this – is he overly dependent on alcohol?" Tom nods toward Lorne's current bottle, half-empty. "Drugs?"

Colin shakes his head, keeping one eye on the bathroom door. "No," he says. "Neither."

"You're sure?"

"About the drugs, no. But he's not an alcoholic. I'm sure of that. He maybe *depends* on it on some occasions more than others – today being a prime example – but he's not *dependent*. Believe me, I see plenty of people who are. I know the difference."

Lorne returns from the bathroom, and the conversation comes to an abrupt halt. Lorne doesn't notice. Colin moves off back down the counter to serve someone else.

It's eight when Tom is able to persuade Lorne to leave the bar. It's dark outside. It's cold. Tom sees his breath misting in front of his face.

"I'm just over here," Lorne says, pointing over the road to the trailer park. "It's not far."

Tom watches him as he walks. Other than his limp, Lorne is not unsteady on his feet. Tom counted that he had about six beers, but they don't appear to have affected him.

It's quiet in the trailer park. They make their way through the warren-like layout. Tom tries to remember the route for future reference. It doesn't take long before Lorne pulls out his key as they reach his trailer.

"Park looks pretty full right now, doesn't it?" Lorne says as he unlocks the door. "With residents, I mean."

"It's pretty big," Tom says.

"Uh-huh. You should see what it's like here when it's skiing season. A lot – a *lot* – of people turn up in their RVs, and we really fill up. You should see this place in the snow, Rollins. It's pretty now, and it's pretty in the summer, but in the winter it's *beautiful*."

"You like it here, huh?"

Lorne looks out across the darkened trailer park. He takes a deep breath. "Yeah," he says, but he sighs as he does so. "Except it's always gonna feel a little dulled for me now. Without Adam, I mean. I don't think it's fully sunk in yet. That I'm never gonna see him again, I mean." He shakes his head, realising how maudlin he sounds. "Anyway. Let's get inside."

The inside of the trailer is just a little bigger than the room Tom had back at the motel. Lorne hurries around, clearing up discarded clothes he has scattered around the place. He dumps them off to one side, closer to the kitchen area. "Take a seat," he says, motioning toward the sofa.

The curtains are open. Before Tom sits, he pulls them closed. He doesn't like people being able to see inside, and he can't see out because of the glare from the lights on the glass.

The sofa curves around the front of the trailer. Lorne takes a seat opposite. "There's a bed under here," he says. "It pulls out. I don't mind sleeping on it. You can take the bed."

Tom shakes his head. "The pull-out is more than enough."

Lorne nods. "You want anything to eat? To drink?"

"No, I'm good. What I wanna do is talk about Adam."

"I figured you would. But I told you, man, it's just a gut feeling. Adam wouldn't kill himself. I can't prove it, but that's how it is. I don't believe for a damn second that he would do himself like that. He was my best friend, man. I would've known – I would've *known*."

Tom doesn't think it sounds like Lorne is trying to convince himself. He speaks with certainty. "Malani didn't see any indication he would kill himself, either," Tom says. "The two of you are in agreement on that. That's why I'm hanging around. I'm going to find out the truth – whether that truth is that someone else killed him, or whether he truly did kill himself."

Lorne nods. "And if you find out it was someone else, what will you do then?"

"I'll find out why," Tom says.

"And then...?"

"I'm not going to commit myself to anything until I find out the why."

"Adam was a good man," Lorne says. "He had his issues. We all do."

"I don't doubt it. And I saved his life once, and now that life has been snuffed out. That doesn't sit right with me."

"You find out who it was, I want to know. I want to be there."

Tom doesn't respond to this. "One thing at a time," he says. Tom looks at Lorne for a long time. Lorne isn't looking back. He stares at the ground, his hands fidgeting. He's lost in thought. Thinking of Adam, probably. Thinking about who could have killed him – if anyone did. Thinking about what he'll do when he finds out who they are.

"What did Adam do for work?" Tom says.

Lorne raises his head. "He worked overseas," he says. "He'd be gone for a couple of months, then come back for a month, and then head out again. Sometimes his schedule fluctuated but that was mostly how it worked out."

"What was he doing?"

"Drilling for oil."

"I hear that pays pretty well."

"I hear that too."

"What countries was he in?"

"Over in Africa, mostly. Few different countries over there, I can't remember which ones specifically. When he first went over, he wasn't drilling. He worked security."

"Oh yeah?"

"Yeah. Keeping the workers and the equipment safe. The next time he went over, though, he was one of the workers. I asked him how come. He said he realised being a worker paid a lot better." Lorne chuckles.

"You know where Olivia lives, right?"

"Yeah, of course. It's where Adam used to live, too, when

they were still together. It's where I stayed when I first came to town."

"Stan live with her?"

Lorne nods. The expression on his face says he dislikes this fact. "Listen, Stan's an asshole, but I don't have any real problem with him. I *do* have a problem with him living in the home that Adam bought. Sleeping in his bed. Cooking in his kitchen. Mowing his lawn. Parking in his driveway. I know it sounds stupid, but I don't like it. It's almost like he's erasing every trace that remained of Adam."

"In the morning, I'll need you to write down their address for me," Tom says. "What about Malani? Do you know where her office is?"

"Samson isn't a big place," Lorne says. "I know where everything is."

"Then add the sheriff's department to that list, too."

"Will do."

They sit in silence for a while. Lorne briefly returns to staring at the floor, but then snaps back into focus like he's just remembered he has a guest. "Should I put the TV on? The radio, maybe?"

"That's okay," Tom says. "Lorne, how've you been doing? I don't just mean recently, I mean for a while now."

Lorne looks at him but doesn't say anything.

Tom waits. Gives him a chance to respond.

Lorne sighs. "I know how I look, Rollins."

"Call me Tom."

Lorne nods. "I know I don't look well. I've got a mirror. I look like a fucking junkie. But I need you to believe – I'm not a junkie, okay? I don't touch drugs, don't go anywhere near the things." He steels himself. "Truth is, I don't sleep too well."

Tom tilts his head. "How come?"

Lorne lowers his face, almost like he's ashamed. "I've got PTSD, Tom. Had it ever since I was discharged. That's the pisser, man – ever since I got back on American soil, I've had fucking PTSD. Not overseas, no. Not over there where all the shit was happening. *Here*. America. Home. Where it was supposed to be all over. Where it's supposed to be safe. Where everything is supposed to be okay and I should be able to goddamn *sleep*. My first night back, my first night back in my own bed, I woke up screaming. Drenched in sweat. I thought I'd pissed myself. And then my hands, man, my *hands*. They wouldn't stop shaking. I was shaking all over. It wouldn't stop. Things should've been cool, and quiet, and I should've been able to sleep, but I couldn't fucking sleep. Things suddenly weren't cool and quiet and calm. I get out of a warzone, and all I can hear is a warzone in my head. Gunshots. Explosions. Constant, yet sudden. All the damn time. And it's all in here." He presses a palm to the side of his head, as if trying to force all the noise out the other side.

"I'm sorry to hear that, Lorne," Tom says.

"I lost a lot of jobs because of it. I couldn't hold down steady work. You ever tried stacking shelves, or working on cars, when your hands won't stop shaking? It ain't doable. And there were some days I couldn't get out of bed. I'd just be pinned to the mattress, couldn't move a muscle, too damn scared to go outside. The bar's the longest I've been able to hold anything down since I left the Army. That's because of Colin. He's a good guy. He's a lot more sympathetic that other bosses I've had. He goes easy on me. He's understanding if I can't make it in or I if need to leave early. He doesn't bust my balls over it." Lorne laces his fingers atop his head and blows out air. "It's not as bad as it used to be. The

PTSD, I mean. But it still flares up, and I don't know when it will or how to keep it from happening." His hands drop and land limp in his lap. "Drinking helps, sometimes. It shuts it up. It calms my hands. But since Adam died..." He shakes his head. "It's been bad, man. I'm not sleeping again. When I do, I wake up like I've been falling. You know that feeling? You ever get that?"

"I think everyone does."

"Yeah, I get it over and over. It's like I've stepped on a mine, and like it's blown me into the air and I feel like I'm falling down from that. You know what I used to see, back when it first started?"

"What?"

"It was when you rescued me. When my leg was broken and all messed up, and the bone was sticking out like that. But it would change up. Like, I didn't break my leg in an explosion. It would be like I was just standing there, and my leg split, and the bone came bursting out. Or another time, I'd be stuck in that ditch – all on my own this time – and a mortar would land in there with me. Or a grenade would get thrown or rolled in. Or the Taliban would be all around me, pointing their AK-47s at me. And then, always at the point of death, that's when I'd wake up, but the feelings wouldn't leave. It ever been bad like that for you?"

Tom shakes his head. "No."

Lorne nods. "Just gets the weakest of us, I guess."

"It's not like that, Lorne," Tom says. "That's not true. It can get anyone. And it fucks people up in all different ways. I've met some real strong people, some of the strongest people I've ever known, who've been cut down with PTSD."

Lorne doesn't say anything.

"It's not late, but I think I'm gonna get to sleep now," Tom says. "I'm gonna get an early start tomorrow."

"Yeah," Lorne says, rising. "Of course. That makes sense. You need a hand with the pull-out?"

"I'll figure it out."

"Okay." Lorne heads toward his bedroom. "You need anything, just shout. I'll still be awake."

"Got it. And Lorne?"

Lorne pauses by his door. "Yeah."

"It's good to see you," Tom says. "Truly. It's been a long time since I last saw anyone from the Army. Hell, I don't think I've seen anyone I served with since I left. You're the first."

Lorne nods. "Speaking of, what *did* happen when you left? After I broke my leg I got discharged pretty soon after, but I spent a while in the hospital out there while I was healing, and I heard some things. There were some wild rumours going around, man."

Tom grins. "That's a story for another time."

7

Tom wakes early the next morning, but he doesn't head straight out. He needs to give the rest of the town a chance to wake up and get to work. Lorne is already up and moving quietly around the kitchen. He draws Tom a rough map of where the people he wants to visit are. Tom already has an idea of the town's layout. He needs addresses. Some directions. He knows where the sheriff's department is but Lorne still draws it on his map. The sheriff's department is closest. It's practically in the centre of town. Tom will go there first. Malani's office isn't too far from there. Olivia lives furthest away. Her home is on the opposite side of town, on the outskirts.

"It's a nice place," Lorne says, marking the house on the spot and noting down the door number. "The whole estate is."

Tom zips up his jacket and heads out on foot. Lorne stays behind. He's planning on going to work today.

"Colin is good to me," he says, "and he gave me a few days off to cope with Adam's death, but I don't want to take advantage of his generosity. You keep me updated, though, okay? I wanna know everything you find out."

"*If* I find anything," Tom says. He wants to keep Lorne's expectations under control.

"Of course," Lorne says. "*If.*"

Tom starts walking. He wants to see the town up close. Being on foot is different to driving by everything. He's moving far slower than if he was in his car. He can see more this way.

The morning air is crisp. The sky is clear. He's surprised there is no frost on the ground. The white tops of the mountains that border the town are tipped golden with the rising sun. The roads are not busy, but he sees plenty of people milling around. He doesn't spot any familiar faces from the funeral. In a way, he's glad of this. He doesn't want to bump into anyone he's planning on talking to out in public. He wants to see them where they live and where they work. Wants to see them on their own turf, where they're likely to be more open and vulnerable. Where he can get a better idea of how they live, and how Adam lived.

Adam's home is also marked down on Lorne's map. Tom isn't planning on going there yet, but he will, eventually. First, he wants to talk to people. Get a feeling for how things were. Paint a picture of his last few days.

It doesn't take him long to reach the centre of town. He glances toward the shop fronts. There's a hardware store and a small bookshop. He sees a few diners, which no doubt see their best business during ski season. There's a large supermarket, too, and most people – on foot and in vehicles – are heading toward it. Tom counts less than a dozen people heading in and coming out. Not many.

Opposite the supermarket is a hotel. Its advertisement is

a classic neon sign that hangs from the side of the building. Tom has stayed in many hotels like this.

As he glances at it, a noise catches his attention. An engine, obnoxiously loud, coming closer. Crossing the road, Tom turns toward the sound. It's two vehicles. Two open-top jeeps, despite the cold air. The jeep at the front holds two men, and the one behind has three. Five, all told. Tom slows his walk to better take in the approaching group. They look like something out of Mad Max. They come roaring down the road, their engines and exhausts sounding in desperate need of a tune-up, or else the whole thing just needs scrapped altogether.

Tom gets a better view of the occupants of the jeeps. They have long hair and thick beards, all of them. They wear shirts, some of them checked and some of them denim. The driver of the second jeep has his sleeves torn off and the guy in the back lounges with his shirt unbuttoned, his pale torso on show. The lead jeep swerves suddenly as it nears the supermarket, crossing the road and pulling to a stop at the side of the building where the dumpsters are. The passenger is standing and aggressively whooping, gesturing and calling out toward the dumpsters. Tom looks and realises someone is there. A couple of kids, teen boys, standing frozen like deer caught in headlights.

Tom pauses and watches. One of the teens was reaching inside the dumpster. He quickly drops its lid back into place and steps back, hands pinned by his sides. The standing passenger jumps from the jeep and stomps over to them, gesticulating wildly and shouting. Tom can't make out all of what he says. He hears the word, "*ours!*" shouted into the face of both boys, accompanied by a jabbing finger.

The other four men get out of their vehicles and saunter

over. Tom notices that they have weapons. A couple of them carry hunting knives on their hips, and one of them has a machete dangling there. Tom spots a Colt 1911 on the second driver.

The two teens are terrified. Tom doesn't understand why these men are giving them a hard time. He looks around. There are other people nearby, but none of them look toward the scene, despite how loud and animated it is. They give it a wide berth. They look the other direction. They pretend it's not happening. Then the passenger pulls out a snub-nose revolver from his waistband and jabs it into the faces of the two boys. They look terrified. One of them is crying.

Tom starts heading over.

Tom is not armed. He left his Beretta and KA-BAR in his bag at Lorne's. He didn't want to go into the sheriff's department with weapons. Be that as it may, he can't leave this to play out. He doesn't announce himself until he's slid through the group and reached the man holding the revolver. Tom takes it from him. He covers the hammer to prevent it from accidentally going off and then twists it out of the man's hand, pushing the barrel away from himself and the two kids. He pushes the man back but keeps hold of his weapon, holding it down by his side, a finger hovering near the trigger.

"What's going on here?" he says, his voice calm as he eyes each of the five men.

They back up, caught by surprise. Their hands go to their weapons, but they don't pull out their knives or machete. The man with the Colt pulls the gun out, however, and holds it down by his side.

"You think you're faster?" Tom says, looking right at the

man with the Colt.

The man falters. He looks from Tom to the man he has disarmed, thinking of how quick Tom was able to take it from him. He doesn't put the Colt away, but it's clear he's unsure how prepared he is to use it.

Behind Tom, the two kids run away. They have skateboards with them. They hop onto them and roll down the road as fast as they can.

The man whose gun Tom has taken smirks. "You crazy, dude?" he says. When he speaks, despite the six feet between them, Tom can smell how bad his breath is. Peering into his mouth, it's no surprise. His teeth are rotten. "You know who we are?"

"A bunch of assholes picking on a couple of kids," Tom says. "I wanna know why you were waving a goddamn gun in their face before I shove this thing down your throat." Tom tilts the revolver toward him so there is no doubt what he's planning on sticking down his throat.

The man with the rotten teeth grins. "They know what they were doing wrong," he says. "Thought we wouldn't catch them, that we wouldn't know – but we *did* catch them. And they needed to know what happens to anyone who looks to take from us."

"Take?" Tom says. "Take what?"

"You ain't from around here, are you?" says one of the other men, the one on Tom's immediate right, a hand upon his hunting knife. "You should just keep moving, stranger. Put down Willie's gun and pray we just decide to let this one go, on account of you not having any kind of idea of what you're involving yourself in."

Tom is outnumbered. He looks the men over. They look like brawlers. They can handle themselves, though he imagines they're more dangerous with a weapon in their hands. The man in front of him, however – Willie – doesn't strike him as any kind of real threat, especially not since he's been disarmed. He's all talk. Backed up by his buddies, he believes he can stand firm against one man.

Tom might have to hurt a couple of them to get them to back off. He's involved himself in this thing now, and there's no other way out. The two teens are gone, and these men are looking to vent their frustrations on someone. Tom knows he needs to strike first.

"You want the gun back?" he says.

"Hand it over," Willie says.

"Take it," Tom says. He makes no effort to offer it. He waits to see who moves first. Tom is done talking.

Willie is first. He lunges forward, reaching for the revolver. Tom deals with him easily. He brings up his knee and buries it under Willie's jaw, rattling his rotten teeth together, knocking some of them loose.

Tom doesn't stop. Before Willie can drop, Tom is swinging the revolver, burying the base of the handle into the bridge of the man on his right's nose, breaking it and knocking him down. Tom turns the revolver upright and points it into the face of the man with the Colt. The armed man freezes as he attempts to raise it. He stares down the barrel of the revolver.

"Hand it over," Tom says.

The man does so. Tom opens the cylinder of the revolver and drops the bullets to the floor. He tosses the weapon to the side, but keeps hold of the Colt for the time being. "You can all get out of here now."

The men hesitate. Willie is on the ground, clutching his jaw and covering his mouth with a hand. Blood dribbles down the side of his mouth and chin from under his hand. He groans, trying to push himself up one-handed. He gestures for the others to rush Tom. "Get him," he says, his words muffled through his palm.

The others hesitate. They look at the Colt. The man on Tom's right nurses his broken nose, his blood dripping onto the pavement. The man with the machete pulls it a little from its sheath, considering. He sees Tom staring at him and decides against it.

Willie manages to get back to his feet. He wipes the blood from his mouth. It smears across his cheek and mats his beard hairs. When he sees that the others are not going to back him up, he falters and steps off. He's a paper man. He will crumple in Tom's hand. They all will.

"C'mon, Rotten Willie," one of the men who hasn't yet spoken says.

"Let's go," the man with the broken nose says, his voice muted from his injury.

"Bear ain't gonna like this," Rotten Willie says. Tom imagines his nickname is in relation to his disgusting teeth. Tom's done him a favour knocking a few of them loose. Rotten Willie jabs a finger toward Tom. "We'll be seeing you again, buddy. You can count on it."

"I don't doubt it," Tom says.

The men back off, then get into their open top jeeps and drive away, roaring their engines as they go. From a safe distance, Rotten Willie flips Tom the bird.

Tom looks around. Still, no one is looking this way. Anyone who is nearby is acting like nothing has happened.

Tom slides the magazine from the Colt and drops the bullets down a nearby gutter. He returns to the dumpster with both guns, lifting the lid to drop them inside. He pauses as he does so, something catching his eye.

Inside the dumpster, there are six boxes placed atop the rubbish. The boxes have lids on them. This is the same dumpster the two teens were looking into when Rotten Willie and friends turned up. Tom pushes the dumpster lid open wider so it props itself against the wall behind. He removes the lid from the nearest box to see what's inside. Frowning at the contents, he removes the rest of the lids, too.

Each box contains fresh produce. Some dried goods, too, as well as candy bars and bottles of soda. Tom checks the dates on the packaging. None of these things are out of date. None of them should be in a dumpster. They're all fresh. It's all sellable.

Tom drops the dumpster lid back into place and looks down the road in the direction the jeeps went. They're out of sight now, though he feels like he can still hear them. He wishes the two teen boys had hung around so he could ask them what was going on.

Tom leaves the dumpster. There are no answers for him here. He continues on to the sheriff's department.

———

8

The sheriff keeps Tom waiting.

The desk is manned by Deputy Anderson. A stocky woman with a friendly smile, she looks only a few years older than Tom. Tom spoke to Deputy Anderson about meeting with the sheriff. She went through to talk to the man himself, then returned and said, "The sheriff's very busy. If it's not an emergency and you still wanna talk to him, you're gonna have to wait a while."

Tom took a seat. "I'll wait."

That was an hour ago. Deputy Anderson is still behind the desk opposite, but she avoids meeting his eye. Her friendly smile has faltered as the time has passed. She looks awkward, now, at having him being kept waiting for so long. She busies herself, with her attention on her computer screen.

The sheriff's department is small. Off to the right, through the window of a closed door, Tom can see two more desks, though only one is currently occupied. The deputy there sits sipping coffee and leaning back in his swivel chair.

Behind him, Tom can see a locked weapons cabinet. Further still, there is another door which leads through to the holding cells. Tom wonders how many holding cells there are. Judging by the size of the building, he'd say three at max, but probably only one or two. Three is being generous.

"Has he forgotten about me?" Tom says.

Deputy Anderson looks up. "No, no, I'm sure he hasn't. Like I said, he's very busy. But Sheriff Rooker hasn't forgotten about you. He'll be with you just as soon as he can."

"Maybe you should give him a little nudge," Tom says. "I don't intend to take up much of his time."

Deputy Anderson doesn't look like she's willing to give Sherrif Rooker any kind of a nudge. "Just sit tight," she says.

The other deputy comes through from his desk. "Hey, Anderson," he says, but then stops as he catches sight of Tom sitting on the bench. Tom sees how he checks to see if Tom is cuffed. Sees that he isn't. The deputy leans over the counter, closer to Anderson. "Who's he?" he says, his voice lowered.

"Just some guy who wants to see the sheriff," Anderson says.

"Why?"

Anderson glances at Tom. She sees him watching them. Listening. She leans closer, lowers her voice still more, but it's quiet in the reception and Tom can make out their whispers. "He's a friend of the guy who killed himself."

"Yeah? What's there to ask about it?"

Tom clears his throat. "Maybe I don't need to see the sheriff," he says. "Maybe I can just talk to the two of you about it. Could save us all a lot of time."

The two deputies turn to look at him.

The door to Tom's left opens before either of them can speak. The sheriff steps into the frame. He's a tall man, lean, with gaunt cheeks and a pinched face. He has a bald pate but hair cut short around the sides and back. He sees his two deputies at the reception. "Anderson," he says. "Norton. Either of you need something?"

Deputy Norton straightens. "No, sir," he says. "Was just seeing if Deputy Anderson would like a coffee while I'm making a fresh pot. Would *you*, sir?"

Sherrif Rooker shakes his head. "No." He turns to Tom. "Mr. Rollins?"

Tom stands.

Sherrif Rooker looks him over, appraising him. He doesn't offer a handshake. He doesn't offer any kind of real greeting. He tilts his head toward his office. "Step inside."

Tom follows him inside. Sheriff Rooker closes the door after them, and then takes a seat behind his desk. He motions for Tom to take a seat opposite.

The office is wood-panelled. On the way in, Tom noticed a mounted deer head on the wall closest to the door. The desk is neat and ordered. The sheriff's name and title are on the desk, right in front of Tom. Sherrif David Rooker.

The sheriff doesn't pay Tom much attention. His eyes are on his computer screen. "What can I do for you, Mr. Rollins?" he says with disinterest.

"I just have a few questions relating to the death of Adam Lineker," Tom says.

The sheriff frowns and turns away from his computer, training his eyes upon Tom now. "Was he a friend of yours?"

"In a sense."

"Army buddies, huh?"

Tom nods.

The sheriff sits back. "I was expecting more of you to come through town," he says. "On account of the funeral. Haven't heard much of that coming to pass, though. In fact, you're the first one I'm aware of. Wasn't much of a turnout?"

"It was disappointing," Tom says. "But a lot of the people we served with directly were killed, and it can be hard to track down others who survived. I just happened to find out by chance. I know for others that when they eventually find out down the road what has happened – if they ever do – they'll be upset that they missed it, and they'll grieve in their own ways. It's nothing personal against Adam. Life is what it is."

The sheriff grunts. "What is it you want to ask?"

"I want to ask about the autopsy," Tom says. "I want to ask about the investigation into the scene – if there were any signs of foul play."

Sherrif Rooker frowns. He places his elbows on his arm rests and tents his fingers. He takes his time before he answers. "What are you talking about?"

"What do you mean?" Tom says.

"What do *you* mean? There was no autopsy. There was no investigation. Everything was cut and dry. He killed himself. There's no case here."

Tom stares at the sheriff. "There was no kind of investigation?"

"Why would there be? There was no sign of a struggle. No forced entry. Even when his little friend found him – Lorne? – he didn't have to break the door down to get to him. He had a key."

Tom feels a tightness in his guts. He didn't know Lorne was the one who found Adam's body. Lorne never mentioned. Tom should have asked.

"Why are you asking this?" Sherrif Rooker says.

"I've had a couple of people tell me that Adam didn't strike them as suicidal."

"So you're taking it upon yourself to look into things? Why? What do you think you're going to find? I'm sorry to be blunt, but your friend killed himself. You're wasting your time." Rooker lets his hands fall. "Who told you they have their doubts? Lorne, right? You know how that sounds to me?"

"It sounds like grief talking," Tom says. "I know that. That's what I thought at first, too. But then I heard doubts from a second source, and knew that if I didn't find out for sure I'd always wonder."

"Who was this second source?"

"I'm not going to divulge that."

Rooker raises an eyebrow. "You know how *that* sounds, don't you?"

"It doesn't matter how it sounds. I'm not going to stop until I know for sure that nothing more sinister happened to Adam Lineker."

"Suit yourself," Rooker says. "But just remember that a lot of people don't seem like they're going to kill themselves until they up and do it."

"And that might be the case here – I have no doubts about that. But I *am* going to find out for sure."

"Like I said, suit yourself. It's your life and your time. But I don't want to hear about you hassling anyone. That clear? I hear you're hassling anyone or causing trouble, I'll lock you up so damn fast you'll wish you'd been one of those Army buddies who missed the funeral."

Tom's eyes narrow at this. He doesn't appreciate the sheriff's tone, or his sentiment. He bites his tongue to stop himself from saying something he shouldn't.

"Will that be all?" Rooker says, his eyes flicking toward the door. He wants Tom to leave, and he's making no secret of the fact.

"I'd like to see the photographs of the scene," Tom says.

Rooker doesn't respond.

"You didn't take any pictures, did you?"

"I told you – there is no investigation."

Tom doesn't hold back anymore. "What kind of ass-backwards operation are you running here?"

Rooker blinks at this, taken aback, but it doesn't take long for his surprise to turn to outrage. Tom sees colour creeping into his face, from his neck up.

"Because you're in a small town where the most action you see is from drunk frat boy skiers, you think you don't need to follow protocol, that you can just do what you want?" Tom is angry, but he manages to keep the tone and volume of his voice level.

Rooker shows his teeth. "Because you're grieving, I'm going to let that go," he says. He jabs a finger. "But don't let me *ever* hear you badmouthing this department again."

"I don't blame the department – I blame *you*. The buck stops with you, sheriff."

Rooker's jaw is clenched so tight Tom sees the sinews dancing in his cheeks. He looks like the top of his head is about to burst.

"I can see you don't have any answers regarding Adam," Tom says, "so let me ask you about something I saw on my way over here."

"I'm not feeling much in the mood to answer anything you have to ask, you little prick."

Tom ignores him. "I saw a bunch of men in two real loud jeeps pull up down the side of the supermarket. Long hair, long beards – looked like mountain men types. They were carrying guns and knives – one of them had a damn machete. Anyway, they pull up, and they start hassling these two kids who were messing around by one of the dumpsters. And everyone nearby, they were acting like nothing was happening at all. Like these mountain men looking types weren't there."

Rooker tries not to react to this, but his whole demeanour changes. The colour drains from his face, and there's a brief twitch in his right cheek. "I'm not aware of anything like that," he says, playing dumb, but it's clear to Tom that he's lying.

"You sure?"

"Listen to me – this is a nice town. A quiet town. A *peaceful* town. The kind of place where families come to settle down. A good place to raise kids. I raise *my* kids here. We don't want any kind of trouble, and what's more is I will not *allow* any kind of trouble. We clear on that? Last thing we need is some outsider coming by and looking for issues where there aren't any. Your friend killed himself, Rollins, and that's all there is to it."

The two men look at each other in silence for a moment, neither of them willing to break their gaze.

The sheriff is the first to eventually look away, turning his attention back to his computer screen. "I'd appreciate it if you'd leave now, Rollins. I'm a busy man, and I can't spend all day discussing tall tales with you."

Tom leaves without another word. He's wasted enough time here. He leaves the sheriff's office door open on his way out. He doesn't respect him enough to close it.

9

Tom leaves the station and composes himself. He's been in the sheriff's department for a long time, and it was warm in there. He reacclimatises himself to the cold. Watches his breath mist as it flares from his nostrils. His hands are in his pockets. He pulls out Lorne's map and refreshes his memory as to the route to Malani's office. If she's with a client, he could find himself with another lengthy wait. He sighs at the prospect.

Raising his head, he starts walking again. As he nears the supermarket, he spots an employee outside, down the side of the building and not far from the dumpsters. She's taking a smoke break. Tom veers toward her.

"Hey," he says, when she's close enough to hear him.

She looks up. She stands with one knee bent and her foot pressed into the wall. She's young, early-twenties, and wears the supermarket's blue uniform vest but nothing heavier to protect against the cold. She blows smoke out the corner of her mouth. "I'm on my break," she says, clearly expecting him to question her regarding the inside of the supermarket. The way she says it, and the look on her face, Tom gets the impression she's been hassled while on her smoke break before.

"I don't want to ask anything about the store," Tom says. He nods at the dumpster where he found the boxes. "I want to ask about the group of wild men who came down here earlier." The woman runs a hand up her face to brush strands of long dark hair out of her eyes and mouth. She clears her throat. "What about them?"

"Who are they?"

The woman looks toward the corner at the front of the shop, and then toward the corner at the back. She has to clear her throat again. "Why's it matter to you?"

"I'm curious," Tom says. "They were carrying weapons, and everyone acted like they didn't exist. I saw them hassling a couple of kids, and–"

Her eyes go wide at this. "Oh, shit – that was *you*? Oh, man, we all saw the footage. We couldn't see your face, though, otherwise I would've realised who you were." She laughs. "Damn, you handed them their *asses*."

Tom says nothing. She's opened up and seems more willing to talk, and he waits for her to get there by herself.

She flicks her cigarette and beckons him closer. "We're not supposed to talk about them," she says. "But the manager leaves boxes of dry and fresh produce in the dumpster for them, and once a fortnight they come into town and pick it up."

"Why?" Tom says.

"So he doesn't get any hassle from them."

"What kind of hassle?"

"Well, if he didn't do it they'd probably kick his ass. Maybe worse. But they'd for sure come instore and start wrecking the place. I never saw it myself – it happened a few years ago, before I started – but I heard about them doing it once before. They were smashing bottles and pushing over shelves. I heard one of them was riding up and down the aisles, swinging a chain above his head." She laughs and pulls her face, like she's not sure how true she finds it but it's humorous enough to share.

"So who are they?"

She shrugs. "I don't know what they call themselves, but they're some militia or whatever – doomsday preppers, something like that."

Tom nods at this. His father was – *is* – a doomsday prepper. The commune he lives on has never gone into town and threatened a supermarket manager, however. "They stay near here?"

"Outside of town, but I don't know where exactly. Other people might know for sure, but I've heard different things – that they live on some ranch, or up in the mountains, or that they've dug a series of intricate tunnels and they make their home down there. They could be beneath our feet right now. Personally, I think the ranch is more likely. Mostly because I *know* that place exists. I've seen it. Didn't notice if a militia was living on it, though."

"And the sheriff's department doesn't do anything about them effectively robbing the store on a fortnightly basis?"

The woman shrugs. "I don't know what to tell you, man. I know first-hand that the sheriff can be quick enough to roll up on a group of kids and chase them off when they're not doing any harm, but when it comes to some real crime like this?" She holds out her hands and blows a raspberry. She checks the time. "Listen, I've got to get back to work. But hey, how about a selfie? The guys inside are gonna shit when I tell them I met the guy who kicked the asses of some militia dudes." She feels at her pockets and realises she doesn't have her phone on her. "Ah, damn. Some other time. You're hanging around, right?"

"Could be."

"All right. Awesome. We'll get that selfie another time. Later, dude." She hurries off, back toward the front of the store.

Tom turns and starts walking slowly, resuming his journey to Malani's office. As he goes, he digests what the woman from the supermarket has told him. About a militia living nearby. Regularly rolling into town. Causing trouble – the kind of trouble the sheriff claims he wants to keep out of the town. Tom isn't sure if the militia could play into what happened to Adam, but it's worth knowing of their existence. At this point, he's not going to cut anything out.

As he walks, he spots a black Honda Accord parked at the side of the road up ahead with out of state plates. Samson is a vacation town. Out of state plates aren't too much of a surprise. This isn't what catches Tom's attention. There are two men inside, both sitting up front. One of them appears to be reading a newspaper, but the other is looking right at Tom. He lowers his head and starts looking at his phone when he realises Tom is looking back at him. He's casual about it. Doesn't fluster. There's no panic in his movements. Nice and calm.

Tom does not hear alarm bells, not yet, but he's always cautious of people he spots sitting in a parked car, especially if one of them is watching him as he walks. He makes a note of the vehicle's details, and stores them away in the back of his mind. It could be nothing, but it could be something. Either way, he's aware.

10

Malani goes over her files.

This isn't the first time she's revisited this particular file in the last week. Adam Lineker's file. They were meeting for a few years. She took a lot of notes. She goes back to the beginning and reads through everything she's written about him. He was an angry man, certainly, and that was why he had to come to see her, but not once did she ever find herself worrying about his physical wellbeing. Not once did he ever make mention of dark thoughts pertaining to himself, or allude that he was going to hurt himself – or anyone else, for that matter. There were no self-harm scars upon his person. No obvious symptoms of alcohol or drug abuse. So far as she could see, he was perfectly fit and healthy.

But still, Malani cannot shake the guilt. Can't shake the feeling that she *must* have missed something.

She failed him.

She failed him, and now he's dead.

She sits in her office, behind her desk, and bites her lip.

Framed on the wall behind her are her certifications. Opposite her desk, against the far wall and facing each other, are the two chairs where she conducts her sessions. She looks to them now and pictures herself in one, the one on her right, and sees Adam in the other, the one closest to the door. The one with the clock on the wall behind his head so she could check the time to see if their session was nearing its end without having to glance at her watch.

She sees Adam sitting there. His arms resting on the sides of the chair. His posture relaxed, as it was in the later years when he was no longer so shut off to her. She sees him in those early days, too, the way he was bunched up, shielding himself. His arms folded. His lips pursed, his tongue probing at his teeth. One leg crossed defensively over the other.

And yet, no matter how open he became with her, how relaxed, he was never truly all the way open. Never all the way honest. He kept things from her, she could tell. There were things he would not discuss. And was it in here, in these silences, where the truth of his mental state hid?

Malani rests her elbows on the table and runs her hands back through her loose hair, letting it dangle through her fingers and hang by the sides of her face. The guilt eats at her. And right beside it is the doubt. The question that asks, how many more of your patients are you failing? How many more of them are close to death and you haven't realised?

She sits back, breathing deep through her nose, resting her head on the back of her chair. Since she found out about Adam's death – about his *suicide* – she's felt like a fraud. Like she isn't qualified to treat her patients, and the framed certificates on her wall are nothing more than bits of paper. She dreads coming to her office. She dreads every single session. She dreads the coming of every new day, fearing that she will wake up to yet more bad news, and another lost patient.

Her receptionist, Laura, knocks at her door. Malani sits up with a start, not expecting to be disturbed. She checks the time. Her next appointment is not for another hour. "Yes?" she calls, quickly scraping her hair back and tying it into a ponytail.

Laura pokes her head around the door. She's frowning. "There's a man here asking to see you," she says. "I've told him that your schedule is full, but he says he doesn't want an appointment."

"Then what does he want?" Malani says.

"He says he just wants to talk to you." Laura hesitates before she adds, "About Adam Lineker."

Malani understands. "What's his name?"

"He said it's Tom Rollins."

Malani nods. "Send him through."

11

T om notices a file already open on Malani's desk. He's standing. There is no chair in front of her desk, only the two behind him, at the front of the room.

Malani sees where he's looking and she promptly closes the file and puts it into a drawer in her desk. Tom notices a filing cabinet nearby, and he sees how each drawer is labelled alphabetically.

"Was that Adam's file?" he says.

Malani gets to her feet, smoothing down the front of her pantsuit. She motions toward the two chairs. "Let's take a seat."

Tom glances at the chairs. "I'm not here as a patient."

"I don't have anywhere else for you to sit," Malani says, going to the chair that faces the clock on the wall. "And I'm not going to rearrange my whole office for a meeting that shouldn't take much longer than five minutes."

"Five minutes, huh?" Tom says, lowering himself into the

chair opposite. "Your assistant mentioned you had a full dance card. I'll try my best not to eat into their time."

"My next appointment is in ninety minutes."

"Ouch," Tom says. "Sounds like you've already made up your mind not to talk to me."

"I told you at the wake that I'm not going to talk to you," Malani says. "Not about Adam, at least."

"That *was* his file, wasn't it?"

She doesn't answer.

"May I look at it?"

"You may not."

Tom grins. He didn't expect her to agree.

"But you already knew I would say that," she says, seeing the look on his face.

"It was worth a try," Tom says. "Who knows? I might have caught you on a particularly sharing day."

"Such a day does not exist." She glances down at his right hand. Tom frowns, turning his hand over to see what she might be looking at. "There's blood there," she says. "Have you hurt yourself?"

Tom sees the dried blood on the side of his hand. He wipes it off on his jeans. "No."

Malani pauses, and then says, "Not yours?"

Tom doesn't answer.

They sit in silence for a moment, looking at each other.

Malani speaks first. "There's really nothing for us to talk about."

Tom holds up his right hand. The hand with blood on it. "You're very observant," he says.

"I suppose I am," she says, though her tone is halting and defensive, like she fears he may be trying to lure her into some kind of verbal trick, as he did at the wake.

"And you've been reviewing your file on Adam," Tom says.

Malani does not respond.

"Checking to see if there was anything you missed?"

She doesn't answer.

"You saw this." He taps the blood. "I get the impression you're thorough. You're certainly observant. I also get the impression that you're concerned about what has happened to Adam. That's why you're reading his file, right? It's why today probably isn't the first time you've gone through it. Am I right?"

Malani doesn't answer his question. "I used to be a deputy," she says, nodding toward his hand. "I was trained to look out for such things."

"Oh really?" Tom sits up. "A deputy? Here, in Samson?"

"Yes."

"I just had a meeting with the sheriff."

"Ah." Malani doesn't say anything more, but Tom gets the impression it's taking all of her willpower not to roll her eyes. "Is it his blood?"

Tom laughs. "No, but I can see you know him."

"There's a reason I'm not a deputy anymore. Where *did* the blood come from?"

Tom tells her. "I take it you're familiar with the militia?"

"Mm."

"Jesus, Malani, I'm hurt," Tom says, grinning. "I could have held back, *not* told you what happened, the way you've held back from me – but instead I was open and honest. Did you see that? Maybe a little two-way action wouldn't be such a bad thing."

"It was your choice to tell me," Malani says. "I never

agreed to share anything, and I've been very clear on that from the moment we first met."

"See, I knew it was a mistake to sit in these chairs."

Malani cracks a smile at this.

"You told me that Adam's death surprised you," Tom says, carrying on undeterred. "That you didn't think he would kill himself. That holds a lot of weight for me, Malani. That's the whole reason I've stuck around. Lorne doesn't believe Adam killed himself, either, and maybe that would have been enough to keep me around, but I would've had doubts, you know? Doubts that Lorne was struggling to come to terms with the truth. But to hear it from *you*, a trained professional, someone who is clearly good at their job. Someone who watches, and listens. Someone who sees things others don't." He holds up his hand with the blood on. "That's not a lot of blood, Malani. But you saw it. The sheriff didn't."

She *does* roll her eyes this time.

"You don't believe that Adam killed himself, do you?"

Malani hesitates for a long time. She looks toward her desk. Toward her certificates. Toward her filing cabinet. Tom watches the side of her face. Watches as she finally turns back to him, having decided how she's going to answer. "No," she says. "I don't believe he killed himself. *But.*" She holds up a finger. "A large part of me does not *want* to believe, either. And I'm aware of that, and I need to acknowl-edge it."

"Because then you'd feel like a failure."

Malani swallows. "Yes."

"If there could be a chance to know for sure that you didn't fail him, you'd want to know, right?"

She nods.

"Then help me. Because whatever happened, I'm going to find out."

Malani takes a deep breath. "In good conscience, I can't reveal details," she says. "But I will give you the *broadest* overview of our meetings, if you somehow think it will help."

Tom holds out his hands. "I won't ask for more."

"Adam was standoffish," she says. "At first. It was clear he didn't want to be here. That it wasn't his choice to come."

"Whose was it?"

"Adam was involved in some street fights. Mostly with out-of-towners, though not always. Deputy Anderson–"

"I've met her."

Malani nods. "She's a good person. She does her best with what she can. Everyone in the department does, insofar as the sheriff will allow them..." She trails off and shakes her head. "I'm getting off-topic. Deputy Anderson knew Adam. She knew he'd been in the Army. She didn't want to have to arrest him. She referred him to me. Made it clear that either he spoke to me, or he would be charged. He came to me, though he clearly wasn't happy about it."

Tom thinks over what she has said. "Random street fights? That doesn't sound self-destructive to you?"

"This was around the time of his divorce."

"Ah."

"Adam was angry, and he needed an outlet for that anger. He wasn't self-destructive, he was just destructive. Momentarily, at least. There were no more incidents. The funny thing is, when we started our sessions and he would talk to me about his divorce, I only ever picked up on a sense of relief."

"Relief that they weren't together anymore?"

"I believe so."

"Did he mention if they had problems?"

"He never said. He was very cagey on certain subjects."

"If he was relieved, why was he fighting strangers?"

"Violence was his outlet. Initially, there probably was some remorse regarding his divorce, before whatever relief he felt could have set in. That could have been why he lashed out."

"Did Adam ever mention being afraid that someone could be coming after him? That they might try to hurt him? Maybe even someone he got into one of those fights with."

"All I'll say to that is, had he ever expressed something along those lines – whether he feared being hurt by someone else, or of hurting himself – I would have passed that on to the relevant authorities."

Tom scratches his cheek. "You said when he first came here he was standoffish, but towards the end he opened up a bit."

"He became friendly," Malani says. "I'm not sure I'd say he ever truly opened up to me. The thing with therapy is, it only works if the patient is honest with both themselves and with me. I can't help them otherwise. They can't help themselves."

"So he could have been lying about everything," Tom says. "He could have successfully hidden how he was truly feeling."

"I don't believe anyone is that good of a liar," Malani says. "Or an actor. There's always a giveaway."

Her eyes are upon Tom. They never leave him. She's always watching, always studying, her brown eyes rarely blinking. Tom gets an idea of what it must feel like to be one of her patients. Of what it must have been like to be Adam.

She sighs. "Or at least, that's what I used to believe."

She's not going to tell him anything else. She won't provide more detail. Tom isn't sure if she knows anything more that could be of use. He starts to stand. "Thank you for your time," he says. "If anything comes up, I'll let you know. Try not to punish yourself, Malani. If he *did* kill himself, that's not your fault. If anyone was there for him, trying to help him, it was you and it was Lorne, and neither of you saw this coming. You did everything you could."

Tom starts to leave, but Malani stops him.

"Tom," she says. Her voice is soft, but it's enough to make him turn.

She doesn't look back at him. She's deliberating. Deciding whether to share.

"There was one subject Adam would open up about," she says. "From day one. He would talk about Lorne."

"Oh?"

"He truly cared for Lorne," she says. "He was concerned for his wellbeing. Adam was more willing to talk about Lorne than he would about himself. He loved him like a brother."

Tom nods, and then he leaves.

12

Tom pauses on the sidewalk outside of Malani's office and runs his hands back through his hair, exhaling. He knows it's only day one, and it's only been a few hours, but he doesn't feel like he's gotten any further forward. He'll go and talk to Olivia, but he's not expecting any great revelations. This isn't for certain, though. She could surprise him. Either way, it's important that he covers all bases.

As Tom starts to turn, he notices a black Honda Accord parked down the road. The same black Honda Accord from earlier, with the out of state plates. Its tail is to him, its hood pointing down the road. Tom can see that there are two men inside. Same as before. He can't see where they're looking, but it would be easy for them to observe him in their mirrors. Tom has watched people like this himself, many times.

Tom crosses the road, and starts walking toward the car. He'll be casual when he confronts them. It could be a coincidence, but he's not sure how much he believes in a coincidence this big, regardless of how small a town like Samson is. He'll ask them if they're lost. If they need directions. He'll get a gauge on them through talking to them.

Except, he doesn't get a chance to talk to them. Doesn't get a chance to get close enough to see what they look like. As he draws nearer, the Honda's engine comes to life and the car quickly pulls away. Tom watches it go down the road. It doesn't speed. It sticks to the limit and then it turns a corner and it's gone.

They saw him coming. Tom knows they did. He saw a flash of eyes spot him in the rear-view mirror, right before the engine was turned on.

Tom is glad he kept the Honda in mind. In a way, he's glad it's here at all. If someone is following him, there must be a reason for that, and the only reason for someone following him in Samson must be to do with Adam's death. Tom wouldn't be here otherwise.

He starts walking again, with renewed purpose now, making his way to Olivia's.

13

In Sudan, it is eight hours ahead of Colorado. It's night. It's dark.

Gunnar Slaughter is armed. He crouches low, behind the wall of a building that has been long-destroyed. It used to be a house. Now, it's ruins. It's cover.

Antoine Fournier is at the corner opposite. Florian Huber is directly behind Antoine, on his six. Gunnar and Antoine look at each other through their night vision. They exchange nods, in position, ready to move in. Gunnar will take the lead. He always does. He leads from the front. He wants to be in the thick of the action, always.

Their enemy is close. Less than half a klick. They can see their encampment, their campfire throwing the shadows of the men circled around it up into the night.

The enemy is a warband, in the employ of a warlord named Abdul Mohamed. Gunnar and his men are in the employ of a rival warlord, called Ibrahim Hussain. Ibrahim Hussain is the richer of the two warlords. He can afford to pay mercenary groups to side with his cause.

There is a lot of trouble across Africa. The Aries Group are kept busy. There's a lot of opportunity for them to make a lot of money in Africa. They're active in many countries here. Gunnar Slaughter is head of the Aries Group. Head, and founder.

Abdul's warband are surrounded. They just don't know it yet. Gunnar gets on the radio. This far out, he doesn't need to keep his voice down. "How does it look from the north?"

A voice comes back into his earpiece. "A dozen."

"Approximately, or precisely?" Gunnar says.

"Precisely thirteen. There were fourteen, one of them on guard, but I've slit his throat."

"Baker's dozen."

"Sir?"

"Thirteen it is," Gunnar says. "Be prepared on my signal."

"Yes, sir."

Gunnar turns to Antoine and Florian. He gestures in hand signals, giving instructions. Antoine is French. Florian is Austrian. The Aries Group is international. His men all understand his instructions, whether spoken or gestured. Gunnar ensures that all new recruits into the Aries Group can speak English. Good English. If not, he won't take them on. Simple. He wants to be able to understand what his men say, and they need to be able to understand him. It's a matter of life and death. He won't take any chances.

Gunnar motions to Antoine and Florian. It's time to move in.

They're armed with AR15s. They advance on the rival warband, weapons raised. They advance from the south. There was a guard in this area too, a fifteenth man, but he's dead also. Florian stabbed him in the heart from behind, covering his mouth to silence him. His body is dumped in a ditch off to the side.

Gunnar reaches the warband first. He drops to a knee and signals for Antoine and Florian to do the same. The three of them raise their rifles. Gunnar picks out a head, silhouetted against the fire. The warband have been careless. The fire is too big. There aren't enough guards. They're not paying enough attention to their surroundings. They're preoccupied with eating, and messing around between themselves. One of them gets up to his feet, gesturing, telling stories. The men gathered around him laugh.

Gunnar does not change his target from the man he has already selected to the man who is now standing. He's an easy target to the men who are north of the group.

Gunnar aims along his sight, to the back of the skull of the sitting man, and opens fire. The man's head explodes.

To Gunnar's right, Antoine picks off his target. To his left, Florian does the same. The men gathered around the fire are stunned at first. The man who is standing is next to die. A shot comes from the north. His skull disappears in a puff of blood.

Gunnar, Antoine, and Florian advance on foot, opening fire indiscriminately. They don't have to be careful. None of the Aries Group are near. The men to the north are not approaching – they hold their line, and they deal with anyone who tries to escape. Gunnar can hear them picking off members of the warband who attempt to run away into the darkness.

The whole thing does not take very long. It's a brief massacre. Within sixty seconds, the thirteen men who were gathered around the fire are all dead. Gunnar confirms the clearance with the north team via his radio.

They rejoin the north team, which is made up of five men. Gunnar motions to one of them. "Radio the forward team," he says. "Tell them we've dealt with the warband and we're on our way to join them."

The man hurries off to do as he's told. Four klicks away, there is a larger team of the Aries Group. Fifty men. A little further than that, there is a village. The village houses Abdul Mohamed's cousin and her family. She'll have an armed guard, but the advance team have told Gunnar it consists of no more than ten men.

Soon, they'll be dead. The armed guard. The cousin. Her family. The whole village.

"All right," Gunnar says. "I want the village taken by midnight, and I want it razed by dawn." He grins at the surrounding men. "For those hours in between, what you do is up to you. Let's go have some fun."

14

The Ford that Tom saw Olivia and Stan turn up to the funeral in is not parked at the house when Tom arrives. The driveway is empty. He knocks regardless, and the door is answered. It's Olivia.

"Hello?" she says. She blinks. She recognises him, but she doesn't know who he is. "You were at the funeral."

"I was," Tom says. "I served with Adam. My name's Tom Rollins."

Her eyes widen momentarily. "Oh," she says. "*Oh.* Yeah, yeah, I know who you are."

"I was hoping we could talk a little," Tom says. "About Adam."

"Uh." Olivia glances back into the house, hesitating, but then she steps aside and holds the door wider. "Sure. Come in. Coffee?"

"A glass of water would be good."

She nods and heads off to the kitchen, and Tom follows. He glances up the stairs and sees framed photographs on the wall. They're all of Olivia and Stan. There are no pictures of Adam, but that is not surprising. From what Lorne said, Adam hadn't lived here for a long time. Tom looks into the living room as he passes. The television is on but muted, no doubt from when Olivia got up to answer his knock. The living room is neat, clean. There is, however, a mostly empty wine glass on the coffee table. No sign of the bottle. A mourning drink.

In the kitchen there is a round table. Olivia motions for him to take a seat, and hands him a glass of water. She pours one for herself and sits down opposite, tying her hair back as she does. She's wearing tracksuit bottoms and a loose blouse. She doesn't have any make-up on. "I'm sorry," she says, "I wasn't expecting any company, otherwise I'd have made myself more presentable."

"That's fine," Tom says. She looks fine as she is. She's a good-looking woman. Not as beautiful as Malani, but Tom doubts many are, especially not in Samson. "You didn't know I was coming. I would have called, but I didn't know your number."

Olivia takes a long drink of water. "What can I do for you, Mr. Rollins? Or can I call you Tom?"

"Tom is fine."

She nods, then glances at the clock on the wall. "Stan is at the gym right now, but he'll be back soon. You wanted to talk about Adam?"

"I want to talk about his death," Tom says.

She recoils at this a little, and Tom thinks maybe he has been too blunt.

"I'm sorry," Tom says, remembering how she was at the funeral and the wake. "I didn't mean for it to come out like that. I know this must be a difficult time for you."

"What do you want to know?" she says, clenching her jaw, steeling herself.

"I want to know if you believe that he killed himself."

She cocks her head at this. Narrows her eyes. "What do you mean?"

"There are people who don't."

She doesn't look surprised. "Lorne?"

"Among others."

"Oh really?" She frowns. "I guess I never really thought about it..." She stares down at her glass of water, her brow knotted. She's silent for a while, thinking about this. She looks back up at him. "What do *you* think?"

"I'm trying to find out."

"I see," Olivia says. She's silent again, looking at her glass of water. She takes another drink and then shifts in her seat. "Have you found anything yet?"

Tom shakes his head. "No. But it's day one. I've kept my expectations under control. Tell me what you think, Olivia."

She bites her lip. She starts to speak but her breath shudders. She can't say anything.

"How did the two of you meet?" Tom says, quickly changing tack in an attempt to put her at ease.

"We met in high school," Olivia says, "but that's not when we got together. We had a few classes together. He was seeing another girl. She was called Carly. She doesn't live around here anymore. She moved away for college and never came back. Me and Adam got together a couple of years after high school, while he was on leave from the Army. We bumped into each other in a bar." She holds out her hands. "It went from there. Next time he was on leave, we got married."

"That's quick," Tom says.

Olivia shrugs one shoulder, both hands wrapped around her glass. "When you're in love, and when you get so little time together because of his job..." She sighs, but it's not wistful. It's filled with regret. "Y'know, I used to think it was exciting that he was in the Army. That he'd been places and he had stories to tell. But that's not what it was like at all. He wouldn't talk about the Army, and it's not like I tried to get him to – he wouldn't *talk*. Full stop. He wouldn't open up to me. We met, and he went off to war. We fell in love, and he went off to war. We got married, and he went back off to war. And then, after going back to war so many times, he came back and it felt like he didn't love me anymore."

"I'm sorry to hear that."

"He was a different man, Tom. He told me what you did for him in Afghanistan. For him and Lorne. After Lorne was sent home, Adam did another tour. It all fell apart after that. Adam came home and he was a completely different man. I barely recognised him anymore. He was drifting for a long time. He couldn't sort his own life out, but he was so desperate to try and fix Lorne's."

"Lorne mentioned that he moved in with you when he first came to Samson."

"That's right. We were suddenly childminders for him, but it never made sense to me. Adam was acting like he had his own life together, and he could fix Lorne's, but he *didn't* have his life together. His life was a mess. It was another few months before he found the overseas work."

"What were you doing for money?"

"I was supporting all of us. Do you know what I did, Tom? I worked in a supermarket. I was a cashier. I was supporting the three of us on a cashier's wage." She shakes her head. "The three of us, and a goddamn mortgage."

"The mortgage was in your name?"

"It was in both of our names, but I was the one paying it off."

"Lorne said that Adam bought this house."

"I'm sure he did. Adam paid it off. Once he was working overseas and he was making more money, he paid off the mortgage. I think it was a make-good."

"For anything in particular?" Tom says.

"Take your pick," Olivia says. She starts counting off on her fingers. "For moving Lorne in without making sure it was all right with me first. For growing distant. For taking a job overseas, but then whenever he was home spending all of his time elsewhere."

"Like where?"

Olivia shrugs. "I don't know. I wasn't invited. I think he was drinking more. He hid it, but I think he was. And by then Lorne had his own place, and Adam would stay over there a lot. It was like he didn't want to come home to me, Tom." She runs her hands through her hair and tightens her ponytail. "I'd seen the signs long before then. That was the point where we were both ready to acknowledge them. To acknowledge that our marriage was over."

"It sounds like you both tried your best," Tom says.

"Sometimes I wonder," Olivia says. "We stayed close, though. We weren't great as a married couple, but we worked out okay as friends."

"You still saw him a lot?"

"I wouldn't say a *lot*, but I always tried to see him when he was back from overseas. He worked hard. He was away a lot. I was glad for him. But it meant I only saw him about four times in the last year."

"When'd you see him last?"

Olivia grits her teeth. She blinks, over and over, trying not to cry. "It was the day he died."

"I didn't know that."

She sniffs and runs a finger under each of her eyes. "He was doing better, Tom. He was doing so much better. Since he started seeing a therapist. He went from his lowest point to finally levelling out."

"When you say he was doing better, do you mean after your divorce, when he was getting into street fights?"

She seems surprised he knows this, but she doesn't say anything. "Yes, but there was more than that. Not everyone saw it, but I did. He couldn't hide it from me. I was his wife."

"What do you mean?"

"He had depressive episodes," Olivia says. "He was prone to them. That distance I mentioned earlier? A lot of it came from his depression."

Tom thinks about this. "He was depressed?"

"I don't know if I'd say he was *depressed* – like, he wasn't always. But sometimes?"

"I don't think depression needs to be a constant thing. It can come and go."

"Oh." Olivia clasps her hands and looks down at them.

They sit in silence for a moment. Tom watches Olivia. She's very pretty. As he thought earlier, not as attractive as Malani, but still very good looking. She looks like she could have acted, if she wanted to. Or modelled. Even dressed down and without make-up, it's clear how eye catching she is.

Tom doesn't think about her like that, though. It's just an observation. She was the wife of one of his Army brothers. By extension, she's family, too.

"Olivia," Tom says. "Do you think Adam killed himself?"

Her breath shudders. She looks Tom in the eye. "I don't know."

Tom nods. He thinks about what she has said about Adam being depressed. He wonders if Malani noticed this, or if he kept it hidden from her. He wonders if Lorne ever noticed.

"Do you know if he had any enemies? If he was worried about anyone?"

"If he was, he never mentioned it to me," Olivia says.

"You said he hid his depression from other people, but he couldn't hide it from you. What about with this? Did you pick up on any concerns?"

Olivia thinks, but then shakes her head. "No," she says. "Not that I can think of."

Tom hears the front door opening.

"Hey, I'm home." A man's voice. Stan Seeger, Tom assumes.

"I'm in the kitchen," Olivia calls to him. "With Tom Rollins."

Stan pokes his head around the doorframe, frowning. "Sorry, who?" He looks at Tom.

Tom gets to his feet and offers his hand. He introduces himself, explains how he knew Adam.

"Oh, right," Stan says, shaking his hand. He has a strong grip. "Army buddy, huh? Like Lorne."

"Yeah," Tom says. "Like Lorne."

Stan is wearing a vest. There is sweat on his collar bone, and at the sides of his head where his dark hair is slicked back. Olivia mentioned he was at the gym. He looks like he works out regularly. He looks strong. Like his muscles aren't just for show. He looks Tom in the eye, unblinking, and won't look away. Tom gets a decent read on him and his Alpha male bullshit. Lorne mentioned his posturing. Olivia's being with him surprises Tom. Tom didn't know Adam as well as he would have liked, but he never saw him like this. The fact Lorne dislikes Stan for this attitude makes him suspect Lorne never saw Adam act like this, either. For Olivia, perhaps she was looking for someone completely different in a new partner as she moved on from her divorce from Adam.

Tom doesn't like the way Stan is looking at him. Trying to size him up. Trying to intimidate him, like he has something to prove. Tom decides to off-balance him. "You and Adam get along, Stan?"

"Huh?" Stan says.

"This was his home, right? Must be awkward living here, knowing he used to."

"Tom?" Olivia says, surprised by his change in tone.

Stan backs up now, caught off guard. He breaks his eye contact. "We got along fine," he says, managing to keep his voice clear. Tom almost expected him to mumble. "We didn't see much of each other. He and Olivia stayed close. That didn't mean I had to have anything to do with him."

"How'd you feel about that? About them staying friends."

Stan casually steps back into the kitchen's doorway. He's able to make eye contact again now that there is more distance between them. He shrugs. "Why would it bother me?"

"Tom, what are you getting at?" Olivia says.

"Nothing," Tom says. "Just getting acquainted." He turns back to Olivia. He smiles. "I've taken up enough of your time, Olivia. Thanks for talking to me."

Olivia starts to stand, but Tom holds up a hand. "It's

okay," he says. "I can let myself out." He turns to leave. Stan steps out of his way. "Nice to meet you too, Stan. Sorry we couldn't talk for longer."

"Will we see you around?" Olivia says from the table.

Tom thinks on everything Olivia has told him. "Maybe," he says. "I'm not sure. You've given me a lot to think about."

15

J ason sits in the Honda. He's parked at a gas station, eating a hot dog. He licks ketchup from his thumb. He's parked far away from where there's a risk of Tom Rollins spotting the car. He's already made them. He's approached them. They're not taking any risks. They're going to have to be careful going forward.

Jason finishes the hotdog and wipes his mouth with the napkin. He can see Harry approaching. Harry comes to the window. Jason rolls it down.

"He was in with the widow a while," Harry says. "But he's on the move again."

"Which direction?"

"Back toward town."

Jason nods. "Can we call her the widow when they hadn't been together for a few years?"

"It doesn't matter. You know who I'm talking about." Harry sniffs. "You had a hotdog?"

"I did."

"From the gas station?"

"Yeah."

Harry pauses. "How was it?"

"It was okay."

Harry glances back at the gas station. He grunts. "I'm not sure I wanna risk it," he says. He comes around the side of the car and gets into the passenger seat. "I know I won't regret this if you start throwing up later. Or shitting blood."

Jason laughs. "It wasn't as bad as that."

Harry looks through the windshield and down the road. "We should call Gunnar."

Jason blows air. "I think I'd rather shit blood."

Harry smirks. "Let's get back to the hotel and place the call."

"Is Rollins clear?"

"He's not on our route."

Jason nods and starts the car. He drives to the hotel and parks around the back, concealing the Honda. They go up to the room and call Gunnar online. It will be late in Sudan. They doubt he'll be sleeping.

The call is answered by Antoine Fournier. Gunnar's right-hand man. His image is momentarily pixelated, but then it comes clear. "Jason," he says. "Harry. What can I do for you both?" His English is perfect, his French accent little more than an inflection.

"We need to talk to Gunnar," Jason says.

In the background, behind Antoine, they can hear gunshots and laughter. Jason catches a brief glimpse of a fire burning in the distance. "He may be busy," Antoine says. "I will go see."

Antoine disappears, and Jason and Harry are left staring

into space. They see men running around. Some men they recognise.

The screen is not unoccupied for long. Gunnar appears, wiping something that looks like blood from the corner of his mouth. "What do you want?" he says, getting straight to the point.

Jason clears his throat. "We want to provide a situation update."

"Is there something to report?" Gunnar says. He stares at them both. Even through the screen, and with thousands of miles between them, his unblinking gaze is cutting. Jason feels his scalp tighten. "I hope it's good."

"A potential issue has arisen," Harry says, leaning forward. "It could be something, it could be nothing, but we thought it best you should know."

"Cut to the chase," Gunnar says.

"An ex-Army buddy of Adam's turned up for the funeral," Jason says. "Name of Tom Rollins. We did some digging on him. The guy's hardcore."

Gunnar looks unimpressed. "And?"

"And he's hanging around," Jason says.

"Staying with Lorne," Harry says.

"He's spent today going around town," Jason says. "He's talked to the sheriff, to Adam's therapist, and to his ex-wife. Three points of interest – and he's obviously talked to Lorne, too, so that's four. We don't know for sure but it seems like he's looking into Adam's death."

Gunnar nods, once. "And you think we should be concerned about this Tom Rollins?"

"There's potential for him to cause us issues," Jason says.

"You've been trailing him today," Gunnar says.

"He made us," Harry says. "We were able to give him the slip. After that, we played it careful. Gave him a wide berth, but we've kept track of him."

"He saw you?"

"He saw our vehicle," Jason says quickly. "He didn't see *us*."

Gunnar doesn't say anything, but he doesn't look happy.

"It looks like Rollins is going to hang around," Harry says. "We wanted to make you aware. Like we said, there's potential for him to cause us problems."

"What kind of hardcore?" Gunnar says.

"We'll send you everything we've been able to find on him."

"There's a lot?"

"He's been busy."

"All right," Gunnar says. There's a scream behind him, a woman's scream, and he glances back over his shoulder toward the sound and grins. He turns back to the screen. "He's staying with Lorne?"

"That's right," Jason says.

"I'm not willing to waste time on this, boys," Gunnar says. "You've been careful so far, but I'm giving you permission to get heavy. That clear? Find out what this Rollins knows. Find out what Lorne knows. You don't need to be gentle about it."

"Understood," Jason says.

"Good," Gunnar says. "I expect results, boys, and I expect them soon. Now I need to get back to the party. I'm sure we'll talk again soon."

He hangs up.

Jason feels a momentary pang, knowing what he's missing out on over there in Sudan.

"Well," Harry says, getting to his feet. Jason knows he's probably feeling the same sense of missing out. "You heard the man. Let's get heavy."

Jason grins. At least they can finally make their own kind of fun. "Rock and roll."

16

Tom gets back to the trailer park, but Lorne isn't home. He's still at work. Tom goes to the bar to meet with him, and to tell him about his day.

Colin is working, too. He sits at the far end of the counter, away from their conversation. He reads a magazine about cars.

"So, nothing solid?" Lorne says when Tom is finished.

Tom thinks about what Olivia said about Adam's depression. He doesn't mention this yet. "No," he says, "nothing solid."

"What did you make of Stan?" Lorne says.

"I thought he was an asshole."

Lorne snorts. "Uh-huh. And then some."

"You said there weren't any problems between him and Adam."

"Not that I know of. Doesn't mean the guy ain't an asshole. I've got no time for dudebros like him." Lorne checks the time. "I finish in like ten minutes. Let's take a drive and talk some more. There's a place I want to show you."

Colin overhears this last. "You can go now if you want, Lorne. It ain't busy. I'm sure I'll manage this horde."

Tom glances back at the room. There are seven people present. Three of them are together.

Tom and Lorne leave the bar and go to Tom's car, still parked nearby from yesterday when he drove to the wake. "Colin live far from here?" Tom says.

"Hell no," Lorne says. "He lives just around the back. You can't see it from here, but there's another building attached. It's just small, but it's only him who lives there."

"I can't imagine there's many people who would like living so close to their work, even if it *is* their own business."

Lorne shrugs. "I don't think he minds. He thinks of it as extra security. He has a shotgun that he keeps close to the door in case he thinks someone's breaking into his bar and he needs to come and chase them off."

"Anyone tried to break into it before?"

"Not so long as I've worked here." They reach the car. "I'll direct you," Lorne says as he gets in. "For now, head east. It's just outside of town."

Tom starts driving. They can talk properly about Adam when they get where they're going. For now, Tom asks, "You know much about the militia around here?"

"The militia?" Lorne says, turning back from the window. "Yeah, I've heard about them. Only seen them a couple of times, though. They don't come to the bar. Why? You heard something?"

"I saw them," Tom says. He tells him about their altercation.

Lorne laughs. "Shit, man, you better be careful. They ain't gonna like that."

"They don't worry me."

Lorne looks at him. "I bet they don't," he says finally.

"Where do they hide out?"

"Some ranch outside of town. They live out there like the Manson family or something." He laughs again. "You get close enough to it, you can hear them shooting."

"Shooting at what?"

"I dunno – just target practice, I think. Maybe coyotes."

"Are we passing near the ranch where we're going?" Tom is curious if they'll see it in the distance.

"No," Lorne says. "That's north – at the base of the mountains."

They leave Samson and Lorne directs Tom where to go. Tells him where to turn off. "A little ways down here, we're gonna park up. Continue the rest of the way on foot."

The road is clearly unused, and seems to lead to nowhere. To Tom's right, there is a field that gradually begins to ascend into a hill. The road becomes cracked and overgrown with weeds. He pulls to the side and kills the engine. Whatever this road led to is clearly not there anymore.

"Where did this road go?" Tom says.

"Abattoir," Lorne says. "But that closed down a long time ago. Decades, in fact. Adam told me. Hell, everything I know about this area I learned from him."

They get out of the car and Lorne leads them up the hill Tom saw forming to his right. At the top, there is a tree. A blue spruce. They reach the tree and Lorne stops. He turns, and there is a sad smile on his face. "This is it," he says.

Tom looks around. "This is what?"

"What I wanted to show you." Lorne lowers himself to

the ground, sitting cross-legged on the grass close to the tree. He looks back the way they've come.

Still standing, Tom turns. He can see all of Samson in the distance and, beyond that, the fields and mountains that surround the town. Far off to his right, at the base of the mountains, he sees something that could be the ranch where the militia lives, or it could be a farm. Whatever it is, it's to the north, and at the base of the mountains, where Lorne said the militia are.

"Take a seat," Lorne says.

Tom does.

"This was our spot," Lorne says. "Adam brought me here. I don't know how long he'd been coming here before that. Not even Olivia knows about it. Not through Adam, anyway. There was one time, the first time he brought me here, my PTSD was real bad. My chest was tight and it was like I could barely breathe. I don't know what made him think of it, but Adam brought me straight here. There's something about this spot, Tom. About the view." He takes a deep breath in through his nose. "The fresh air. The smell of the tree. The feel of the grass. It's peaceful. It brings *me* peace."

Tom looks at him and realises there is a tear rolling down his cheek.

"This is my first time out here," Lorne says, "since..." He closes his eyes for a moment, and keeps them closed. When he opens them again, he says, "He was like a brother to me, Tom. I was closer to him than I was to my real brothers. I've got two, and I can't remember the last time I spoke to either of them. But I wanted to come back here. To mine and Adam's spot. We used to come here all the time, to just drink and shoot the shit. To look at the view and to watch the stars. I wasn't brave enough to come here alone. Not for the first time. And I wanted to show it to you." Lorne motions to the view before them. It's early evening and the sun is going down. Everything is golden. "It's very beautiful here. I love it here. Samson isn't where I'm from, but it feels like home to me now. Even with Adam gone, I can't leave."

They stare at the view in silence for a while. Tom takes it all in. He imagines looking at it through Adam's eyes. Imagines him sitting here with his friend, in a place of peace while simultaneously plagued with depressive thoughts that he refused to share.

"I didn't know that you found Adam's body, Lorne," Tom says, his voice soft. "I'm sorry you had to go through that."

Lorne sniffs. He doesn't say anything. Tom looks at him. He's grimacing. Remembering. Tom doubts he'll ever forget.

"As soon as I saw him, I knew it was too late," Lorne says suddenly. "I knew there was nothing I could do. I didn't try to hold his legs and prop him up or anything, didn't try to save him, because there was nothing *to* save. There wasn't a breath left in him. I've seen enough dead bodies to know when a person is well and truly dead." He runs a hand down his face. "I called the cops. It was all I could do."

Lorne takes a long, deep, shuddering breath. Tom gives him a moment. He looks toward Samson and considers his next moves. He's starting to doubt that there was anything nefarious in Adam's death. All he has to go on are Lorne and Malani's doubts. Malani might be a trained professional, but she could still be wrong. Tom needs concrete proof. Thus far, he hasn't been able to find anything. No mention of enemies. No mention of Adam's fears. The only potentially concrete thing he's been given has come from Olivia – that Adam was prone to depression. Of course, not all depressed people kill themselves, but the fact appears to be that *this* depressed person could have.

There is, however, the black Honda Accord with the out of state plates. The car that has been following Tom around town. The car that quickly fled when he attempted to confront it. This disturbs him. Makes him wonder about Adam's death, and if the men in the car are involved somehow. Or if they had nothing to do with it at all. If they're here for Tom. If they're from *his* past, and they're going to be a future problem for him. It wouldn't be the first time. He's made plenty of enemies.

Tom's investigation isn't over. He's not ready to give up on the possibility that Adam did not kill himself just yet. There are still some stones left to turn.

The sun is getting lower, and the view is no longer golden. It will be dark soon. By the time they get back to Samson, it will be dark enough for what Tom must do next.

He turns to Lorne. "You have a key for Adam's house, right?"

Lorne clears his throat. "Yeah. Why?"

"Because I want to go there," Tom says. "I haven't been getting anywhere talking to people who knew him. I want to see what his home can tell me."

17

Adam's house is on the outskirts of Samson. The opposite side of town to where Olivia lives. Tom and Lorne go to the back door, and find that they don't need to use the key. The glass has been smashed, and the back door has been unlocked. Tom and Lorne exchange looks.

"Someone's broken in," Lorne says.

"It could have been kids," Tom says. "Knowing that the house is empty. Using it as a place to hang out, or seeing if there was anything they could steal."

Lorne looks furious.

"Go wait in the car," Tom says. "Keep an eye on the street. If it looks like anyone is coming, call me."

Lorne nods, but he has to drag himself away.

Tom pushes open the unlocked door. It leads him into the kitchen. There are signs of weathering on the floor – the linoleum is damp, and leaves have blown in. Tom takes a knife from the rack and steps further into the house.

"If anyone's in here, show yourself now." He waits for a

response. The house is still. He keeps hold of the knife anyway, just in case.

Tom starts his search upstairs. On his way up, he spots where Adam was hanged from and he pauses. The paint on the railing above, on the landing, has been scraped away where the rope was anchored. Beneath the banister, at the wall, there are dark marks where the rope has swayed. On the ground below there are dark markings that have stained the carpet. Tom wonders who cleared this up. Who cut down the rope, and who mopped up the released bodily fluids. If it was the sheriff's department, or if it was Lorne.

Tom stares at the space for a moment. He can see Adam hanging there, his limp body swaying slightly, the sound of the railing above creaking. All alone at the end of his life. All alone in an empty, dark, cold house.

Tom moves on.

Everything in the house is mostly intact, but there are signs that a search has already taken place. Subtle things. Missing items – the kind of things Tom would understand being gone if there was an investigation, but since there's not they should be here. Things like a cell phone. A laptop. In Adam's bedroom, at the foot of his bed, there is a desk, but no computer upon it. These items could have been stolen, but then in one of the drawers of the desk Tom finds an address book. He flicks through it. A page has been torn out. A page in the E section. Tom thinks. He hasn't come across anyone with an E surname. Again, it could be nothing, just an address that Adam no longer had any use for, but it's worth looking into. Tom can see indentations in the page following on from the one that is missing. A small block of detail.

In another drawer, Tom finds a pencil. He traces over the

indentations to see what the torn-out page said. He reads a name and an address. The name is Gabe Elcoat. The address is in Boulder. Tom tears this page out and folds it before slipping it into his pocket. He flicks through the rest of the address book. There's nothing that catches his eye. Names of people and places he's already aware of.

There is a spare room next to Adam's bedroom. It has a weapons locker bolted to the wall. There's nothing else in the room. There's nothing in the weapons locker, either. The lock has been picked and the weapons have been cleared out. Again, this could be thieves. This robbery doesn't appear to have necessarily been targeted at Adam in an effort to conceal anything after his death.

Tom looks the rest of the house over. There's nothing to find. But he notices there are some things that haven't been taken that he would expect a thief to take. The television, for a start. A record player, and the record collection to go with it. Tom flicks through the albums. It's a decent selection. Led Zeppelin, AC/DC, Jimi Hendrix, The Beatles, The Doors, Janis Joplin, Jefferson Airplane. Stuff that would easily sell, either out the back of a car or online. There's a small Blu-ray collection, too, in a cabinet next to the television. Most of them are Westerns, along with a couple of samurai movies. Again, these are untouched.

Tom returns the knife to the rack in the kitchen. He has searched the house thoroughly. There's nothing else here for him to find. Tomorrow, he'll find out who Gabe Elcoat of Boulder, Colorado, is. Find out what his connection to Adam was. After that, other than the men in the Honda, Tom is all out of leads.

18

"Did you find anything?" Lorne says as Tom gets back into the car.

Tom starts the engine, but he doesn't drive yet. "Hard to tell," he says, looking down the road. It's quiet. He can see someone out walking their dog, but they're far off down on the sidewalk and walking in the opposite direction. "The place hadn't been tossed, but things had been taken. Some things you'd expect to be gone, they were gone. Some things you'd expect to be stolen, they were still there."

"What was taken?"

"Laptop, cell phone, guns."

Lorne tilts his head. "They took his guns?"

Tom nods. "What did he have?"

"Hunting rifles, mostly. Couple of handguns." Lorne pauses. "So what do you make of it?"

"It didn't look like regular theft," Tom says. "Like I said, it's hard to tell. The place hadn't been ripped apart, but I could see that it had been searched. I don't know what it looked like beforehand so I can't say if things were out of place."

"You want me to go in and take a look?"

Tom remembers seeing the space where Adam hanged himself. He doesn't want Lorne to have to see that again. He has no idea how it could affect him. "There's no point," Tom says. "For all we know, the sheriff's department could have taken a cursory look at the place. There's no investigation, but that doesn't mean they didn't perform a minor search. The place could look different to you, and it's nothing more than them not putting things back where they found them."

"Okay," Lorne says, "so what next?"

Tom starts driving, getting them away from outside of Adam's house, and away from his neighbourhood. "I found a name, and an address. It could be nothing, it could be something. Tomorrow, I'll look into it. For now, we go back to the trailer and we rest up. It's late. Nothing more we can do."

They reach a crossroads. The lights are red. Tom stops the car. Nothing comes through. It's late and the town is quiet. Tom can see lights on in some of the nearby buildings. Apartments. People in their homes. Other than this, there are few other signs of life. The small businesses beneath them – cafes, a hardware store – are long closed. The town is winding down for sleep. Closer to the centre, where the bars and restaurants are, and the main supermarket, there are probably more signs of life. But not here on the outskirts.

The light turns green. Nothing came through all the time it was on red. Tom pulls through the intersection.

From the left, a parked car suddenly comes to life, its lights off, and it roars toward Tom's car. Tom sees it out the corner of his eye. Lorne spots it soon after.

"Holy shit!"

Out the corner of his eye, Tom sees the dark blur heading their way. It's coming fast. In the split-second before impact, Tom attempts to speed his car clear, stamping the pedal to the floor. It's not enough to get them through. The car is upon them.

It is, however, enough to get Tom clear of the immediate collision. The speed the car is coming at them, it would likely kill him. Instead, it makes impact with the door behind him. Metal crumples. Glass shatters. The charging car keeps coming. Tom's car begins to rise, and to topple. Everything feels like it's in slow motion. The car rolls onto its roof, and then onto its side. Tom feels his body thrown around. He bangs his head. Flying shards of glass cut him across the cheeks and nose. He tastes his blood. The car rolls onto its side, and finally ends right way up.

Tom is dazed, but he knows he needs to stay alert. His vision is blurred. He slaps his bloodied cheeks, blinking hard, trying to focus. His vision gradually clears. He feels nauseous. Beside him, Lorne is breathing hard. His eyes are closed tight. Tom looks to him. He's hyperventilating. He can't move. He's having a panic attack.

19

Tom manages to force his door open. The car is wrecked. It won't drive. He falls out, his legs weak, but manages to get back to his feet, using the side of the damaged car to drag himself up. He looks over the top of it, searching for the car that struck them. It's still driving, but slow. It's been damaged, too, its front end crumpled and dragging along the ground. It passes beneath a streetlamp. Tom is not surprised to see that it's the black Honda Accord.

Tom leans back into the car, trying to get Lorne's attention. "Lorne! Lorne, come on, we need to go!"

Lorne's eyes remain tight shut. His breathing hard and panicked. He can't hear Tom.

"*Shit.*"

Tom hurries around the car to Lorne's side. He glances back at the Honda. The men aren't out of it yet, but Tom knows they're coming. They're not going to stop at a crash. They're going to want to finish the job.

He tears at Lorne's door, managing to yank it open. He

reaches in and unbuckles him from the seat. He looks back again while he works, blinking blood out of his eyes. The Honda's door has been pushed open. The men inside are moving slowly. They've been dazed by the collision, too.

Lorne can't move. He's pinned to his chair. Tom can't communicate with him. Doesn't have the time to calm him. All he can do is get him clear. He pulls him forward, gets him out of the car, and slings him over his shoulder.

The two men are out of the Honda now. They're carrying weapons. They're too far and it's too dark, and Tom doesn't have time to hang around and study them to see what they're packing. They look handheld, and automatic. With Lorne over his shoulder, Tom starts running.

There are gunshots behind him. Automatic, as he thought. They tear into the road behind and around him. Tom runs to the nearest building, hoping his legs don't give out beneath him. They don't. They can't afford to. If he falls, he's dead. He and Lorne both.

He reaches the building and disappears into the darkness of the alleyway between this building and its neighbour. He gets to the end and he cuts left. He thinks about stopping, about finding a dark place to hide and launch an ambush when their pursuers get close enough. Tom is unarmed, but he can get the drop on them. Disarm at least one of them and turn their weapon on the other.

He can't, though. Not with Lorne suffering a panic attack. Right now, he needs to get clear. Needs to get Lorne somewhere safe.

He keeps running.

20

Jason follows, armed with a MAC-10. Harry is behind him, covering his rear in case of ambush, carrying a Steyr TMP. Jason fired upon Rollins and Lorne as they made their escape. He wasn't trying to kill him, just to get them to stop. To surrender. They were too close to the alleyway, though. They kept running.

Or, to be more precise, Rollins kept running. It was hard to tell if Lorne was still alive, slung over his shoulder. He could have been badly hurt. Regardless, Jason and Harry are on the hunt for them both. Jason is already thinking how they might need to kill Rollins outright. He's too dangerous. Too strong. Could be a better idea to keep Lorne alive and talk to *him*. Find out what he knows, or what Rollins might have found. Rollins won't talk. Lorne might. He'll be the easier of the two to break. Jason and Harry are aware of his PTSD. Aware that he is already a broken man.

"J," Harry says. They will not use their names. They don't know who might hear.

Jason pauses halfway down the alley, turning back.

"A car passed the crash," Harry says. "There's people at the windows in the apartments nearby. Any of them could call the cops. They probably already have."

Jason grits his teeth. "Go back and get the car. Circle around to the end of the block. I'll continue the search. If I don't have them by then, we'll get clear."

Harry nods and turns, then sets off at a run back to the Honda.

Jason continues on down the alleyway, more cautious now. He listens as he goes, stepping lightly. He can't hear any footsteps. Can't hear any running. Behind, far behind, he can hear Harry driving the wrecked Honda. Can hear its front scraping along the road as he clears the crash site.

Jason sticks close to the wall as he nears the end of the alleyway, keeping the MAC-10 raised. He's ready to open fire as soon as he comes face to face with Rollins. He won't take any chances. He looks around the corner opposite, and peers around the corner at his shoulder. It's clear. It leads out onto the road. Jason steps out, weapon raised. The area is empty. He presses on. This is the only way Rollins and Lorne could have come out. He sticks to this side of the road, but he looks to the other side. There are trees there. Rollins and Lorne could have disappeared there. Jason can't think of anywhere else they could have gone to have disappeared so fast.

"*Fuck.*"

He wants to follow, but he hears sirens approaching. They're coming from off to his left. He can see their red and blue lights coming closer. Jason turns right. He runs down the sidewalk toward Harry and the Honda, though he remains alert, knowing Rollins could be anywhere.

He reaches the car and dives inside. Harry drives. He

goes as fast as the car is able. It's not very fast. It's too damaged.

"Get us out of town," Jason says. "The cops will be held up at the crash site."

Harry takes side roads out of town, avoiding the main route. "We're going to have to tell Gunnar," Harry says. "He won't be happy. Rollins knows for sure we're coming after him."

Jason is all too aware of this. He doesn't respond, not at first. After a while he says, "He knows we're after him, but he doesn't know who we are. He doesn't know who we're with."

Outside of town, they dump the Honda in a field. Jason goes to the trunk. He takes Adam's hunting rifles out and hands them to Harry. "Go bury them," he says. "Away from here." He takes Adam's handguns – a couple of Glocks – and keeps them, tucking them both down the back of his jeans. He'll give one to Harry when he returns. Jason burns the car out. The Honda was stolen. There is no record of their having had it. They'll steal another one from another town and return to Samson.

Jason is already walking down the road when Harry catches up to him. The car burns brightly behind them.

"That was a fucking disaster," Harry says.

Jason grunts. He presses on. They have a long way to walk. "It won't happen again," he says.

21

Tom checked himself and Lorne into a motel. Tom washed the dried blood from his face. There were two cuts on his left cheek, one longer than the other, and another across the bridge of his nose. Another on the right side of his neck, quite long and quite deep, which could have proved problematic if it had gone any deeper. The cuts were all scabbed over and didn't require any kind of dressing. After he was able to calm Lorne down, to get his breathing back to normal, Tom stood on guard. Unarmed, still, but at least if he saw anyone coming they had a chance to get a head start.

In the morning, as the sun begins to rise, Tom goes into the room, expecting to find Lorne asleep. Lorne is not asleep. He's sitting on the bed, his knees drawn up to his chest and his arms wrapped around them. He's pale. His face looks hollowed out, and his eyes sunken. He's ghostly.

"I'm sorry, Tom," he says, looking up as Tom enters. Lorne shakes his head, ashamed. "I fell apart... I'm sorry... I'm so fucking useless..."

Tom places a hand on his shoulder and squeezes. "That's not true. You're not useless."

"I couldn't do anything!" Lorne says, shrugging his hand off. "I couldn't even get out of the car! You had to carry me! You had to carry me like I was a fucking child…"

Tom puts his hand back on his shoulder. "Lorne," he says, his voice firm. "Look at me. You're not useless."

The two men stare at each other for a long time. Neither of them speaks.

Eventually, Lorne nods. He squeezes Tom's hand.

"Let's move," Tom says. "Back to town. Back to your trailer. We need to make sure no one's been by there."

"Shit," Lorne says, "I hadn't considered that."

"Let's hope they haven't either," Tom says. "Because I don't want to remain unarmed in this town a minute longer."

They walk across town, back to the trailer park and Lorne's home. When they get there, there are two cruisers parked outside. The sheriff is present, along with Deputy Norton and another deputy Tom doesn't recognise. When they're close enough, Tom sees that his name tag reads Lowell.

"Rollins," Sheriff Rooker says, adjusting his belt and stepping forward. He looks both men over. "Lorne. I was wondering when the two of you might show up."

"We kept you waiting long, Sheriff?" Tom says.

"Not long," Rooker says. Norton and Lowell flank him, sticking close to their cruisers. "Ten minutes, give or take. I understand you were in a car accident last night, Rollins."

"Hit and run," Tom says. "The other driver sped off. We didn't get a chance to exchange details."

Rooker looks him over, checking the cuts on his face and neck. "Looks like they hit you hard."

"It wasn't a gentle tap."

"And what about the gunshots? Witnesses at the scene saw one of the men of the crashing car pursuing two other men and opening fire. One of the fleeing men had the other over his shoulder." He glances at Lorne. "We've found the bullets. Some of them are still embedded in the tarmac. I assume the men fleeing were you?"

"The shooting took us by surprise, too," Tom says. "I'm not sure what we did to piss them off. *They* hit us."

Rooker is silent while he takes a step back. He appraises them both. "A car hits you, the drivers shoot at you, and you don't call us?"

"I was worried Lorne was hurt," Tom says. He's not going to tell the sheriff where they hid out. He's not going to give the sheriff too much information. This is Tom's business, not his. "I took him straight to a hospital. I haven't had time to call anyone."

Rooker looks Lorne over. "You look in worse shape than Lorne is, Mr. Rollins."

"They took a look at me, too," Tom says. "You don't need to worry."

"Mm. You get a good look at the shooters?"

"No," Tom says. "Did your witnesses?"

Rooker doesn't answer. "We found the car they were driving a couple of miles outside of town. It had been burned out."

Tom keeps a mental note of this. Next time the men come at him, they won't be driving the black Honda Accord with the out of state plates. That makes them more dangerous. He'll have to be extra vigilant.

"What do you make of that?" Rooker says.

"What do *I* make of that?" Tom says. "I'm afraid I can't do your job for you, Sheriff. What do *you* make of it?"

Rooker gives him a hard look. "It sounds like trouble, Mr. Rollins. And I warned you against making trouble."

"Then we're both in luck, because I wasn't making it. I just got caught up in it is all. You want my thoughts? Fine, I'll share them with you – free of charge, because I think you could use all the help you can get. I think it was joy-riders. Not necessarily from this town, but they were joy-riders and that was a stolen car. I'm sure you're looking into that yourself already, right? Maybe you already know it was a stolen car."

Rooker says nothing.

Tom continues, planting seeds to throw the sheriff off the scent of what really happened. "They likely stole it at gunpoint. The same guns they used to fire on us. And then they burned it out, to erase all trace of themselves. How does that sound to you, Sheriff?"

Rooker says nothing. His face is hard, and his jaw is set. He takes a deep breath. "What hospital did you go to?"

"The only one in town."

"And if I pay them a visit and ask about you, they'll remember your being there?"

Tom calls his bluff. "I assume they will. It looked like it was a quiet night for them."

Tom holds Rooker's eye while Rooker studies him. Tom doesn't believe he'll go to the hospital to check. There's nothing to be gained from it. Either Tom is lying or he's telling the truth. Either way, it doesn't provide him with any kind of answer as to what happened at the crash, or who the shooters were.

"Sheriff, I want to go into my home," Lorne says. His voice is shaky. He's fragile. He looks it, too. "If you need a statement or something, can we do it some other time? It was a long night."

Rooker's eyes never leave Tom. "Sure," he says. "But let me make something very clear, Rollins. I told you back at the station – I don't want any trouble in my town. If I find out you've come here looking for it, or if you're making it, I swear to God I *will* escort you out of here."

Tom stands his ground. "What is it that you're afraid of, Sheriff?"

Rooker blinks at this. He's caught off guard. "I'll be keeping an eye on you, Rollins," he says, preparing himself to leave. "No more issues. No more trouble. No more noise. You've been warned." He turns and motions to his deputies. They get into their cruisers and turn to go.

"Your sheriff's an asshole," Tom says to Lorne. "And he's hiding something."

"What do you mean?" Lorne says.

"Why's he so desperate for me to leave?" Tom says. "All of his threats. All of his warnings. His constant reaffirming that he doesn't want any trouble here in town. Why?"

"It's his job to not want trouble," Lorne says.

"Sure, but why does he keep directing that at me?"

"'Cos you beat up the militia and got into a car crash, which was followed up by a shooting," Lorne says. "Maybe that's why?"

Tom laughs. They watch the cruisers leave. "I still think there's more there," Tom says. "Something has scared him. I can see it in his eyes. He's trying to conceal it with bravado, but it's still there."

"Why'd you lie to him about last night?" Lorne says, unlocking the trailer door.

"Because someone took a shot at us," Tom says. "And I don't like that. It could have something to do with Adam, or it might not. Either way, we're going to deal with it ourselves."

"I don't think I'm in much condition to be of use to you, Tom. I wish I was but... I fall apart."

Tom doesn't get a chance to respond. As the cruisers leave, another car comes into view. A familiar car. A blue BMW.

Malani.

22

M alani gets out of the car and strides over. She wears a charcoal grey pantsuit. Her hair is tied back. Her face is focussed. "Can I talk to you?" she says, her eyes burning into Tom. They narrow when she sees the cuts and scabs on his face, but she doesn't question them.

She looks angry. Tom isn't sure why it seems to be directed toward him. "Sure," he says, turning toward the trailer.

"In private," Malani says, cutting her eyes toward Lorne.

Lorne holds up his hands. Tom notices that they're trembling slightly. "I need to sleep," Lorne says. "I have a shift in a few hours. Supposed to start just after lunch. If I wanna make it, I need to get some rest."

Tom steps away from the trailer while Lorne disappears inside.

"In my car," Malani says, tilting her head.

Tom follows her. He gets into the passenger seat. Malani glares at him, unblinking.

"I'd say it's a nice surprise to have such a beautiful woman come and search me out like this," Tom says, "except you look furious to have found me."

Malani ignores him. "I'm going to ask you a question," she says, "and I want you to answer truthfully. And I want you to understand that I will know – I will *know* – if you are lying."

Tom frowns. "Okay."

Malani stares at him a moment longer before she asks her question. "Last night," she says, "did you break into my office?"

"No," Tom says.

Malani studies him. Tom doesn't look away. His gaze is steady. Malani takes a deep breath and turns to the side, slamming her steering wheel with the flat of her hand. "Damn it," she says.

"What was taken?" Tom says, though he thinks he already knows.

"Files," she says.

"And Adam's was one of them," Tom says. "That's why you came here. To find me."

She nods.

"Multiple files?"

"Yes."

"If a handful of files were taken, that was likely to disguise the one they were truly after."

Malani nods again.

"How much damage did they do? They smash a window?"

"Damage to the office was minimal. Luckily. They kicked the door open. I've got someone out there now, replacing what they've broken. They shot open the lock on my filing cabinet, though. I'll have to get a new one. The files, however, are irreplaceable. In some instances, they represent years of work. Years of sessions. Years of breakthroughs."

"You don't keep digital records?"

"Of course I do. I back everything up. But the folders are what I work with in the sessions. I have them right in front of me. The issue isn't that I've lost my records, Tom. I've lost *their* records – their *privacy*."

"And you thought it was me who took them."

"You had a lot of questions about Adam. You very much wanted to see his file."

"Did you see the sheriff's cruisers leaving as you pulled into the park?" Tom says.

"They were hard to miss."

"They were here to see us. Me and Lorne. We were attacked last night. My car was totalled. They took a few shots at us, too."

"Jesus," Malani says, turning back to him. "They do anything worse than I can see?"

"No," Tom says. "Just these cuts."

"You get a good look at them?"

Tom can sense the ex-deputy in her coming out. "No," he says. "But I'm guessing whoever they were, they were the same two men who broke into your office and stole your files. Stole *Adam's* file."

"If that's true, what's their interest in him?"

"I'm going to find that out," Tom says. "I have a lead. In Boulder." He looks at her. He's hoping to play on her ex-deputy curiosity, and her commitment to Adam. "I need a ride."

Malani thinks about this. She checks the time. "Boulder?" She considers. "I've had to cancel all my appointments for this morning because of the break-in. Because of that, I don't have another session until late afternoon. I could probably make it there and back in time. How long do you think it'll take?"

"I don't know," Tom says.

"Who or what is your lead?"

"Start driving and I'll tell you." Tom grins at her.

"All right," she says, starting the engine. "Are you going to tell Lorne where we're going?"

"He might be sleeping already. I don't want to disturb him. I'll message him, let him know that way."

"What about the men that attacked you both last night? Are you concerned they might come back for Lorne while you're gone?"

"In a few hours Lorne will be at the bar," Tom says. "He'll be surrounded by people he knows. Colin will be nearby, if not in the bar beside him, and I've heard he packs serious heat. And I don't think our attackers will come back just yet. Firstly, it's daylight. They're more likely to strike in the dark. Secondly, the sheriff said they've burned out their own car. They'll need to find another one to get back here. I doubt they're going to steal one from a town as small as Samson. It'd get spotted too quick."

Malani nods. She pulls out of the trailer park. "All right," she says. "Tell me your lead."

23

Tom has punched Gabe Elcoat's address into Malani's satnav while she drives. The voice starts talking. Giving them directions.

"Mute it for now," Malani says. "I know the way to Boulder."

Tom does as she says and sits back in the passenger seat. It's very comfortable in her car. Very spacious. "A BMW," he says. "I take it therapy pays better than being a deputy."

"Everything about it is better than being a deputy in Samson," Malani says.

"Speaking of, did you report the theft of your files?"

"I reported the theft," she says. "I don't expect anything to come of it."

Tom watches the side of her face. She's annoyed. Personal information she has been entrusted with has been stolen.

"Whatever they're looking for, they're going to be disappointed," she says. "There isn't much in Adam's file."

"You said he was standoffish."

"Exactly."

They drive in silence. As well as the satnav being muted, the radio is off. The only sound is the well-tuned engine. Tom looks out the window, across the fields and toward the mountains. It's another clear day. Clear and cold.

"You worked with the sheriff," Tom says. "Tell me about him."

"What do you want to know?"

"You're clearly not a great admirer of his work."

Malani sighs. Her shoulders lower a little. Some of the stress she has been carrying since the break-in leaves her. "He used to be a good sheriff," she says. "He *is* a good man. At least, I *think* he is. Somewhere, deep inside. When he was first sworn in, he was good at his job. He took it seriously. But then the militia arrived."

Tom sits up, intrigued. "The militia?"

"He's scared of them, Tom," she says. "I don't know if something happened between them, and if so, I don't know how bad it could have been. That fear has rendered him useless. He's not fit for the job anymore. From the second the militia moved onto that ranch, he's been no good to anyone. He won't let anyone else go after the militia, either. I know that for a fact. I tried."

"Yeah?"

"Militia went in the supermarket and wrecked the place. Beat up the manager. Stole some goods. Well, not *some* – a *lot* of goods. The manager wanted to press charges. I tried. The sheriff refused. Told me to forget about it."

"How'd he explain that away?"

"He didn't. He just refused to discuss it further. Most he would say was that the security footage at the store had somehow been wiped, and no one who'd been present was willing to say what they'd seen – other than the manager. We had arguments. Many arguments. The incident at the super-market was the start of it for me. There were further issues after that. Eventually, it became untenable for me to stay there. I toughed it out while I did my training to become a therapist, and then I left. I wasn't doing my job there anymore anyway. I wasn't a deputy if I wasn't upholding the law. I couldn't tolerate that."

"What about the deputies?" Tom says. "Do you get along with them? You mentioned Anderson yesterday."

"I don't see much of them, but yes. I know they do the best they can."

"It seems like the town is accustomed to the militia by this point."

"They don't have any other choice. But they know that if they don't do anything to piss the militia off, then the militia *should* leave them alone. Doesn't always work, but people do the best they can."

Tom digests this. He looks ahead. Checks the time left of their journey on the muted satnav. Fifty minutes to go. They've been driving for just over an hour so far.

"I know a lot about your professional life, Malani," Tom says. "I haven't heard much about your personal life."

Malani smirks. "Are you flirting with me now, Tom? Don't think I missed you calling me 'beautiful' earlier."

"It's a long drive," Tom says. "And your being beautiful is just a plain fact."

She laughs. After a pause she says, "I don't have much of a personal life to speak of. I stay busy with work. Feels like I've stayed busy with work for as long as I can remember now."

"I can see you're not married," Tom says, nodding at the

lack of a wedding ring on her finger, "but what about a boyfriend?"

Malani blows air. She has to think about it. "It's been six months now."

"That's not so long."

"Well, he wasn't really a boyfriend. We were dating briefly. He was a ski instructor, so it's not like he would have been hanging around Samson for long. Anyway, it didn't work out and he moved on to his next gig."

"Sorry to hear that."

Malani smiles. "I don't think you are."

Tom grins. "I find it hard to believe that a *beautiful* woman like you struggles to find a partner."

She laughs. "That's very flattering. Thank you. And it's a small pool to pick from, Tom. But the pool isn't necessarily the issue. Like I told you, I'm always busy." She glances at the satnav. "What about you? A handsome man like you, are you seeing anyone?"

"Who knew you could be so charming, Malani? And no, not since I got to town."

"Wasn't that just a couple of days ago?"

"Not for a few months before that, either."

"Sounds like we're in the same boat."

"Yeah," Tom says. Neither of them says anything for a moment. Tom scratches at the scab across the bridge of his nose. "Yeah," he says again. "Sounds like we are."

24

Gunnar stretches his body, twisting left to right and then reaching for the sky, both arms high above his head. It's late afternoon. He slept in. He didn't intend for them to still be at the village this time of day. It was a late and busy night, though. It was a good time. He and the rest of his men deserved their rest. He had men on guard though, of course. He's not as slack as the warband they eliminated last night.

He runs his tongue around the inside of his mouth. He can taste blood, but it's not his. Grinning, he looks around the village. At the dead bodies that are strewn across the ground. At the pools of blood that are baking on the sand. Some of the bodies are charred. His men tied a few villagers to the ground with stakes embedded deep, leaving them three feet of slack on each of their ropes. Then they doused them in gasoline and set them on fire. Laughed and cheered as they desperately tried to put themselves out. They screamed until the fires burned away their nerves. It didn't take long before they collapsed to the ground and burned to blackness.

The only members of the village still living are badly wounded. Some of them try to drag themselves along the ground, but they're not able to get far. They moan in pain. They have broken bones, or bullet or knife wounds. Gunnar sees at least one man with some of his intestines hanging out. Antoine is close to this man, leaning against a gutted home while smoking a cigarette. Bored, he watches the man crawling. Watches the effort he's putting in, while leaving a trail of dark blood behind him. When the man is close enough, Antoine steps forward, pulling a Glock from his waistband, and puts a bullet through the back of the man's head.

Gunnar is topless. He scratches at the sides of his stomach with both hands and then reaches back to his coffee mug. His body is not shredded with rippling muscle, but he is strong. Field strong. Work strong. He's not a model. He doesn't need muscles. He's a fighter. A killer. He takes a long drink. He has his coffee black. No sugar. He scratches his crotch, and thinks about the woman he took last night. Abdul Mohamed's cousin. She was Black too, and she didn't need any sugar. She was more than sweet enough. They had a good time together. Well, *he* had a good time. He doesn't give a shit whether she enjoyed herself or not. She won't be able to enjoy herself anymore. She's in the house behind him, her throat cut from ear to ear. Gunnar did it himself. He went so deep he nearly decapitated her. Felt the blade of his knife grating against her vertebrae. She died fast. Gunnar sat back and watched her dead body as the blood slowly leaked out of her. She was a good-looking woman and it was a shame to kill her, but this is what he's being paid to do.

Besides, it's not like he can take her away with him. Sure, he could keep hold of her while he's in Africa, keep her in his camp and pay her nightly visits, but he'd have to eventually put her in the ground before he returns to America, whenever that might be.

He and his men will move out soon. Continue on their mission. They'll be setting off late, but they don't need to be anywhere fast. When they leave, they will destroy the village. Anyone who is still alive will be executed. The remaining buildings will be burned down. There will be nothing left. Gunnar yawns and takes another drink of coffee.

Florian comes to him. "There's a call for you."

"Who is it?" Gunnar says.

"Jason and Harry."

"Is it good news?"

Florian just looks at him, and this is answer enough.

Gunnar grunts, and empties what is left of his coffee onto the ground. He follows Florian to his laptop, and sees Jason and Harry waiting for him. Their heads are close together so they can both see. The last couple of times he's spoken to them, they were in a hotel room. Here, it looks like they're in a car, talking to them via their phone, judging from the way they both squeeze into frame.

Gunnar doesn't sit. He leans toward the laptop, balling his fists and pressing them into the table on either side of the computer. "What's happened?"

Harry speaks. "We failed," he says. "No other way to put it. Rollins and Lorne got away."

Jason is quick to follow up, shooting Harry a look. "We already knew that Rollins is dangerous, but now we've seen him up close. We know he's fast. We know he's fighting fit – he had Lorne slung over his shoulder and he still managed to evade us. Don't get me wrong, we didn't underestimate him, but he still managed to surprise us. We won't make that kind of mistake again."

Gunnar doesn't say anything for a long time. He stares at them both. He can see his shoulders and his chest rising and falling with his breathing, so they know that the connection has not frozen.

Jason and Harry look uncomfortable. They shift in their seats, almost knock heads. Harry clears his throat. He says, "We broke into the therapist's office. We got Adam's file." He bites his lip.

"And?" Gunnar says.

Harry shakes his head. "Nothing that can help us. There was very little in the file."

"That's not true," Jason says, clearly not wanting to appear as a complete failure. "It said he was close with Lorne. That he cared about him. Worried about him. That Lorne was about the only person Adam was close with. *Lorne* is the key. Lorne is gonna have answers for us, I'm sure of it."

Harry nods along with this, agreeing with what Jason is saying. "He's probably our best option. We just need to take Rollins out so we can actually get to him. With Rollins still in the picture, if we take Lorne he's going to come after us."

"This is a discussion for you to have among yourselves," Gunnar says. "I don't need to hear it. What I *do* need to hear about are *results*. Is that clear?"

They both nod and mumble that it is.

"*Good.* I've been patient, boys, but my patience is wearing thin. By this point, I'm sure that's understandable. I want what is mine, and I want it back *yesterday*. I thought you could be trusted. Jason, Harry – I thought I could rely on you. Either the two of you deal with this situation, or else I will come over there and deal with it myself. You will not like it if I have to come over there. The town of Samson will not fucking like it if I have to make my way there."

Jason and Harry do not speak. There's nothing for them to say.

"We're done here," Gunnar says. He doesn't give them a chance to respond. He ends the call.

25

The address that leads them to Gabe Elcoat is not a house address. It's an office.

Tom and Malani sit parked on the other side of the road from the office. It's glass-fronted and easy to see inside. Gabe Elcoat's name is printed on the glass in a crescent shape, and beneath that, in a straight line, it gives his occupation: accountant.

"We came all this way for an accountant?" Malani says. She's reversed into the parking bay so they can see straight over the road. Tom would have pulled into it normally and watched through the mirror, but it doesn't matter right now. He's not planning on observing the office for long. Soon, he's going to go inside. "Adam worked overseas," Malani continues. "It would be more of a surprise if he *didn't* have an accountant."

"The page had been torn out of his address book," Tom says.

"He might have gotten a new accountant."

Tom nods. He knows this could be the case. "It's a loose end," Tom says. "It's worth tying it up, to know for sure."

He can see who he assumes to be Gabe Elcoat inside, sitting behind his desk. He's on a phone call, his landline tucked between his ear and his shoulder, while his hands mash at the keys of his computer. At one point he glances at his cell phone, too. Gabe is overweight, and he appears to be overworked, too. He looks to be in his early forties. Balding, but his hair on the left side has been allowed to grow longer than the rest and scraped over his scalp in a terrible, greasy combover. His white shirt is dishevelled, and hasn't been ironed in a few days.

Tom starts to get out of the car. "I'm going to talk to him," he says.

"I'll come with," Malani says. "I didn't drive you all this way just to sit out here."

Outside the car, Tom says, "I'll do the talking. You hear him say anything you want him to expand on, follow my lead."

Malani nods.

They cross the road to his office and walk straight inside. Gabe is still on a call. He glances up as they enter. Tom notices he doesn't have a secretary or a receptionist. He's the only person that works here. The office is just this one room, with a door to the left of the desk that probably leads to a bathroom. The floor is thickly carpeted, and Tom feels his boots sinking into its pile. Behind Gabe's desk, a radio gently plays classical music. Tom doesn't know much about classical music. It's not his thing. There are two chairs in the corner for waiting, next to the window, and two more in front of the desk, but Tom doesn't sit. He steps in front of the desk and watches the accountant. Malani stands next to him.

Gabe glances from Tom to Malani. His fingers slow at the keys. Up close, his combover appears even more ridiculous than it did from across the road. Tom wonders why he's bothered.

"Listen," Gabe says into the phone, "I'll call you right back. I dunno, give me ten minutes or something." He takes the phone from his shoulder and hangs up. He looks back to Tom and Malani, eyes narrowed. "Can I help you?"

Tom smiles. "I understand you know a friend of mine."

Gabe looks at him blankly. He shrugs. "Maybe I do. I know a lot of people's friends."

"Adam Lineker."

Gabe blinks. He clears his throat. He makes a show of furrowing his brow and looking to the ceiling. After a protracted moment he says, "It's not familiar."

Tom stares at him. Waits until he's uncomfortable and squirming. "You sure about that?"

Gabe grits his teeth. Tries to look sure. "I've never heard that name before."

Malani nods her head at his filing cabinet in the corner. "That's a big filing cabinet," she says. "And it's probably full, right? Maybe you should check. Just to make absolutely certain."

Gabe doesn't move. "I don't need to check it. I know the names of my clients. I've never heard that name before, and he's certainly never been any client of mine. I'm sorry, who are you? Both of you."

"I'm not sure if that matters anymore," Tom says. "If you're not familiar with my friend. Maybe I've misunderstood and we've come to the wrong accountant."

"Are there many other accountants in this neighbourhood?" Malani says. "This is the address he gave us, I'm pretty sure of that."

"I'm the only one on this block," Gabe says. "The next accountant is a few neighbourhoods over."

Malani nods at this. She stares at the filing cabinet. "I'm amazed you've memorised the details of every single person you deal with. That's very impressive."

"I didn't say I'd memorised their details," Gabe says. "I know their names. It's a big difference."

Tom tilts his head a little, like he's struggling to believe Gabe doesn't know who Adam is. "And you're *sure* you've never heard of Adam Lineker? You've never so much as filed a tax return for him?"

"I'm *certain*," Gabe says with finality. He laces his fingers on the desk. He wants them to leave, and he isn't trying to disguise the fact. His face looks like he's tasted something that doesn't agree with him. "What is it the two of you do, exactly? I have a full workload at the moment, but I could potentially recommend you to a peer."

Tom takes a step back and waves a hand like it doesn't matter. Gabe is trying to find out who they are, where they came from. Some clue as to what they might want. Tom looks around the office. "Just you in here? Must get lonely."

"I'm too busy to be lonely," Gabe says. "I'm sorry, but you've taken up a lot of my time and you still haven't told me your names, or what you do, or why you're here – other than telling me I was recommended by a person whose name I've never heard before."

"Feels like that would be a waste of everyone's time," Tom says, catching Malani's eye and tilting his head toward the door. "We've clearly got the wrong place – if you've never heard of my friend Adam Lineker, that is." He looks at Gabe, looks him right in the eye and holds his gaze long enough to let him know that Tom knows he's lying. "Goodbye, Mr. Elcoat. Enjoy the rest of your day."

Tom and Malani return to Malani's car. "He was lying," Tom says, strapping himself in.

"That was clear as day," Malani says.

"Pull down the road – he's watching us," Tom says, keeping his face lowered so Gabe doesn't see him looking straight back.

"I saw him," Malani says. She pulls out of the bay and down the road, parking again around the corner and out of sight of Gabe's office. "He knows exactly who Adam was," she says.

"But why was he hiding it?" Tom says, thinking out loud. "Why not just admit to knowing Adam? It's not a crime to know a person. What was he trying to hide?"

Malani checks the time. "What now?" she says.

"I'm going to stay in Boulder," Tom says. "I'm going to come back here tonight and break in. I'll take a look at his files, see if there's anything. If he didn't want to talk about Adam, there must be a reason for that."

Malani raises an eyebrow.

"I'm more than capable of breaking into places," Tom says. "I just didn't break into yours."

"I know. I believed you, didn't I?" She looks around. "You're going to have a lot of time to kill in Boulder. What are you going to do?"

"I'm going to start by getting something to eat. And then I'm going to watch Gabe's office from somewhere he can't see me."

"How will you get back to Samson?"

"I'll find a way."

"Call me," Malani says. "I'll come get you."

"You're sure?"

"I'm sure. I want to know what's happening here too, Tom. I want to know if there's anything worthwhile in Gabe's files."

Tom nods. His phone begins to ring. It's Lorne. He gives Malani a look before he answers.

"Tom, you need to get back to Samson," Lorne says.

"What's up?" Tom says, the tone in Lorne's voice putting him on high alert. "Has something happened?"

"There's someone here you need to talk to," Lorne says.

Tom looks at Malani again. She's confused. She can't hear Lorne's side of things. Tom puts the call on loudspeaker. "Who is it?" Tom says. "Who do I need to talk to?"

"Do you remember John Breen? You saw him at the funeral."

Tom remembers him. An older guy. He left the wake abruptly. There was something in his appearance that stuck with Tom. Something harried, and haunted. "I remember."

Lorne takes a deep breath. Tom hears him down the line. He and Malani look at each other over the top of the phone.

"You need to get back here, Tom," Lorne says. "John says he knows who killed Adam."

26

J ason and Harry find a cheap roadside motel to hide out in. The place is a dump. A shithole. It's not as nice as the rooms they had at the hotel in Samson. They're sharing a room here. They don't intend to be here for long.

They've stolen a car already. It was their first port of call after walking all through the night and finally managing to hitch a ride to the nearest town of Fraser. It's a red Toyota. It's parked around the back of the motel, out of view of the road in front.

After the noise they caused last night, Jason and Harry need to keep a low profile. Jason sits in a chair by the window, rocking back and forth on it. He watches the road, thinking. Planning their next move. Behind him, Harry is lying on the bed, fingers laced behind his head.

Jason turns his chair around so he can see Harry. "I hope you're thinking about what we're gonna do."

"Of course I am," Harry says without looking at him. He stares at the ceiling.

Jason works his jaw a moment. "You should've let me do the talking with Gunnar."

Harry looks at him now, an eyebrow raised. "That was hours ago. Why you bringing it up?"

"Because it's important. You told him too much. You should let me do the talking."

"I'm not a fucking child, Jason," Harry says, staring at him. "You ain't ever gonna tell me what to do. We clear on that?"

Jason holds up his hands. "Cool down, partner. We're on the same side here. I'm just saying, is all."

"Well, just *don't*."

Jason rolls his eyes. "Forget it. We've got more important things to talk about."

"Agreed," Harry says, settling back on the bed. "So what are you thinking?"

"All right, hear me out, and then if you think you've got a better idea we'll compare notes."

"I'm all ears."

"We've been taking things carefully so far. We're getting close to the time where we need to throw care out the window."

"We weren't careful last night," Harry says. "We royally fucked up last night."

"Uh-huh – I said hear me out. We stay careful just a little longer. We've shaken the nest – let's wait and see if Rollins is able to dredge anything up."

Harry props himself up on an elbow. "You think he could find the money?"

"He's spending a lot of time with Lorne," Jason says. "And I think Lorne is our key. I said as much to Gunnar, didn't I? I meant it. Either they already know where the money is, or they're gonna figure it out. For now we wait, and we see if they find anything. After that, we get in and we get out, same as we would on any other mission. And we don't worry about care, or about noise, or any other shit like that. We come down *hard*."

Harry nods along. "No notes," he says. "That seems like our best course of action."

"In that case, we stay here. Hide out. Let them do their thing. But first we're gonna have to go back to Samson and get our bags from the hotel."

"Straight in, straight out. Ain't gonna give him a chance to see us."

"That's right," Jason says.

"Then let's go get it," Harry says, sitting up. "And then we'll give Rollins a little breathing room to find what we can't."

27

M alani stops her car in front of the bar.

"Do you need to go?" Tom says, looking at the time.

"Are you kidding me?" Malani says. "Someone says they know who killed Adam? No. I'm coming in. I still have some time before I need to get to my appointment."

Lorne wouldn't tell them on the phone whom John Breen is accusing of Adam's death. He said it was a long story, and better that they heard it from the man himself. They go inside. Lorne is behind the bar. Sitting at the stool directly in front of him is the older man that Tom recognises from the funeral. John Breen. He looks up nervously as Tom and Malani enter.

Lorne and John watch them both as they approach. Lorne is surprised to see Malani with Tom. To Tom, he says, "Are you sure you want her to hear this?"

"I want to hear it, Lorne," Malani says.

Tom holds out a hand toward John. "Mr. Breen," he says.

John looks at his hand, and then tentatively shakes it. His grip is weak, frail. Tom notices that his arm is trembling. The man is afraid. Tom takes the stool next to him. "You told Lorne you know who killed Adam," he says. "Do you want to tell me about it?"

John swallows. The glass in front of him has water. He takes a drink, and then decides it isn't strong enough. He asks Lorne for a shot. Lorne pours him a whisky. John downs it and then stares at his hands on the counter, waiting for them to stop shaking. They don't.

Tom doesn't rush him. Gives him time to gather himself. He feels Malani beside him, standing close. She places a hand on his shoulder, waiting. All eyes are on John Breen.

He takes a deep breath. "I don't know that they killed him for sure," he says, "but I think they might have. Timing-wise, it lines up. I came in here today and I was talking to Lorne here, and I mentioned how much Adam's death surprised me. I thought it was strange that Adam would kill himself, especially so soon after he and I had been talking. I found it hard to believe. Lorne told me how he didn't believe it, either."

"What were you and Adam talking about?" Tom says.

John looks back over his shoulder, checking the bar. It's empty. They're the only people present. He looks toward the entrance. It's closed. No one is coming in. Still, he lowers his voice. "You know about the militia, right?"

Tom nods. "I know about them."

"They have my daughter," John says.

Tom leans closer. "What do you mean? She's a member?"

John shakes his head. His eyes are moist. "They took her."

Tom glances back at Malani. Her eyes are narrowed, watching John.

"What happened?" Tom says.

John takes a drink of his water. "Their leader, Bear – she started dating him. This was about four months back. I didn't like it. It worried me. I knew about the militia. Who around here doesn't?"

"How did they meet?" Tom says.

"I don't know," John says, shaking his head. "She said they met at a bar, but I don't know if that's true. I've never heard about the militia coming into town for beers, but I guess it might happen. Anyway, however it started, they were dating for about a month, and then Heather disappeared."

"And Heather is your daughter," Tom says.

John nods. "And they took her to that disgusting ranch of theirs. At least, I think that's where she is. I went out there. I tried to get her back. But I couldn't see her, and they caught me when I was trying to look in their windows and see where she was. I just wanted to know that she was all right – they could have done anything to her out there. She could have been dead for all I know – she *could* be dead..." His voice chokes. He covers his eyes with a hand and takes a moment to recover. He coughs, and takes a drink. "They found me. They have people on guard. And they beat me within an inch of my life. And I never found Heather. I never saw her."

"What happened then?" Tom says.

"They drove me back to town and dumped me by the side of the road. I spent a couple of days in hospital. When I got out, I went to see the sheriff."

"And he didn't do shit," Tom says.

John purses his lips and nods grimly. "He said there were

no signs that Heather was in trouble, and that technically I was trespassing when I went out to that ranch, so the only people in any position to press charges were the militia themselves."

Malani makes a sound of derision.

"It felt like there was more to him refusing to help," John says. "I couldn't understand why he wouldn't help me, or help Heather. It was like he didn't even want to hear me out. It didn't make any sense."

"I've met the sheriff," Tom says. "I've seen his disinterest firsthand."

"Heather is all I have left," John says. "Since my wife – her mother – died, it's just been the two of us. I need to know that she's okay. And if she's not, I need her back. I knew that Adam was ex-military, so I went to him."

"When was this?" Tom says.

"It was a week before he died. I knew he worked overseas. I'd had to wait for him to get back home."

"How was he when you spoke to him?"

"He was...fine, I guess. He invited me into his home. He listened to what I told him. He was more interested to hear what I had to say, and to hear my concerns, than the sheriff was. He agreed to help. He said he would go out to the ranch and make sure Heather was there, and if she was, he said he'd bring her back to me."

"And then?"

"I don't know. He went out to the ranch, and the next I heard he was dead. And that sounds suspicious as hell to me. He promised me he would bring back my daughter. I don't believe he would break that promise. I don't believe he would kill himself right after he made that promise, either. He didn't strike me as that kind of man."

Tom runs a hand down his mouth. He looks at Lorne. Lorne looks back. "If the militia killed Adam," Tom says, "they might have worked out who I am. They see me arrive in town for the funeral – they might think I'm here looking for revenge. It could have been them who ran us off the road."

"What about when you saw them behind the supermarket?" Lorne says. "Did it seem like they knew who you were?"

Tom thinks on this. "No," he says. "It didn't seem like it. But if they want to keep the element of surprise, it would make sense for them to play dumb."

"What are you going to do?" Lorne says.

Tom looks at Malani, and then at John. "I'll go out there. I'll see if Heather is there, I'll see if she's in danger, and if she is I'll bring her back." John's face lights up. He looks hopeful. "And I'll find out what the militia knows about what happened to Adam."

"Thank you," John says, "thank you so much." He reaches into his pocket and pulls out his wallet. He takes a picture from it and hands it to Tom. "This is Heather. This is what she looks like. My baby girl."

Tom looks at the picture. "How recent is this?" It's taken at a birthday party. Heather's, presumably. There are a pair of golden balloons behind her that read '27'. She's laughing, and holding up a glass of champagne to pose for the camera. She's pretty. Flashing perfect teeth. Her hair is long and brown.

"That was from her birthday the year before this one," John says. "It's up to date. She should still look like this."

"Can I keep hold of this?" Tom says. "For now."

"Yes, of course," John says, "please do. Just please, bring her back to me."

Tom nods, slipping the photo into his pocket. "I'll do my best." He makes no promises. For all he knows, Heather could be dead. John said he didn't see any sign of her when he went to the ranch. Tom has to be realistic.

"When are you going out there?" Malani says.

"I'll need to find some gear," Tom says. "Weapons, binoculars. But once I've got them, I'll head straight out. Few hours, maybe. Where around here can I get guns?"

"What kind?" Malani says. "There's a hunting store, which has some rifles, and a general gun store."

"Automatic rifles. The general gun store."

"They'll have decent binoculars there, too," Lorne says. "I'll give you directions. It's not far."

Malani looks at her watch. "I wish I could go with you," she says. "I want to know what happened to Adam just as much as you do. And you know how I feel about the militia."

Tom takes Malani gently by the elbow and leads her to the side, nodding to Lorne and John that he needs to speak to her in private. "I don't know how long I'll be out there," Tom says. "Could be a couple of days. It'll depend on how things go. I'll leave you my number, in case you need me. While I'm up there, I need a favour from you."

"Sure, what is it?"

"When you can, swing by, make sure Lorne is okay. I need to be sure no one comes after him when I'm not around. I'm not putting all my hopes on the militia. There could be others out there coming for us."

"No problem. Anything comes up, I'll let you know."

"Likewise."

"And when you get back we can catch up. Maybe dinner?"

"That sounds good," Tom says. "I'll look forward to it."

Before Tom can turn, Malani places a hand on his arm. "Those guns you're going to buy – those automatic rifles – they're just for protection. Right?"

"Of course," Tom says. "I don't know what they're packing out there, but I'm not going to turn up short."

Malani nods. "Good." There's a look in her eyes. She's no fan of the militia already, and hearing that they may have kidnapped a woman and are holding her against her will flares up a new kind of hatred. "If they come for you, Tom, remember to stand your ground."

"Always do."

———

28

Gunnar travels in the back of a Humvee with Antoine and Florian. His high command. The village burns behind them, belching black smoke into the blue sky.

"What are you thinking?" Florian says.

Gunnar stares out the window at the passing landscape, stroking his chin. The Humvee jostles them as it passes over uneven terrain. Jeeps and other Humvees drive ahead and behind them, heading to their next deployment. He answers without turning. "I'm thinking about Jason and Harry," he says, "and I'm thinking about Adam Lineker. Most of all, I'm thinking about Tom Rollins." He turns now, sees the two men looking back at him. "Jason and Harry sent me information on him, but I reached out to some contacts in America, learned a little extra. Rollins has some fans higher up."

"What do you mean?" Antoine says.

"Someone in the government likes him. Most likely it's a senator by the name of Seth Goldberg. Rollins saved his and his family's life from a bomb attempt. Unofficially, he's almost untouchable. The senator hears about anything he's been involved in, he pulls some strings to keep Rollins out of any major trouble."

"Shit," Florian says. "He has a guardian angel?"

"So long as he doesn't go too far," Gunnar says, "it would seem so. So long as he stays on the side of the angels."

"Is that gonna cause a problem?"

"Goldberg isn't watching over him at all times. If he hears something, he takes an interest. As of now, there's nothing for him to have taken an interest in. If we're fast enough, he'll never know that his golden boy is dead."

"You want him dead?" Antoine says.

"What other choice do we have? He's too dangerous. And frankly, his presence has pissed me off. It's complicated things. It shouldn't have gone on this long."

"The blame for that could potentially be lain at the feet of Jason and Harry," Florian says.

"I'm aware," Gunnar says. "I'm *very* aware. I thought they could be relied upon, but they've proven to be a great disappointment."

Gunnar looks at Antoine and Florian. They weren't with him at the beginning, but they joined him soon after. They rose through the ranks of the Aries Group. Became his most trusted confidants. Gunnar does not have friends, but these two men are who he considers himself to be closest to. He trusts them both – insofar as one mercenary can trust another. If Antoine is his right-hand man, then Florian is standing resolute on his left.

Twenty years ago now, since Gunnar started the Aries Group. He'd been in the US Army, but it didn't suit his style. The training was useful, but Gunnar didn't like following orders. Court martial followed court martial. Out in the field, war crime followed war crime. Gunnar went AWOL. If he hadn't, he would have been put under arrest when he returned to America anyway. He stayed active overseas, starting up the Aries Group, allowing things to cool off stateside. He's careful when he goes back. Rarely returns via an airport. Uses a fake passport on the occasions when there is no alternative.

Usually, though, he's abroad. He's in the action. It's where he prefers to be. In battle. Bullets flying. Blood on the ground.

Those first two years as the Aries Group were tough. Gunnar recruited a dozen fellow Americans and a handful of Brits, all with a similar outlook to his own. Men who couldn't go home. They started out in Africa. The Aries Group operate worldwide, but they've always gotten most of their work in Africa. It's where they made their wealth. After those first two years, that was when they started to get noticed. When they started to make real bank. And it all started when Gunnar saw the opportunity to raid and take control of a small diamond mine. No one paid them to do it. It wasn't a target. Gunnar saw an opportunity, and he seized it.

With the diamond mine in their control, they stripped it of all it was worth. It allowed them better funding. Better equipment. Better soldiers. It opened the whole world to them. And now they're five thousand strong, worldwide, and they're in regular demand.

Gunnar grins to himself, thinking on all he has built. He's not going to let someone like Tom Rollins ruin it. He's not going to let a small town like Samson ruin it. He's not going to allow his lost money to remain out of his reach for much longer. It's *his*, and he will get it back, one way or another.

"What happens next?" Florian says.

Gunnar looks at him, dragged out of his memories. "We wait and see how Jason and Harry do out there," Gunnar says. "And if they fail..." He looks at Antoine and Florian. "If they fail, then I'll deal with Rollins. I'll go over there myself. I'll deal with Samson. And I'll get my fucking money back."

29

Tom watches the ranch through binoculars he purchased at the gun store. He bought a rucksack too, and travelled out here on foot with it slung over his back. He gave the ranch a wide berth, passing it on foot, and made his way up into the mountains, concealing himself behind a boulder and under the shade of a bush. The rucksack contains water and some provisions, as well as the weapons he purchased. He hasn't eaten anything yet. He's not hungry. He's been here a couple of hours so far. Watching. Getting an idea of the ranch's layout. Examining the people down below, and who they could be.

He thinks he's picked out Bear. His name is apt. He's a large man – six foot five, easily three hundred pounds. His hair is long, and his beard is thick. Broad-shouldered, barrel-chested, big-bellied. He wears a vest and sits to one side on the porch steps, sipping from a beer. There are a few other men gathered around him. One of them is standing. He's tall and thin, and smoking what could be either a roll-up cigarette, or a joint. There are two men sitting on the ground near to Bear. Tom recognises them both from his altercation behind the supermarket. Neither of them is the man with the rotten teeth. Rotten Willie. Tom hasn't seen him yet.

Tom puts down the binoculars and reaches into the rucksack for a bottle of water. He takes a long drink, blinking while he looks over the lay of the land. It's quiet out here. There's a road, but no one comes down it. The bushes on either side are overgrown, and the road is cracked and weedy. It reminds Tom of where Lorne took him on the outskirts of town. The spot with the tree. Lorne and Adam's spot. The road there was in similar disrepair. The bushes beside the road also line the property immediately surrounding the ranch house. They're thick and evergreen, and afford much privacy.

The militia's vehicles are parked close to the road, on the grass next to the driveway that leads up to the ranch house. The ranch house used to be red, but its paint is peeling and its natural wood mostly shows through. There are some tents pitched on the ground outside. Some are bigger than others. A couple look like they will only shelter one or two people, while others look like they could hold up to six people each. The members of the militia are moving a lot, coming and going in and out of the house and the tents, and it's hard for Tom to gauge how many of them are down there. He registers their faces, and tallies them. So far, he's reached fifteen. He doesn't think there can be many more.

This place used to be a farm, clearly, but it has not been farmed in a very long time. The fields surrounding it have turned to scrubland. The grass around the house looks like it gets cut, but it has been trod down and is as close to dead as the fields.

There are women below, only a few, but none of them are

Heather. Tom checks the photograph of her that John gave him for reference. Reminds himself of her face. The women he sees look to be a part of the militia. They look more than happy to be there.

If Heather finally turns up, and if she looks as comfortable down there as the rest of the women, Tom wonders how John will take that. Tom won't take her back if she's settled. If she's in danger, that's a different story. But if there's no danger, there's no reason to rescue her.

Tom still needs to talk to the militia, though. Find out what they know about Adam, and if they were involved in his death. If they're now targeting him and Lorne. Tom has been watching the people below, and picking out the ones he thinks are most likely to talk. Bear is a no-go. Likewise the tall guy that stands by him. Tom could break them, but it would take too long. It's not worth the effort. Rotten Willie, however, Tom is confident that he will answer any questions Tom has, and Tom might not need to apply any kind of pressure. Willie is the kind of man who is all talk, and even then he needs to be surrounded by his buddies.

Tom returns the water bottle to the rucksack. There's an M4 inside. Whether he'll need to use it or not remains to be seen. There are a couple of M67 grenades, too. Again, just in case he needs them. If not, he'll return them to the gun store. They were not an over-the-counter purchase. Tom is sure he can persuade the owner to refund him, if necessary. Also in the bag is a set of NVGs, and magazines for the M4, and some for his Beretta, too. The Beretta is in the bag with the M4 for now. His KA-BAR is sheathed on his hip.

Returning the binoculars to his eyes, Tom sees movement. Rotten Willie has risen from his tent. It's one of the single-sleepers. He wears a stained vest. He rubs at his stomach and then runs his hands through his wild hair, smoothing it out. He kneels and reaches back into his tent and pulls out a beer bottle. He drinks from it, swirls it around the inside of his mouth, and then spits some to the side. Then, he takes another drink. This time he swallows it.

Tom adds one more to his tally.

Tom sees a group of the militia go off to the side, behind the house. There are straw men hanging from a rack. The people that have come here practise knife work upon the straw men. Bear leaves the porch steps and is watching over them, arms folded. The knife practise goes on for a while. They're using hunting knives, KA-BARs, and machetes. Tom scans the rest of the area. He sees Rotten Willie talking to the tall man. Willie is smoking a cigarette.

The others don't look particularly busy. They smoke, and they drink. A couple of them are barbecuing. Tom can faintly smell the charring meat. He looks back to Bear and the group with knives. They've switched to guns, now. They put some distance between themselves and the straw men and open fire upon them with AR15s. Tom keeps their weaponry in mind. He's noticed that a lot of them are carrying handguns.

Bear leaves the people shooting, heading toward the house. He motions for the tall man to monitor the shooters. The tall man does as he's told. Bear goes inside the house. When he returns, he's dragging a woman out, roughly, by the elbow. The woman stumbles. She looks smaller than everyone else here, and she looks tiny in comparison to Bear. She's unsteady on her feet. Bear shoves her and she falls, losing her footing. She lands on her hands and knees. Tom can't see her face. Her hair is darker than it should be –

unwashed and dirty – and it hangs down, covering her features. Strands of it have entwined with dirt and grease. She's skinny. Malnourished. The way she moves, Tom thinks she's high, or coming down.

Tom already knows who she is before she brushes the hair out of her face. It's Heather. Heather Breen. Her cheeks are gaunt, her eyes sunken. Her skin is sickly pale. But it's her. She stays on the ground and shuffles forward, like a dog. There is washing in a basket on the ground, with a tin drum full of water next to it, and a washboard. Heather, remaining on her knees, gets to work washing the clothes. After each item, she hangs it to dry on a nearby line. Bear monitors her for a while, watching her work. He scratches at his cheek through his beard. He doesn't speak to her. Tom doesn't see anyone speak to her. After a while, Bear walks away. He gestures to someone, motions for them to take his place watching over her. The man that steps forward has a holstered revolver on his hip. He keeps a hand on its handle, staring at her.

Tom watches her while she works, occasionally glancing around the grounds to see what everyone else is doing. He can hear the firing of their guns.

He sits back, reaching into the rucksack and bringing out one of his snacks. A protein bar. He eats it while continuing to watch without the binoculars. He can't see details, but he can see Heather while she works. It looks like they're guarding her. She doesn't make any attempt to escape, but where could she go? She isn't in any kind of condition to run. Even if she attempts it, they could easily run her down, either on foot or in their jeeps.

They have her drugged. She may have started out taking them of her own will, but judging from her armed guard, and the way that Bear was manhandling her, Tom assumes whatever she's on now is being administered. Or at least put into her hand and encouraged into her body.

Tom looks at the sky. It'll be early evening soon. A couple of hours after that, it's going to be dark. Tom will continue to watch. He'll plan. When it's dark, and the ranch is sleeping, it'll be easier for him to formulate how to get both Heather and Willie out.

Tom *is* going to get Heather out of there. The danger she's in is not immediate, but it *is* present. He can't leave her there. If he leaves her there, she will die there. Tom is going to take her home.

30

Malani's mind roams as she makes her way around the supermarket. She thinks about the militia. About when they raided this very supermarket, and she was called to the scene. She thinks about them out at their ranch. She thinks about Tom, too. He's there. Watching them.

Malani wishes she could be out there with him. Heading out now, trying to catch up with him, would be a bad idea. She doesn't know where he is, where he's hiding, and she can't risk calling him. Can't risk trying to find him physically, either. Doing so runs too great a risk of exposing him. She hopes things are going well. She hopes Heather is out there. That Tom has spotted her. That soon he will bring her back to town and to her father.

She saw her last patient an hour ago. It was an online appointment. Malani wrote out her notes and came to the store. She's trying to keep herself preoccupied. It's not working. She thinks of Tom, but mostly she thinks of Adam. Of the very real possibility that she did not fail him. She does not find much comfort in this. All it serves to do is lead into the awful horror of what really happened to him. If he *was* murdered, she needs to make sure that whoever killed him does not go unpunished.

As she reaches the tills, she realises she hasn't been paying much attention to what she's been putting in her cart. She casts a quick gaze over the items. Random groceries – fruits and vegetables and tinned goods. They'll do for the week. They'll get her through. Anything she's missing, she can always come back another day.

Malani pays and makes her way out, back to her car. As she leaves, she sees a familiar face loading things into the back of her Ford, just a couple of bays down from Malani's BMW. Olivia. Stan is with her.

Malani knows who she is, but she's not sure if Olivia knows who *she* is, and what she was to Adam. However, Olivia turns and sees her. "Malani," she says, seemingly surprised at her presence.

Malani nods. "Hello." She can see into the open trunk of the Ford. There are a couple of grocery bags, but also a couple of brand-new holdalls that were presumably bought in the supermarket.

Olivia turns to Stan. "This is – *was* – Adam's therapist."

"Oh," Stan says. "Okay." He doesn't sound like he cares.

"How are you doing?" Olivia says, turning back to Malani.

"I'm okay," Malani says, leaving her cart at the back of her car and stepping closer to Olivia so they can converse easier. "How are you? Are you doing all right?"

Olivia nods, looking around the parking lot. "I'm…I'm good, all things considered."

Malani nods. She doesn't say anything. She can see that

Olivia wants to say more. Stan, on the other hand, looks bored. He's ready to leave.

"It's just..." Olivia says. "It's just that things have been very hard recently. Since...since Adam died." She swallows. Malani hears a dry click in her throat. Her eyes are glassy. "It's hard to be here. It's hard to pass by his house. I avoid it when I can. I'll drive all the way around the town just to avoid his home. And I know that sometime – probably soon – someone else will move in there and make it their own, and I don't know if that makes it better or worse."

Malani shows her sympathy. "I'm sorry for your loss," she says. "I know that you would have done as much as you could for him. I know that if you'd known what he was going through, you would have been there for him." She doesn't share Rollins and Lorne's suspicions, or what they have since discovered. Doesn't share that she too is starting to agree with them.

"Did he..." Olivia hesitates. "Did he ever say anything to you?"

Malani shakes her head solemnly. "I'm afraid not."

"Did he ever say anything...about me?"

Ordinarily, Malani would tell her that she can't discuss anything a client confided in her. Truthfully, Adam very rarely talked about his ex-wife. Malani struggles to remember anything he ever said about her. Nothing of real importance. She was a character in his life, and he referred to her as such. But he talked mostly about the present, and she was a larger presence in his past. She can see Olivia's pain, though. Her grief. So she lies. "He cared about you very much. He just wanted you to be happy." Malani hates lying, even a white lie. She looks purposefully at the holdalls in the trunk, finding a way to change the subject. "Are you going on a trip?"

Olivia blinks at her, as if her mind has suddenly gone blank. She looks at the holdalls. "Oh," she says, "those. I mean, yes. Yes, we are." She glances back at Stan. "We're going on vacation." She turns back to Malani. "I need to get away for a while." She bites her lip. "I'll be honest with you, we might end up leaving town altogether. I don't think I can stay here any longer. Everything I see, it all reminds me of Adam." She sniffs and then scratches the side of her nose under her right eye. She holds back her tears.

Stan closes the trunk. "We should get going," he says.

Olivia nods, then looks at Malani apologetically. "We really should be on our way," she says. "It was good to talk with you, Malani. I don't think we ever have before. When I would see Adam, though, he'd mention you. He said you were helping him a lot." She holds out her hand and they shake. "Thank you for everything you did for Adam."

Malani steps back as Olivia gets into the Ford. Stan is driving. Malani thinks on what Olivia told her Adam said about her. It's not often Malani hears how she makes her patients feel. Sometimes they'll send her flowers, or a thank-you card, but most often she just has to hope that she's helping. She returns to her car and unloads her cart into the trunk as the Ford reverses and pulls out of the supermarket. Stan drives too fast through the parking lot and out onto the road. If Malani were still a deputy, she'd pull him over. But she's not anymore, so instead she just winces as she watches them speed off down the road and out of sight.

31

I t's getting dark at the ranch. Tom drains the last of his bottle of water. He'll be going down soon, once the dark has settled. Once everyone is asleep. John Breen said there were guards posted when he came out. Tom can sneak past them. If not, he's sure he can subdue them. Then he'll hotwire one of the jeeps to get Heather and Willie back to town.

Heather is still outside. She finished washing the clothes and hanging them up to dry about an hour ago. She's just sitting on the grass now, picking at it. She looks dazed. Now that her work is finished, she doesn't know what to do with herself.

She's still under guard. It's a different man now, sitting on the porch of the ranch. He has a shotgun across his lap. He's picking his nose while he watches her.

There hasn't been any sign of Bear in a while. He's been inside the house, along with the tall man and a few others. Rotten Willie has been left outside. He's been lying on the grass and drinking beer. It doesn't appear like he has much to do around here. He hasn't practised his knife work or his shooting. From what Tom saw of him behind the supermarket, he should probably work on both, as well as his hand-to-hand combat.

Tom readies his gear while it's still light. As he works, he spots movement down below. It's around Heather. He raises the binoculars.

Bear has emerged from the house. He's made his way to Heather, and he's dragging her to her feet. He's not gentle. He holds her face in his hand and looks into her eyes, checking how cognizant she is. Bear shakes her. He's rough. Backhands her. At no point does Heather object. She doesn't fight back. Bear grins and drags her back up to the house. Willie has propped himself up where he lies, and he's watching. He starts to sit up. A lot of the other men are watching, too. They're smiling, laughing. Someone whoops, though Tom can't hear it from up here, just sees the shape their mouth makes.

Bear drags Heather into the house. They don't return. Tom feels his stomach tighten. He has a bad feeling about what is happening. He puts the rucksack on his back and pulls the strap tight. He's left the M4 out. He carries it on his shoulder and carefully makes his way down the mountain. He wants to get closer, to be sure of what he thinks is happening.

He moves carefully, being sure not to knock loose any rocks that could tumble down the mountain and alert the people below to his movements. He pauses every few metres and looks through the binoculars and makes sure no one is looking his way. No one is. With darkness coming, a lot of the people are settling down for the night. A couple of them are lighting a fire. Some have gone into their tents. The women of the militia are with the fire-makers. However, a group of men – four men – stand around on the house's porch. They look like they're waiting. Waiting to go inside, perhaps.

Or else waiting their turn.

Tom moves as fast as he is able. He gets closer. He can hear the murmuring of the militia's distant voices. He can't hear anything coming from the house, other than the laughter of the men on the porch. He can't hear any screaming. Heather didn't look like she would scream. She looked numb. Numb to everything. Even this.

Tom reaches the base of the mountain and pauses to check the area. Bear is outside of the house, now. He's on the porch with the others. Another of the men has gone inside. Tom ducks low and continues on. He makes his way to the camp. From what he could see when he was higher up, no one is standing guard yet. He makes a wide circuit around to the house. He's running now. He's on grass, and concealed behind the bushes that line the property. They won't hear him, and they can't see him.

When Tom is parallel with the ranch house, he gets down low and crawls under the bush. Its branches conceal him, though they snag at the rucksack on his back. He can hear better from here. Except, there's nothing *to* hear. Not from inside the house.

He slides the rucksack and the M4 from his back and hides them in the bushes. He checks that no one is looking, that the way from the bushes to the house is clear, and then he pulls out his Beretta and crawls out from under the branches. He pauses once he's out from under them, up on one knee, Beretta held in both hands. No one is close to his position, and no one looks his way. Clear, Tom monkey-runs to the house, stopping beneath the closest window. It's too high above him for him to peer in. Nearby, there is an old, rusted oil drum. Tom checks how sturdy it is, then uses it to stand on. The window looks into an empty room with an unmade bed. There are a couple of empty wine bottles on the dusty, exposed wood floors. There are posters on the walls of naked women stretched out on the bonnets of cars, or else in fields and up against trees. Some of the posters are torn. There are stains on the walls that look like spat-out chewing tobacco.

Tom does not linger on this window. There's nothing to see. Nothing worthwhile. He hops down and checks the area remains clear still, and then he continues on to the next window with the oil drum. He climbs back up and looks inside. As he gets closer to the glass, he can hear sounds in this room. He's careful as he peers over the frame. There are people inside. Heather is one of them. The other is one of the men from the porch. Heather lies on the bed at the opposite side of the room. The bed is wide. A double king-size. Tom assumes this room is Bear's. The floor is the same as next door, but the walls here are devoid of nudey posters. There is, however, a Don't Tread On Me banner on the wall at the head of the bed.

Heather lies still. Her face is turned up, her empty eyes staring sightlessly at the ceiling above. The man has long hair, and it hangs down into her face. She isn't wearing any clothes. Tom can see them in a pile by the side of the bed. Her limbs are thin. He can see her ribcage. She's malnourished. Her lips are slightly parted, though not with pleasure. She doesn't feel anything. Her expression is completely blank. The bed rocks as the man atop her thrusts. The door at the foot of the bed is wide open. The man still wears most of his clothes. Only his jeans have been pushed down around his knees.

Tom feels sick at the sight before him. It's as he feared. His sickness turns to anger. Tom gets off the oil can and puts it back where he found it. He returns to the bush, grinding his teeth. He stays careful, though. He can't allow his anger to make him careless. Out the corner of his eye, he spots movement at the porch. He hides himself in the bushes again and watches. Bear has stepped down off the porch. He makes his way down the side of the house, past where Tom has just been, lighting a cigarette. Tom stares at him as he reaches into the rucksack, and pulls out both of the grenades. He places them within easy reach while he readies the M4, strapping it across his chest so the rifle is down by his right hip where he can quickly bring it to action.

On the porch, there is movement. The man who was with Heather is stepping back out, buttoning up his jeans. Another man claps him on the shoulder and then heads inside. It's his turn. Tom grits his teeth. He doesn't want to give him a chance.

He looks to Bear. Bear scuffs dirt with his boot, blowing smoke. He looks into the distance at the back of the house. Tom feels intense hatred for him. For what he has done to Heather, and what he has put her through. Tom slips the grenades into his jacket pockets. They won't be there for long. It's dark now. He pulls on the NVG and lights up the night.

Tom makes his move.

32

He gathers speed, gaining on Bear. Tom has his weapons, but he doesn't bring any of them to bear. Not yet. As he passes the rusted oil can, he scoops it up. Bear hasn't heard his approach. He hasn't turned. Tom swings the oil can hard. It crumples against the back of Bear's head.

Bear drops to a knee. He almost chokes on his cigarette, and coughs until he spits it up. He's wavering, dazed. Tom brings the oil can down again, swinging it wide. Bear falls face first into the dirt. Tom doesn't think he's dead, but he doesn't care if he is. Either way, for now, he's subdued. Tom will come back for him later.

He gets back on the now dented oil can and looks into the room. Heather is still on the bed. She hasn't moved. The man hasn't started with her yet. He's undoing the clasps on his dungarees. Heather moves her hand in front of her face, and watches her fingers with flickering eyes. She's drugged. She has no idea what's going on.

Tom pulls out his Beretta. He presses the barrel to the

glass and takes aim at the man still standing in the open doorway. Tom raises a hand to protect his eyes and then fires, twice. The glass shatters. Both bullets catch the man in the chest. Blood sprays out of his back and he stumbles through the doorway before landing flat outside the room. Heather does not register the gunshots. She remains flat on the bed, staring at her hand.

The men on the porch hear them, though. Tom steps down off the oil can. He's already prepared for them as they come running. He pulls a pin and rolls a grenade their way. It explodes as they come into view, blowing one of the men off his feet and knocking another sideways back onto the porch. The explosion tears chunks of wood out of the house. Tom brings the other grenade from his pocket and makes his way toward the corner where the first one exploded. The pin is pulled. He throws it deep into the camp, and then shoulders the M4. As the grenade explodes near the tents, he opens fire upon the rest of the men on the porch. He downs them all, and then turns his fire upon the rest of the camp.

This is not how he intended to raid the militia. This is far louder than he expected. But he didn't expect to witness them taking turns with Heather, either. He didn't expect to see a gang rape. He was never going to just stand by and allow it to happen. Fuck the noise. He doesn't care about it. They're too far out for anyone else to hear.

Tom watches the militia scatter as he fires upon them. They're disorganised, and not prepared for his attack. They don't know how to react. Some of them attempt to fire back at him, but they don't have the AR15s. They're back in storage. The most they have are their handguns. Tom keeps moving, making himself a more difficult target in the darkness. He's able to easily pick off anyone who fires upon him.

Some members of the militia flee toward the jeeps. Tom would have crippled the vehicles if he'd had the time. Things have moved faster than he anticipated. A handful of the militia gets away. The tall, thin man is with them. He jumps behind a steering wheel and speeds away with a full vehicle.

The magazine empties. Tom drops to a knee to replace it, continuing to scan the area. He sees Rotten Willie, cowering on the ground, covering his head with his hands. He's close to his tent. Tom sees three members of the militia charging. They've grabbed the AR15s. One of them attempts to fire while she runs. She isn't wearing any NVG. She can't see what she's shooting up. Her bullets tear up dirt, far from Tom. Her bullets land closer to Willie than they do her intended target.

The M4 is loaded. Tom shoots the three of them down. The area is quiet now. The only survivors of the militia are the ones who were able to reach the jeeps. Seven of them, Tom counted, spread across two of the vehicles. One of the jeeps remains.

Tom makes his way to Rotten Willie. Willie looks up. Tom wonders what Willie can see of him in the dark. Tom strikes him in the temple with the stock of the M4, knocking him unconscious. Tom leaves Willie where he lies for now and makes his way back to the house. To Heather. As he does, a large figure stumbles into view from the side of the building. Bear. Still alive. He spits blood. He sees Tom coming his way. He growls, and beckons him, his meaty fists raised.

Tom removes the NVG and waits for his eyes to adjust. He puts down the M4 and slips the rucksack from his back. It would be so easy to gun Bear down. To destroy him in a hail of bullets. That would be too quick. Too easy. It isn't what Tom wants. Instead, he pulls out his KA-BAR.

Bear is sluggish after the headshots. He takes a right swing at Tom, but Tom easily ducks under and slides through on a knee. He jabs the tip of his knife into the back of Bear's right hamstring. Bear loses balance but he does not go down. He's growling. He spins and lunges for Tom again, swinging his fists carelessly. Tom avoids all of his blows. Bear is too dazed and too slow. Tom stabs at him, burying the KA-BAR in inches at a time into his arms and his thighs, and into his sides.

Bear stops swinging. Blood is pouring out of him. He folds his arms in front of himself, trying to plug up his torso wounds. He falls to his knees. He coughs blood. He looks up at Tom. He tries to speak.

"Who...who are you?" His voice is deep and gruff. He sounds exactly how Tom expected him to.

Tom doesn't answer.

Bear looks down at himself. At the bleeding. He winces. "Why?"

Tom takes a handful of his hair and yanks his head back. He presses the knife to his throat. "Because you're a rapist piece of shit," he says, "that's why." He slides the knife into Bear's throat.

He leaves Bear bleeding out, dying in the dirt, and goes into the ranch house. He holds out his Beretta and goes room to room, making sure the house is clear. Heather is the only person inside. She lies on the bed, still. She hasn't moved. She doesn't so much as raise her head when Tom enters the room. He puts the Beretta away and gathers up her clothes. He can smell them from the ground. They're filthy. He can't put her back in them. He looks around. There is no wardrobe in the room. There is a pile of clothes in the corner, on a chair, but none of them look like they belong to Heather. They look like they're Bear's.

There's a blanket on the bed. Tom wraps her in it and scoops her up. She looks up at his face, blinking, but there's no light behind her eyes. There's nothing in her face. Tom carries her out of the ranch house and heads toward the remaining jeep. Willie has stirred. He's started to crawl along the ground, but he's slow. He won't recover before Tom gets back.

Tom places Heather gently in the front passenger seat of the jeep. In the back, he finds some rope. He takes it and returns to Willie. Uses it to hogtie and gag him, then drags him across the ground. He dumps him in the back of the jeep. He doesn't have keys so he hotwires it. He looks at Heather. She looks back at him, her head pressed into the seat. Tom opens his mouth to speak, but he doesn't say anything. She doesn't look like she'd understand, and nothing he could say right now would matter. His words cannot undo the last few months of hell she has gone through. Instead, he turns the jeep around and he leaves the ranch.

33

L orne isn't sleeping. It's late, and it's dark, and he's been trying for a while, but it will not come. Instead, he lies awake and stares through the darkness, and he listens to the trailer park outside. He has his window open so he can better hear if a vehicle or if anyone on foot starts to approach. He's heard plenty of cars, but none of them have come to his home. They've all headed deeper into the park.

Occasionally, sleep will take him, but only for a brief time. It's never long enough for him to feel like he's truly been unconscious, or like he's rested.

John Breen had sat with him at the bar for a few hours after Tom left. The poor man was in pieces, clearly. It was taking everything he had to hold himself together. Lorne gave him a beer, on the house, to try and calm his nerves. John's hands were still shaking when he finished drinking it.

"She's all I've got left," he kept muttering. "I can't lose her too. Not my Heather. She's all I've got left."

Lorne felt pained for the man. Felt a tight clenching of sympathy in his chest. He thought about Adam. Without Adam, who does Lorne have left? When Tom is done in Samson, and he moves on and continues with his life, Lorne will be left truly alone.

He'll have Colin, he supposes, but Colin is his employer, not his friend. Lorne tries not to dwell on these things. He knows what he wants out of life. He wants friends. He wants to find a woman he can fall in love with and settle down with. Have some kids. And he wants to sleep through the night, every night, without fear that he will wake up soaked in a cold sweat, the sound of artillery and bullets resounding in his ears.

He can't have any of the former until he fixes the latter. Until he's able to control his PTSD, he can't find anyone to love. He's too scared he might hurt them in his sleep and awaken with no memory of what he has done. And as broken as he is, he can't have children for the same reasons. He needs to know that they'll be safe around him.

Lorne isn't sure if he'll ever be fixed. He feels like he'll be broken forever.

He watched John staring into his drink, and understood his pain. It was quiet in the bar. It never really got busy today. A few people came and a few people went.

"Tom will find Heather," Lorne said finally, stepping closer to John. He knew he shouldn't make any kind of promise. He knew it wasn't his promise to make. But he hated seeing the man in so much hurt. "He'll bring her back."

John looked up at him with drooping eyes. "How can you be sure?"

"I'm not," Lorne said. "But we have to have faith, don't

we? And I have faith in Tom. He saved my life, once. He carried me on his back through a warzone from behind enemy lines. If Heather is out there, Tom will bring her back."

John nodded at this. He didn't look hopeful, but he didn't look as entirely distraught as before, either.

"You should go home, John," Lorne said. "Waiting here isn't doing you any good. Go home and try to get some rest. I know it's not going to be easy, but we don't know how long Tom is going to be out there. It could be a couple of days. Sitting here isn't going to bring him back any faster."

John took Lorne's advice and left the bar soon after. Lorne stayed on shift until the bar closed. It never got busy. Clean-down didn't take very long. He took the takings around to Colin and then he came home.

And now he's in his bed, wishing he could take his own advice. Lying awake won't bring Tom back. Lorne wonders what it's like out there, at the ranch. Wonders what Tom has seen. Wonders if Heather is there. If he's found her. Lorne hopes for John's sake that she is, and that she's willing to return with Tom.

Lorne rubs at his left leg. It aches. It particularly aches when he's struggling to get to sleep.

Finally, he feels his eyes growing heavy. He doesn't fight it. Lets them close. His limbs grow heavy, too. They sink into the mattress. His breathing thickens. Lorne welcomes sleep. It's been a distant friend for too long.

He's brought back to consciousness with a start. A banging upon his trailer door.

Lorne scrambles from his bed and stumbles through the doorway, his feet tangled up in the bed sheets. He kicks them loose and then pauses by the door. "Who is it?"

"It's me, Lorne," Tom says.

Lorne throws the door open. Tom is not alone. On the ground behind him, a man is hogtied and gagged. Beside Tom, supported by his arm, is a woman wrapped in a blanket. She looks cold and ill. Her lank hair hangs in her face. After a moment, Lorne realises that she is Heather.

"Holy shit," he says, taking Heather by the hands and bringing her into the trailer. He guides her to a seat and gently lowers her. She's shaking all over. Her face is blank, but there's some recognition in her eyes. She looks around the trailer, probably wondering where she is and how she came to be here. Lorne turns back to Tom. "What's happened to her?"

"She's coming down," Tom says.

"From what?"

"I don't know."

Lorne looks back into her face. "Heather? Heather, can you hear me? Are you okay?"

She tries to speak, but her words are slurred. She can't form them fully. Can't construct a sentence.

"Lorne," Tom says.

Reluctantly, Lorne leaves Heather where she sits. He goes to Tom. The hogtied man is struggling on the ground, to no avail. Lorne notices a jeep nearby that he has never seen before.

"Call John," Tom says. "Tell him his daughter is here. By the time he gets here, I'll be back to talk to him."

"Back?" Lorne says. "Where are you going?"

"Is there anyone in the bar?"

"What? No. What time is it? It's two am. It's been empty for hours."

"Good. I need your keys."

34

Tom takes Rotten Willie down into the basement of the bar. He leaves the gag in and binds him to a chair. Ties the rope tight at his wrists and ankles. He's not going anywhere.

Tom finds plastic sheeting and spreads it out on the ground beneath Willie. He drapes it over the nearby kegs, too, and anything else that is close by. Willie watches him with wide, terrified eyes. Tom was right. It will be easy to make him talk.

After what Tom has seen, he's not sure he wants it to be easy.

"I'll be back soon," Tom says, placing a hand on Willie's shoulder and looking down into his eyes. Tom wonders how many times Willie took his turn with Heather. He sneers. "Don't go anywhere."

He drove the militia's jeep from Lorne's trailer over to the bar with Willie in the back. It's parked out front. He leaves it where it is for now. After he's done with Willie he'll get rid of it. At a light jog, he returns to Lorne's trailer. Heather's father has already arrived. Tom steps inside and sees him clinging tight to his daughter, crying hard, holding her close to him. She's crying, too. She's not dazed anymore. The drugs have worn off. She's alert, and she's aware. She remembers everything that has happened to her, and now she's crying it all out.

Lorne stands to one side, gnawing his bottom lip. He looks to Tom as he enters the trailer.

"Mr. Breen," Tom says. "John. *John.* I need to talk with you."

John does not want to let his daughter go. Tom goes to him. It doesn't matter if Heather hears. Tom takes a knee beside them. "Some of the militia are still out there," Tom says. "Not as many as there were, but you should get out of town for a couple of weeks. Do you have somewhere you can go?"

"Uh, I, uh, I have a sister in Burlington," John says, having to swallow so he can speak. "We can stay with her."

"Okay, good. Go to her, and don't come back until you hear from either me or Lorne. We'll tell you when it's safe to return."

John nods. He looks at his daughter, brushing the hair out of her face and stroking her cheek. "She can't talk," he says.

"She's probably dehydrated," Tom says. "And she'll be tired. She's been through a lot."

"What..." John hesitates, not sure if he wants to ask. "What was it like out there? What did she go through?"

Tom looks at him. He shakes his head, just a little. "You don't want to know," he says. "If ever she feels ready, she'll tell you herself. But don't force her."

John's face is solemn, and Tom knows he never would. He's just glad to have her back.

"She'll need a hospital," Tom says, standing. "The sooner the better, but she'll last until you reach Burlington." Tom turns to Lorne. "Go with them to their house, help them pack. Send them on their way."

"What are you going to be doing?" Lorne says, concerned. "What about the bar?"

"The bar will be fine," Tom says. "There won't be any mess. There won't be any sign that anything has happened there that shouldn't have. But you can't come over, Lorne. It's not for you to see."

Lorne understands. "Okay," he says. He turns to John and Heather, knowing that the best he can do is help them.

"Thank you, Tom," John says. "Thank you so much. You brought my daughter back to me."

Tom nods. He thinks of what he saw at the ranch. He wishes he'd known about Heather earlier. That he could have gotten her out of there sooner. "I need to go," he says, and he leaves the three of them in the trailer.

He returns to the bar. To Willie.

The chair has fallen. Willie is on his face. The plastic sheeting is bunched up beneath him. He's tried to break free. Tried to shuffle the chair forward and work his way out of the binds. Tom pulls the chair upright. He brings out his KA-BAR. He slides it under the gag. "I'm going to ask you some questions," he says. "You make any noise other than what I permit, I'll smash what teeth you have left. That clear?"

Willie nods, cutting his cheek a little on the knife.

Tom cuts the gag loose. Willie works his mouth, stretching it out. "Jesus Christ," he says. "You killed them all–"

"I haven't given you permission to talk," Tom says.

Willie clamps his mouth shut. He swallows.

"I'm going to ask questions, and you're going to answer. That's how this works. That clear?"

"Yes," Willie says.

"Good. Adam Lineker. What does that name mean to you?"

Willie frowns. His eyes dart left to right, thinking, trying to remember. "I don't – I don't know him," he says.

Tom stares at him, waiting, giving him a chance to break.

Willie doesn't break. "Man, I'm telling you, I don't know who he is. I'm sitting here and I'm thinking, and I've never heard that name before. Who is he?"

Tom doesn't answer. He changes up. "That's a hell of a name you've got. Rotten Willie. What brought that? Your teeth?"

Willie grins, showing off his namesake. "That, and the syphilis."

Tom straightens, thinking of Heather. "You have syphilis?"

Willie tries to shuffle back in his chair, seeing the fire in Tom's eyes. "Used to," he says. "I caught it early. Wiped it out with antibiotics. But the name stuck. Didn't matter that I never got a serious symptom. The name stuck, and people used to joke that my dick was rotten."

"Is your name even William?"

"It is, but no one ever calls me *William*. Just Will or Willie."

Tom settles back down, leaning against a couple of kegs piled atop each other. He folds his arms. He still has the KA-BAR out. Willie's eyes settle upon it. He can see his blood on the blade from where his cheek was nicked. "Who ran the militia?" Tom says. "Bear?"

"Yeah," Willie says. "He dead? You leave anyone alive?"

"I ask the questions," Tom says.

Willie silences.

"Who was the tall man in your camp? Tall and thin."

"You've been watching us?"

Tom stares at him.

Willie swallows. "That sounds like Skinny Long."

"Is that his real name?"

"Only name I've ever known him by."

"He got away. Where would he go?"

"I don't know. Hey, I swear! He could've gone anywhere. Skinny Long was Bear's right hand."

"He's gonna come for revenge?"

"Probably." The corner of Willie's mouth twitches. Tom spots it.

"Spit it out," Tom says.

"Spit what out?"

"Don't make me hurt you." Tom knows he could make Willie scream very easily. Down here, Colin won't hear him. No one will. "I don't like you, William, and I have no problem with making you hurt."

Willie bites his lip.

"What are you keeping from me?"

"After you beat me up behind the supermarket, Skinny came into town to find out who you are. He only caught glimpses of you. He didn't wanna get too close. But he found out where you're staying. He found out about Lorne out there. And he managed to find out your name, Rollins." Willie grins.

Tom straightens and slaps the look off his face. "Tell me what happened to Adam," he says. He grabs a handful of Willie's hair and presses the blade of his knife to his hairline. "Start speaking or I'm gonna scalp you."

"Shit, shit – I told you! I told you I don't know who he is! I don't even remember his last name!"

Tom presses in with the blade. A line of blood runs down the middle of Willie's face. "Adam *Lineker*," Tom says. "What did you do to him? What happened?"

The feel of his blood panics him. "I don't know! I've never heard of him, I swear to fucking God!"

"Did the militia run me off the road?" Tom says, keeping the knife in place and pulling on his hair. "Was that Skinny Long? Did he take a shot at me?"

"No! No one from the militia took a shot at you! They were going to, but it hadn't happened yet, I promise!"

Tom looks down at Willie. Watches his eyes. Sees the blood that runs down his face and drips from the tip of his nose. Tom believes him. Believes that the militia did not kill Adam. Believes that they don't know who he was and had nothing to do with him. Believes that the militia did not run him and Lorne off the road. It was someone else. There's still another problem out there that needs to be dealt with, and whoever they are, they're most likely the people involved with Adam's death.

"All right," Tom says, removing the knife from Willie's hairline. "I believe you didn't do anything to Adam."

Willie breathes hard. He gasps, catching his breath and filling his lungs. He blows blood from his lips.

Tom gives him a moment. Allows the relief to flood his system. He leans down closer to Willie, next to his ear. "But that doesn't matter," he says, "because I know what you were all doing to Heather."

He cuts Willie's throat.

35

Jason and Harry have heard about what has happened out at the militia's ranch. The whole town is abuzz with it.

"You thinking Rollins?" Jason says.

They're in their room. Jason paces the floor in front of the television. Harry is at the table, on his laptop. He nods. "Who else? We saw him get into it with them by the supermarket."

"He went out there solo," Jason says. "No back up."

"Last time I saw him on the cameras, he was alone. And he was heading out of town at the time. On foot. Right after he'd been to the gun store."

Jason shakes his head. "The guy's a machine."

"He's dangerous," Harry says. "Too dangerous. We need to deal with him."

Jason nods his agreement. "We've given him a chance to shake something loose, and it hasn't happened. Right now, it's feeling like he's just gotten in our way. We were doing fine before he turned up. We would have what we were sent here for by now if he wasn't slowing us down."

Harry grunts. He's typing. Jason doesn't need to ask what he's writing. He already knows. It's an email, for Gunnar. It's telling him about Gabe Elcoat.

Gabe got in touch with the Aries Group. Since Jason and Harry were closest to him, the call was forwarded through to them. Gabe told them how Rollins and the therapist had turned up at his office, asking questions.

"I didn't tell them anything," Gabe said, and just from the sound of his voice it was clear he was sweating hard. He was worried. Panicked. Paranoid that they could turn back up. "But they didn't believe me, I could tell. They might come back."

"Sit tight," Jason told him. "You're not going to have to worry about him for much longer."

Harry finishes his email and sits back. He looks toward the window. The sun is bright outside. "Still a while before it's dark," Harry says.

Jason nods. They're waiting for the night. It's still too early to busy themselves preparing to go out. "I'm gonna take a nap," he says, getting off the chair and going to the couch. He takes a seat and laces his fingers across his stomach. "You get a bead on Rollins's whereabouts. Wake me if he's on the move."

Jason needs his rest. They both do. Tonight, they're done with being careful. Tonight, they go in hot.

36

Tom wants to get back to Boulder, to Gabe Elcoat, but he knows he shouldn't leave town. Not while some of the militia is still out there. Skinny Long will want revenge. Willie said as much. And they know where Lorne's home is. They know where he works.

Tom sticks with Lorne. Sits in a dark corner of the bar while Lorne works. He has a glass of water. He watches the door. Nothing but customers so far. It's busy.

Rotten Willie's dead body is nowhere near here. There's no sign he was ever down in the basement, nor that he died there. Tom wrapped his bled-out body in the plastic sheeting and drove his corpse out of town in the jeep he stole. He found an isolated spot to bury Willie, then drove halfway back to town and dumped the jeep. He burst all the tyres with his knife, including the spare, and tore out the starter engine. He continued on foot, leaving the vehicle behind to rust.

Lorne comes over to see him. "You don't have to babysit me, Tom," he says.

Tom doesn't respond. "It's busy today."

"Uh-huh. You know why, right?"

"I haven't been making conversation."

Lorne sits down beside him, and keeps his voice low. "It's because of what happened out at the ranch. With the militia. Everyone's talking about it."

Tom nods. "How much do they know?"

"They don't know who it was," Lorne says. "The theory is that they either got into a fight with some other militia, or they just got into it among themselves. Like a civil war kind of thing." He leans closer. "No one's suspecting you. No one knows anything about John and Heather, either."

"Good," Tom says.

The door opens. Malani steps through.

"Well," Lorne says, seeing her, "*someone* knows."

It takes Malani a moment to spot them in the dark corner. She waves and then comes over. It's the first time Tom has seen her not in a pantsuit. Instead, she's wearing high-waisted jeans and a white T-shirt tucked into them. Her hair is tied back in a ponytail. Tom almost didn't realise it was her at first, before he saw her face. She has an unforgettable face.

"I better get back to work," Lorne says. He nods hello to Malani as he stands, and then goes back behind the bar with Colin.

Malani takes a seat opposite Tom. "I heard what happened," she says.

"Seems like everyone has," Tom says.

Malani glances over her shoulder. "How much do they know?" she says, turning back.

"Not enough."

"Good. Was Heather there?"

Tom tells her what happened.

Malani listens intently. Her face is grim at some of the darker details. "I'll find some way to help them when they come back to town," she says. "I have contacts, people who can provide her with aid through this."

"She'll need it," Tom says. "She's messed up."

"They've put her through hell."

Tom looks at her. "I've told you everything that happened," he says. "I didn't keep anything back. You used to be a deputy, but you don't seem to be disturbed by what I did."

She looks straight back. "I'm not a deputy anymore," she says. "And I knew when you went out there that what happened was a very real possibility. And frankly, after what you've told me, I'm glad you did what you did. They deserved it."

"That's not therapist speak."

"No, it's not. But I'm not talking from a professional standpoint right now. I'm talking from a personal one."

"Speaking of professional and personal," – he nods at what she's wearing – "I almost didn't recognise you."

"I don't have any appointments today."

"A day off?" Tom says, raising an eyebrow.

"It's a rare occurrence, but it does happen."

"You look nice."

She smiles. "Thank you. You don't like the suits?"

"Actually, I *do* like the suits. Very much so. There's nothing wrong with variety."

"I'm flattered. Has the sheriff been by?"

"I haven't seen him," Tom says. "I'd like to keep it that way."

"Wouldn't we all? Did you leave any evidence at the ranch? He's probably out there right now."

"I gathered up my shell casings before I left, but I can't guarantee I got them all."

"You bought the guns in town," Malani points out. "And there are security cameras."

"I'm aware. But I paid cash, and I kept my face away from the camera. I don't think the owner will say anything, though."

"Why not?"

"Because he sold me some things he shouldn't have been selling."

"I see. Smart."

"Necessary," Tom says. "I didn't know if I'd need the grenades or not, but I knew I'd rather head out there with them, just in case."

"Oh, I bumped into Olivia and Stan, by the way," Malani says. "They're going on vacation." She tells him of seeing them at the supermarket and noticing their holdalls.

"Did they say when they're going?" Tom says. "And where?"

Malani shakes her head. "No. She just said soon. I forgot to ask where. I'm not so sure they know themselves. Olivia is torn up about what has happened. I don't blame her for wanting to take a break from here."

Tom grunts. "Her boyfriend's an asshole."

"Mm," Malani says, raising her eyebrows. "I got that impression."

They sit in silence for a moment. Tom watches the door. He glances at Lorne. Sees him laughing at something Colin has said.

"Do you have plans for today?" Malani says. "Or are you lying low in here all day?"

"I'm watching out for Lorne," Tom says. He looks at her. "Do you have plans?"

She shakes her head. She pauses, then says, "Are you hungry?"

"I could eat," Tom says. "Give me a minute." He goes to Lorne at the bar, tells him he's going out. "Call me if anything comes up," Tom says. "If anyone so much as walks in here that you don't like the look of, call me."

"You don't need to worry about me, Tom," Lorne says. "I'll be fine. The bar is full. Colin is here. It's all cool." He sees the look that Tom gives him, then adds, "But okay. If anyone gives me a bad feeling, I'll call you."

Tom turns back to Malani and waves her over. They leave the bar together.

Tom and Malani go to a diner and take a seat at the back. Tom has his back to the wall. He can see out the window, and he can see the entrance. The place is full, nearly all of the booths and tables occupied. Tom glances at the other people present, casting his eyes over them. No one is looking back at him and Malani. No one is checking them out.

Tom stays alert, but he settles back a little. The waitress comes to take their order. They both get burgers. Soon after, the waitress brings their drinks. Tom has water. Malani has a soda.

"Have you had a chance to eat in here yet?" Malani says. "I imagine you've been pretty busy since you reached town."

"I've just grabbed what I could," Tom says. "Stuff from the supermarket, mostly. Is the food good here?"

"Yeah, it's good. I come here often enough. Every other Friday. A treat to myself."

Tom smiles. "So I take it the burgers are good?"

"Well, I didn't want to oversell it, but if I'm being honest, they're the best."

"I've eaten a lot of burgers."

"Look at me, Tom. Do I look nervous?"

Tom laughs. While they make small talk he looks out the window, watching the road. He checks the cars that are parked out there. Makes sure they're as empty as they look, and that he's not being followed and observed.

"I'm just going to check in with Lorne," he says, pulling out his phone.

Malani gives him a moment to send his message. "You really care about him, don't you?" she says after he hits send.

Tom keeps the phone face-up on the table while he waits for a response. "I should have kept in touch through the years," he says. "With Adam, too. If I had, maybe things would be different right now, for both of them."

"We can't be sure of that," Malani says. "And you shouldn't blame yourself. Life moves fast. I'm sure you've been busy. You strike me as a man who keeps himself occupied. Next thing you know, a year has gone by, and then two, three, so on. I know I have friends who I haven't spoken to as recently as I would like."

Tom's phone buzzes. He checks Lorne's response.

> Everything good here. Don't worry about
> me. Enjoy your date.

There's a winking emoji at the end. Tom grins. He slides the phone back into his pocket.

The waitress brings their burgers. Tom takes his first bite. Malani watches expectantly. She waits for his verdict.

"It's all right," he says. "I've had better."

Malani laughs and shakes her head. "Asshole."

"For real, though, it's good."

Malani picks up her own burger and they touch them together like clinking glasses. "Cheers," she says.

They eat in silence for a while. Someone enters the diner. A man, middle aged. Tom keeps an eye on him. He doesn't look around the diner. Isn't searching anyone out. He goes straight to the counter and smiles at the waitress there. They talk like he's a local placing his regular order. He's no one for Tom to be concerned about.

"Adam looked out for Lorne," Malani says. "He took care of him the same way you are."

"Like I say, I wish I'd kept in touch," Tom says. "I wish I'd got to know them better. I didn't know them well enough when we were in the Army together."

Malani takes a deep breath, bracing herself. Hesitating before she reveals something. "Adam told me about you," she says. "He told me about how you saved him and Lorne."

"Oh yeah?"

"Yeah. He said you kept to yourself. He said that the day you saved them, you were the last person he expected to turn up in that ditch."

"What did he mean by that?"

"He said you struck him as the kind of person who only looked out for themselves. He said that if he already knew that you'd survived the attack, he would have expected you to clear out of there and leave anyone else behind."

"Maybe that's how it seems sometimes. That's not how it is."

"I can see that. I asked him why he thought that about you. When he got deep down into it, he figured it was because he didn't really know you. He could only judge you from how you presented yourself."

"And how did I present myself?"

"As a loner. Standoffish. You weren't looking for friends. You were more comfortable by yourself."

Tom considers this. He can understand why Adam would think that. "Some things don't change," he says.

Malani laughs. She takes a bite from her burger and they both fall silent.

Tom scratches the skin around the scabs on his cheek. It itches while it heals. He's careful not to pick at it. Doesn't want it to bleed. He finishes eating.

"There's something else about Adam," Malani says, "something else I've been thinking about a lot." She's almost finished eating, too.

"What is it?" Tom says.

"Just a feeling he gave, sometimes, especially towards the end. Adam was often quite vague, and sometimes I had to infer things. I got the impression he was unhappy in his work, which surprised me because he didn't really talk about his job."

"Did he say why?"

"No. The clearest thing he said was that he was hoping to give it up soon. To find something different and closer to home."

"Maybe he'd saved enough from all those years working overseas," Tom says. "Maybe he could afford something smaller scale." He pauses, thinking about what Olivia said about him being depressed. He shares this with Malani.

She listens. "He never gave me that impression," she says. "But perhaps it could have been to do with his job dissatisfaction."

"Maybe."

"What are you planning going forward?" Malani says.

"How do you mean? With looking into Adam's death?"

She nods.

"The only lead I have left right now is Gabe Elcoat. When I can be sure things are copacetic here in town, I need to go back to Boulder. He was lying to us. He was keeping things from us, and I'm going to find out what they were."

"But that's not going to be today." Malani wipes her fingers on a napkin and takes a sip of soda.

"Unfortunately not."

"Or maybe not so unfortunate," she says.

Tom tilts his head. He doesn't understand.

"We've had a good time so far," she says. "I've enjoyed spending time with you. It would be a shame to bring it to a close so soon."

Tom pays the bill, and then they go to Malani's home.

38

J ason and Harry know where Rollins is. They've tracked him as far as possible via the town's cameras. When he was in the diner with the therapist, they parked a couple of blocks away in their stolen Toyota. Jason was driving. Harry sat in the passenger seat with the laptop balanced on his knees.

"What are they doing?" Jason said. "You think they're on a date?"

Harry shrugged. "I can't see inside the diner. Could be they're just eating. Folks have got to eat."

Harry woke Jason from his nap back at the hotel to tell him Rollins had left the bar with Malani. They promptly followed, figuring they could be attempting to return to Boulder, and to Gabe. They were surprised when they just went to a local diner. The same diner where Jason and Harry have eaten more than once. The same diner with that pretty little waitress Jason liked the look of.

He'd forgotten all about the waitress. He thinks of her

now, though, as Rollins and Malani go into her house. Jason
sucks his teeth, his mood dark. Looks like Rollins is getting
to do what Jason wanted to do with the waitress.

"What do you make of that?" Harry says, looking toward
Malani's home. He's put his laptop away. There aren't any
cameras around here, and it can't do them any good. They're
parked on the far corner at the end of Malani's street, out of
view of the windows of the house. It's a different car, but they
know Rollins is cautious. He made them last time. They
weren't careful enough. They won't make that mistake
again.

Harry turns when Jason doesn't answer.

"I said what do you make of that?" Harry says. "A little
afternoon delight?"

Jason shrugs. "Looks that way," he says.

"Son of a bitch," Harry says, shaking his head. "She's a
real looker, the therapist."

"Never fuck a psychiatrist," Jason says.

Harry laughs. "You speaking from experience?"

Jason winks at him.

Harry looks back at the house. "We should go in now," he
says. "While he's distracted."

"No," Jason says. "We stick to the plan. We go when it's
dark."

"If he's hitting that, he's not gonna be thinking about us."

"Damn it, we're not risking it, Harry," Jason says, glaring
at him, losing his patience. "You thought that maybe they
ain't fucking at all? That maybe he knows we're here?"

Harry doesn't respond.

"He saw us last time, didn't he? And we were being
careful then. We're being even more careful now, so let's not

fuck things up. This could all be a ruse, to draw us out, to draw us into the house where he can trap us." Jason raises a finger in the air. "We ain't taking chances. We wait until dark. He ain't gonna see us coming."

39

Tom makes his way downstairs to the kitchen for a glass of water. He hydrates standing at the sink, looking out at the backyard. The light is fading, but Tom can make out enough. There's a loveseat in the far-right corner, and a grill on the patio beneath the window. The grass is neatly trimmed.

He puts the glass into the sink and steps through into the living room. He wears only his underwear, but he brought his phone down with him. He checks the screen. There are no messages from Lorne. No missed calls. While he and Malani were busy, Tom kept his phone on the bedside table, and kept an ear out for its vibrations. There were none. He checks now just to be sure.

The living room is large, its walls covered in bookshelves. Tom didn't get much of a chance to look down here when they first arrived. They promptly made their way upstairs. He looks now. The books are a mixture of fiction and psychology textbooks. There are two sofas in the living room. There is a television in the corner. The floors throughout the downstairs of the house are exposed wood. In the centre of the living room floor is a rug, and atop the rug is an oak coffee table. There's a fireplace, and on the mantelpiece there are some framed photographs. Tom inspects them closer. Malani with her parents. Malani in her deputy uniform. Malani with friends.

Malani is still upstairs, in the bed. Tom returns to her. He lies down beside her. She rolls onto her side. Tom strokes her hip. "Hanging around town today has had its perks," he says.

She laughs and presses a hand to his chest, then kisses him. "Have you heard anything from Lorne?"

"Nothing," Tom says.

"That's a good sign."

"I hope so."

"Is he still working? Do you want to go along to the bar and see him, make sure everything's all right?"

"Yeah," Tom says. "I think I will."

"I'll come with," Malani says.

They get dressed and leave the house. They get into Malani's car. She drives them to the bar. It's dark now. Getting late. The bar will be closing soon.

It's quiet inside. A lot quieter than it was earlier in the day. Tom counts only four men in the bar. They sit around a table together, talking and laughing. Lorne and Colin are behind the bar counter. Tom and Malani approach. Lorne gives them a knowing grin.

"How was lunch?" he says, then makes a show of checking the time.

"Best burger I've ever had," Tom says, and Malani laughs.

"See?" she says. "I knew it."

"How's it been here?" Tom says, taking a seat on the stool. Malani sits beside him.

"It only started to quieten down around an hour ago," Colin says, looking out at his remaining four patrons. "What happened out at the ranch has really got people talking." Colin does not give any indication that he knows Tom was out there. To be sure, Tom shoots Lorne a look. Lorne shakes his head. "Hopefully that'll be the last we see of those assholes," Colin says, returning his gaze to the people closest to him. "I never had any trouble with the militia myself, but I know plenty of people around town who did. We shouldn't have to live under constant intimidation like that. Hell, we're lucky they've never troubled our tourist trade. It could've been just a matter of time, though. Best we never have to find out for sure."

"Today's been a good day," Lorne says. "Especially takings-wise."

"I'm not sure anyone else around town will have benefited like we have," Colin says. He laughs. "People came here to gossip. They love a good story. Want to trade notes and theories. Of course, no one knows what really happened, but it's fun to hypothesise, ain't it?"

"I'm sure it is," Tom says.

"What was it like at the diner?" Lorne says.

"It was busy," Malani says. "Height of tourist-season busy."

"Sounds like they might have benefited, too," Colin says.

Lorne yawns and stretches out. "We gonna close soon?"

Colin nods toward the remaining table. "Gonna give them a couple more minutes to finish their drinks, then I'll send them on their way."

The door into the bar is off to Tom's left. Almost as soon

as the words have left Colin's mouth, Tom notices the door begin to open.

Colin spots it, too. He turns to tell them that he's closing up soon.

The door is opening too fast. It's been kicked open. Tom spots weaponry. Two figures. "Get down!" he calls, as he throws himself to the right, toward Malani, and knocks her off the stool and to the ground, he on top of her. He shields her as the men entering the bar open fire.

40

Two men. Tom looks back, braced. He makes out that their weapons are a MAC-10 and a Steyr TMP, just as they open fire. The sound of gunfire fills the bar, drowning out any other noises. The four men at the table are peppered with bullets by the man on the right with the MAC-10. Their bodies shake and tremble and blood sprays from them. They slump onto the table or fall to the floor. The gunshots sound familiar to Tom. These are the same men who fired upon him and Lorne after running them off the road.

The man on the left fires upon the bar. Bottles and glasses smash and shatter. Drinks spray. Tom can't see Lorne and Colin. He can only hope they were able to duck in time. The bullets from the Steyr TMP tear chunks out of the wooden counter.

Tom and Malani can't remain stationary. He gets off Malani and she is already turning onto her front so they can both crawl away. Tom pulls out his Beretta. He fires back at the two men, causing them to scatter. They pause in their firing as they dive behind cover. Tom rolls onto his back and sits up, gun outstretched in front of him, looking for a clear shot. Malani continues on, crawling around the corner of the bar and behind cover.

The man with the Steyr TMP takes a shot at Tom. Tom is prepared for him. As soon as he raises his head from behind the booth, bringing forward his weapon, Tom shoots him twice. Both bullets hit him in the face. He crumples to the ground, dropping his gun. Blood and bone from his skull splash upon the wall behind him.

The other man doesn't go wild. He doesn't react to the death of his friend. It seems like they might not actually be friends. This is professional. This isn't the militia. Tom saw how they reacted out there. As he shot them down, they tried to help each other. They struggled, in the dark, but they still tried. They called out the names of their fallen friends. They showed emotion.

That's not what is happening here. The man with the MAC-10 is careful. He doesn't rise wildly from his cover as Tom hoped he would, ready to promptly shoot him down. This is professional, but not *too* professional. They've burst in guns blazing. Careless. They should have killed the power first. Killed the lights. Come in wearing NVGs. Even in a small town like this, Tom knows they're available. Someone should be outside covering the exit, too, but judging from how they've come in, Tom doubts anyone is.

Tom doesn't stay where he is like a sitting duck. He doubts his opponent is, either. Tom gets to his feet, careful not to make too much noise. He steps back, keeping the Beretta raised. He risks peering over the counter. He sees Lorne, Colin, and Malani sheltering there. Colin lies flat, covering his head. Lorne sits up, his back against a refrigerator. His breathing is hard, but his eyes are bulging and a hand is at his throat like he can't fill his lungs. His face is red. Malani is beside him, a hand on his shoulder. She's trying to calm him.

Tom hears movement and spins. One of the dead men at the table is sliding off. He falls to the ground.

The man with the MAC-10 has heard the same noise. He rises from behind the booth, probably thinking Tom is trying to sneak up on him but has tripped on a chair. He opens fire. It's likely a fresh magazine, now. He's aiming at the table. Where the noise came from. He plants bullets in the corpses and shoots up the table. It doesn't take him long to realise that Tom is not there. He doesn't stop firing. He turns as he scans the room. He turns toward the counter. Toward Tom.

Tom dives to his right, away from the arc of fire. He knows he can't escape it. It will catch up to him. He keeps a tight grip on his gun. He stays calm. When he lands, he lands hard on his ribs. The air is knocked out of him. He doesn't think about it. He stays focussed. Aims down the length of his arm. Aims at the man who is aiming at him. Tom fires. His first shot misses, but only just. The bullet goes over the shooter's left shoulder. Tom corrects. Fires again. The next bullet goes through the shooter's left cheek. The next goes through his mouth.

The MAC-10 falls dead. The shooter falls dead.

Tom gets to his feet, catching his breath. He searches both dead men, keeping them covered while he works. It's unlikely they're still living, but there's never any harm in being careful.

Neither man has identification. The man with the MAC-10 has keys for a Toyota. Tom takes the keys, but before he can step outside to find and search the car, the sound of blaring sirens screeches to a halt out front. He hears doors open. The sheriff and his deputies don't come straight in. They stay outside. They can hear the shooting has stopped, but they don't know that it's over.

The sheriff gets on the megaphone. Tom isn't listening. He goes to Lorne and Malani. Hops over the bar. Colin is crouched on Lorne's other side now. Lorne is coming down now, but slowly. He can breathe again.

"Stay low when the sheriff and the deputies come in," Malani says. She's talking to everyone. "They're not used to things like this. They might come in with itchy trigger fingers. Everyone stay down here until they get a chance to cool, and then let me do the talking."

41

The sheriff is not happy to see Tom. He motions to deputies Norton and Lowell. "Put him in cuffs."

Tom doesn't struggle while they cuff him.

"What are you doing, Sheriff?" Colin says. He stands by Lorne, who is slumped on a stool. Lorne is pale. He looks sick. His hands are shaking. His hair is slick with sweat.

Rooker ignores Colin. He looks straight at Tom. "I warned you," he says. "No one can say I didn't. I warned you more than once."

"Rollins didn't do anything," Colin says. "He saved us. Hell, if it wasn't for him, we'd all be like those four men right now."

"Where are your weapons?" Rooker says to Tom.

Tom shrugs.

"Search him."

Lowell pats him down. "He's clean."

"Uh-huh. Then what did you kill these men with, Rollins? A toothpick?"

Tom doesn't answer.

The Beretta and the KA-BAR are concealed behind the bar. Malani knows where they are. She steps forward. "Sherrif Rooker, why are you placing Mr. Rollins under arrest?"

Rooker looks at her, running his tongue around the inside of his mouth. "Malani," he says. "Been a while."

"Uh-huh. Why are you placing Mr. Rollins under arrest?"

"He's not under arrest," Rooker says. "I want to question him. I want to find out what's happened here."

"Then why's he in cuffs?"

"Because he's dangerous." Rooker folds his arms. "I don't need to explain myself to you, Malani. You forewent the privilege of questioning me a long time ago."

"You never gave me answers back then, either."

Rooker ignores her. He motions to his deputies, Norton and Lowell. "Take him out to the cruiser – and keep an eye on him. Anderson, take witness statements."

The deputies take Tom out to the car and put him in the back. The bar door is open, and Tom can see Malani complaining to Rooker inside. Outside of the bar, a small crowd is gathering. A couple of deputies whom Tom doesn't know are keeping them back. Norton and Lowell stay by the cruiser. Ten minutes go by, and then Sherrif Rooker comes out. Malani follows him to the door. She continues to protest, but Rooker is not listening. Malani signals to Tom. She mouths that she'll get him out.

Rooker gets into the front of the cruiser and starts the engine. He looks at Tom in the mirror. "I told you not to make noise," Rooker says. "One damn thing. Don't make any trouble. Yet here we are, six men dead, and a lot of spent shell casings." He turns to look at Tom now. "And so soon after the militia are attacked out at their ranch? I assume you heard about that. Seems like everyone has. You know anything about that?"

Tom doesn't answer.

Rooker shakes his head and turns back around. "You'll talk to me," he says. "You'll talk soon enough."

42

The Aries Group have set up camp. They're less that twenty miles from Khartoum. They sit tight, waiting to hear from Ibrahim Hussain. They're expecting retaliation from Abdul Mohamed after what was done to his cousin's village. So far, nothing has been heard. If he's going to retaliate, he's taking his time about it.

Gunnar glances at his watch. Works out the time difference between here and America, and what time it is over there.

They've set up a small seating area outside the Humvee. It's just after dawn. The sky is lighting. Gunnar did not sleep last night. He sat and listened to the sounds of distant battle. Looking through binoculars, he could see flares and strobing through the night sky. He felt a pang, wishing he could be amidst it.

Florian is nearby, on a laptop. Gunnar turns to him. "Have we heard anything from Colorado?"

Florian double-checks the emails. "Nothing," he says.

"How long has it been?"

"They didn't specify when it would happen. They said they'd wait until dark."

Gunnar drinks from a water bottle. He swirls it around the inside of his mouth and spits some to the side, into the dirt. The sun is coming up and already it's getting hot. Gunnar pours some of the water over his head in an attempt to cool off. He's thinking. "It's been hours," he says. "More than long enough. We should have heard from them by now."

"Should I call them?" Florian says.

"No," Gunnar says. "If anything has gone wrong, their phones and laptops may have been compromised." He falls silent, thinking. He turns and stares at Florian's laptop. "Search the news for the local area. Samson, Colorado."

Florian nods and gets to it. Gunnar turns away, leaving him to work. The sounds of last night's battle are practically non-existent now. His binoculars are in his lap. He raises them to his eyes and looks around. There's nothing to see. Nothing of interest, at least.

Off to his right, he sees Antoine emerge from his tent. He wears his camo trousers and boots, but nothing on top. He yawns and stretches, his arms reaching out wide. He squints toward the horizon, and then makes his way to Gunnar and Florian.

"Good morning," Gunnar says.

Antoine grunts.

"Another beautiful day in paradise," Gunnar says.

Antoine chuckles. "There is nowhere I would rather be."

"Not even Paris?"

Antoine snorts. "Fuck Paris."

Gunnar laughs.

The rest of the camp is subdued. The men make coffee.

They cook and eat breakfast. They wander aimlessly, waiting for the next action. Some of them are still sleeping. There is a muted quality to the air here. Gunnar recognises it. This is not the calm before the storm. This is the wait before the calm. They all hate the waiting.

"Have we heard anything from America yet?" Antoine says.

"Nothing," Gunnar says. "Florian is looking into it."

Antoine calls to him. "Florian. What have you found?"

Florian turns. His face is grim. "There's nothing official yet," he says, "but I've found posts from social media in Samson, and people are talking about a shootout in a bar there. Six dead."

"Any names?" Gunnar says, setting his jaw.

"Not yet. But people are saying that two of the dead are the attackers."

"*Fuck*." Gunnar gets to his feet. The binoculars fall from his lap to the ground. He ignores them. He paces.

"There is also mention of a militia having recently been attacked," Florian says. "People are wondering if it's connected."

Gunnar waves a dismissive hand. "Our boys have nothing to do with any militia."

Antoine and Florian say nothing while Gunnar continues to pace. They let him think.

Gunnar halts and stares off into the distance. The sun is above the horizon now. He feels its hot rays upon his face. He breathes deep and turns back. "If you want something done right," he says.

"You're going to go yourself?" Antoine says. "We can send men there."

"I'm handling this," Gunnar says. "Enough is enough.

And besides, all this we've heard about Tom Rollins, I want to see him myself. See him up close. Iron sharpens iron, boys. Been a while since I was able to put myself to the test."

Antoine nods, understanding.

"Antoine, gather me a team. Ten men. No. Eleven. Florian will be one of them. Find me ten more. In my absence, you're in command. I'll relay this to Ibrahim Hussain before I go." He turns to Florian. "Contact some of our men, whoever is closest to Boulder, and send them to Gabe Elcoat. Make sure he's protected until we can get there and deal with things. Then organise our flights. ASAP. Once that's done, kit up and get ready to move out."

Antoine and Florian both know what they must do. They get to it. Gunnar spits onto the ground. He notices the water he spat out earlier has already dried. "It'll be cold in Colorado," he says, mostly to himself. The cold will be a welcome reprieve from the heat here. From the sweat. He'll go over there, and he'll deal with what Jason and Harry failed at. He'll get his money back. He doesn't anticipate it will take long. And then he will come back here, to the heat, and the sweat. To the action.

He thinks about Tom Rollins. The man who has caused them this trouble. The man who has likely killed Jason and Harry. He sounds tough. He sounds like a challenge. Gunnar is looking forward to meeting him.

43

Tom has not been taken to a cell. He's been deposited in the interrogation room, and left alone for a couple of hours. He's cuffed to the table. He can't move around the room. He sits facing a wood-panelled wall opposite. To his left is a mirror. Two-way glass, no doubt. No way of knowing if anyone is behind it, watching him. To his right, in front of him, is the door he was brought through. It has remained closed and locked since Tom was brought in. No one has come in to see how he's doing. To question him. To offer him a drink, or a bathroom break. He needs neither. He sits still and stares straight ahead, his hands clasped. He waits. He doesn't like it. There are more important things for him to be doing. He *can* do this, though. Stronger men have tried to break him. They've all failed.

There is no clock in this room. No way to tell the time. At a guess, Tom thinks it's two in the morning, or thereabouts. Hard to be sure. There's no source of light in here other than the glaring, buzzing strip-light overhead.

The door unlocks. Sherrif Rooker enters. He offers no

apology for Tom's wait. He offers no explanation, either. He sits, and he stares at Tom. Tom stares back. Neither man blinks.

"What did you kill them with, Rollins?" Rooker says.

"A gun," Tom says.

"Don't get smart with me."

"Then don't ask stupid questions."

The sheriff's nostrils flare. "All right. *Where* is the gun you killed them with?"

"I don't know. It was chaos back there. I'm not sure what happened." Tom keeps his face blank. He looks straight ahead. He looks through the sheriff.

"Where did you get it from?"

"It's my own. I'm very attached to it. Have you found it?"

Rooker says nothing. He takes a deep breath.

Both men sit upright. Neither of them lounges. Both have their hands on the table.

"Tell me what happened," Rooker says. "As you remember it."

"Two men burst into the bar and started firing. They killed the four guys at the table, and they started firing upon us. I pulled my gun and I shot them both."

"It doesn't sound so chaotic to me."

"A gunfight is always chaotic. I'm surprised you don't know that."

"What I mean is, your account is very straightforward."

"I'm giving the condensed version. You don't have anything to hold me on, Sheriff."

Rooker ignores him. "Did you know either man? Recognise them?"

"No."

Rooker pauses, and then says, "They weren't militia."

There is something about his pause. Tom doesn't respond. He studies the sheriff. For the first time, Rooker looks away. He looks down at his hands. He fiddles with his wedding band.

Tom takes a different approach with the man. He softens his tone. "You played dumb when I asked you about the militia."

Rooker doesn't look up. He looks tired. Tom sees his shoulders sag, like some of the fight is going out of him. Tom can't be sure, but he thinks he looks almost relieved. This confuses him.

"Did you have trouble with the militia?" Tom says.

Rooker finally looks back up. "Who were the men that attacked you in the bar?"

"I don't know."

"I'm pretty certain they were looking for you."

"Why?"

"Who else would they be there for? You're a stranger in this town. I told you not to make trouble, and yet trouble has been made. It's almost like it's following you around, now."

"That still doesn't mean I knew who they were. A lot of people shoot at me, and I don't always know who they are, either." Tom grins.

The sheriff chuckles lightly, shaking his head. "I knew it," he says. "You're a yahoo, ain't you? A goddam cowboy, looking for trouble wherever you can find it."

"I just came here for a funeral. I didn't know there would be a militia, or crazed gunmen shooting up a bar."

"What happened to the militia, Rollins?"

"How should I know?"

"Because I know you beat a few of them up," Rooker

says. "Because I know they had John Breen's daughter, and I know John Breen came to see you."

"Sounds like you've taken a great interest in the militia."

"It's my job."

Tom attempts something. Drops a name. He watches closely to gauge the sheriff's reaction. "John had some interesting things to say about the militia, and especially about the man running it. What was his name again?" Already the sheriff has stiffened in his seat. "Bear?"

Rooker is trying hard not to react. Not to flinch. His teeth are gritted tight. He has to clear his throat before he speaks. "I believe that's right."

"I think you *know* that's right." Tom watches the sheriff. Tom is starting to feel like something happened between the sheriff and the militia. With Bear in particular, perhaps. Tom remembers what Malani said about the sheriff. That when he first took the job he was good at it, but after the militia arrived, it was like a switch was flipped.

"Let me ask you something," Tom says.

"You're not in a position to ask me anything."

Tom ignores him. "I understand the militia root around in the dumpsters at the supermarket to get their food and other supplies. And I've been told that they threatened the manager into putting fresh produce out there for them."

"This isn't a question," Rooker says.

"I'm getting to it," Tom says. "Let me illustrate my thinking process for you. It'll all make sense. Because of how they were getting the supplies, I get the impression the militia didn't have a lot of money. I've heard they weren't growing anything out there at the ranch." Tom doesn't mention that he saw this for himself. "So it's not like they were farmers and making their money that way. Any money they did get, they probably put it back into getting weapons and ammunition."

"Will you get to the point."

"My point is this – I don't think they could bribe you. They didn't have anything to offer. So my question is this – did they threaten you?"

Rooker looks like he's been slapped. His mouth works, but he doesn't say anything. He bites his lip. He has to look away from Tom.

Tom doesn't speak. He waits the sheriff out. Tom thinks he's right. That the militia threatened the sheriff. An isolated place like this, it was probably easy to do. The sheriff could have called on back-up, though. He could have fed this information to state police, or the FBI.

Rooker finally looks back at Tom. "I can see you're not married, Rollins," he says, nodding at the lack of rings on Tom's left hand. "But do you have children?"

"No," Tom says.

"I've got two daughters," Rooker says. "Oldest is ten. Youngest is seven." He pauses. Hesitates. Looks Tom in the eye. "Bear threatened me, sure," he says. "Put a gun to my head. But he also threatened *them*. Threatened my wife, too. I didn't worry so much about myself. That kind of risk comes with the job. But I *did* worry about my family. Bear made it very clear – I was all alone out here in Samson, and they could get to me and my family any time they wanted. He...he used much more colourful language than I'm using right now. He told me what he and his men would do, and they'd make me watch."

"Why'd he make those threats?" Tom says.

"So I'd keep my nose out of his business," Rooker says. "So that when he hassled the town, I'd leave him be. He was running his own little settlement out there at the ranch. He said he wanted peace and quiet, and so long as I provided that, he wouldn't cause me any real issues in town. I just had to leave him alone. I...I told myself I could do that. That I could live with that, with not doing my job, so long as it meant my family were safe."

"Did you try telling anyone? FBI? Do your deputies know?"

Rooker shakes his head. "Didn't dare. Couldn't tell anyone. Couldn't take the chance."

Rooker lowers his face. He's ashamed. He's never admitted this to anyone. The silence returns. Tom watches the sheriff. Rooker can't look back. He stares down at his hands, though he doesn't really see them. His mind is elsewhere. Remembering.

"I've heard," Tom says, and Rooker looks up, "that Bear isn't someone anyone needs to worry about. Not anymore."

Rooker doesn't say anything for a long time. He's still thinking, except now he's thinking about what Tom has just told him. "You sure about that?" he says finally.

Tom shrugs. "I heard he's dead. I heard most of the militia are dead. I heard they had it coming, too."

Rooker clenches his jaw. "What were they doing to Heather Breen?" he says. He looks like he doesn't want to know.

"Whatever they wanted," Tom says.

Rooker closes his eyes tight. He knows what this means. "I'm sorry," he says, though it's not clear whom he's talking to. Tom does not think this apology is for him.

The sheriff gets to his feet and paces for a few moments with his back to Tom. He rubs at his eyes. Composes himself. He sniffs when he sits back down. Sucks his teeth. "How many members of the militia are left?" He pauses, then adds, "If you've heard."

"Half a dozen," Tom says. "Give or take. Guy called Skinny Long could be leading them."

"And they could be anywhere right now," Rooker says.

Tom nods.

"Is...is Bear really dead? For sure?"

Tom looks at him. Doesn't respond. This is answer enough for Rooker.

"Tell me what happened at the bar."

"I already have," Tom says.

"Who were the men?"

"I don't know."

Rooker waits. "That's the truth?"

Tom nods. "I'm going to find out."

Rooker sighs. He starts to laugh, softly. "I don't suppose there's any point in asking you not to?"

Tom spreads out his cuffed hands, wrists pressed together. "Couldn't hurt," he says. "But it would just be wasted breath."

"Where's the gun you killed them with?"

"I don't know where it ended up," Tom says. It's a half-truth. He has a pretty good idea where it is, and the fact Rooker keeps asking about it tells Tom that his deputies were unable to find it when they searched the bar. "Did you find any ID on them?"

"No," Rooker says.

"Did you find their vehicle? Search it?"

"We did," Rooker says. "There was nothing worthwhile in it. A couple of burner phones. An encrypted laptop. I've been told that if we get the password wrong too many times it's likely that the software will be wiped. I don't hold out much hope that we'll access it."

Tom notices how the sheriff is more open with sharing information now than he was the other day.

There's a pause. It doesn't seem like either has anything to say or ask the other anymore.

Rooker takes a deep breath. He holds it in his lungs for a couple of seconds, staring at Tom, appraising him, then slowly releases it through his mouth. He takes a key from his pocket and undoes Tom's cuffs. "Sorry I kept you waiting for so long earlier," he says.

Tom supposes this apology is better late than never.

"On behalf of the sheriff's department and the town of Samson, I'd like to thank you for your heroic efforts in the bar." Rooker stands, and he offers a hand.

Tom stares at the hand. He stands and takes it. They shake.

"And thank you for – for the *news* of the militia," Rooker says. "I can't say I'll miss any of them. In the meantime, I'll increase patrols of the town. We'll keep an eye out for the survivors, make sure they don't attempt any kind of retribution."

"That would be smart," Tom says. He rubs at his wrists where the cuffs were a little tight. "Now's the time for some real policing."

The sheriff nods grimly, his earlier shame still apparent. He stands a little straighter though, with a renewed sense of resolve. With purpose. "You're free to go, Rollins."

44

R ooker leads Tom through the station and to the front. Lorne and Malani are there, waiting for him. Lorne sits slumped in the same spot where Tom first waited to meet with the sheriff a few days ago, and Malani is at the counter, talking with Deputy Anderson. They both look up as Tom enters. Lorne still looks pale and shaken. He looks like he needs some sleep. He rubs at his left leg. It's where he had the break back in Afghanistan. Tom appreciates him coming here to wait for him, despite his traumatic experience and his body's response to it.

Malani's face brightens when she sees Tom. She notices he's not cuffed. She steps forward and looks at the sheriff. "He's free?"

Rooker nods. "He's free. Thank you for your cooperation, Mr. Rollins."

"Any time," Tom says.

Rooker turns to leave, but before he goes he places a hand on Tom's arm and squeezes. He leaves the foyer, returning to his office.

Malani looks confused at the gesture. She watches Rooker go. She glances back at Deputy Anderson, who looks equally surprised. "What was that about?" Malani says, turning back to Tom.

"I'll tell you later," Tom says.

Malani embraces him, and then Lorne gets to his feet and does the same. They leave the station. Lorne drags his left leg behind him, wincing with every step. So long as Tom has been in town, he hasn't seen Lorne's limp look this bad.

It's dark outside. The night is quiet and still. Their breath billows in front of their faces. Malani tells him it's almost three in the morning. Her car is parked over the road. They go to it. Once they're inside, Tom starts talking.

"I'm starting to get real tired with how things are going," he says. "Whoever they were who attacked us, it must have had something to do with Adam. That's all I can assume. They weren't militia. They didn't look it, and the sheriff verified as much."

Malani starts her car and turns the heaters on. "It looked like the two of you got almost friendly."

"We found some common ground," Tom says. "And it made him more talkative."

"Yeah?" Malani remains surprised by this. "You're going to have to tell me what happened in there. Did he know who the two men from the bar were?"

"He didn't. But I'm going to find out. I'm going to find out today, if I can help it. I'm going to find out what their connection to Adam was, and why they're coming after us."

"What's the plan?"

"I need to borrow your car," Tom says. "I'm going back to Boulder. To Gabe Elcoat. He's going to talk, and he's going to tell me everything he wouldn't before."

"You can use my car," Malani says, "but I'm coming with."

"It could be dangerous," Tom says.

"I've been in dangerous situations before," Malani says. "Tonight included. I can handle myself."

Tom nods. "It could take a while. I want to get answers today, but I can't guarantee that I will. Today or tomorrow or the day after – whatever it takes."

Malani nods. "If it comes to that, I'll tell Laura to let my patients know I can't make it but I'll make it up to them."

"You're determined to come," Tom says.

"I want to know what's happening too," Malani says. "And I want to know what happened to Adam."

"I want to know, too," Lorne says from the back of the car. His voice is very small. "But I don't want to come to Boulder. I – I'm sorry... I just can't. I need to sleep. I need to – I need–"

"You don't need to explain yourself to us," Tom says. "We can drop you off at the trailer. But be careful, Lorne. Okay? Anything comes up, call me. Find a place to hide out if you need to. Some of the militia is still out there, and we don't know who the other two were with, or how many of them there could be."

Malani starts driving, heading back to the trailer park.

Tom watches the sheriff's department disappear behind them in the side mirror. It's the only building on the block still lit up at this time of day. "Where are my weapons?" he says, turning from the mirror.

"Glove compartment," Malani says.

Tom pulls them out. "They see you take them out?"

Malani grins. "They didn't see a thing. Why would they suspect me of smuggling anything out of there? I almost feel bad for tricking them like that."

"Almost?"

"Well," Malani laughs, "not as much as I should."

45

L orne hates being this way.

He hates how weak he has become. He hates how shaken he still feels, despite the hours that have passed since the shootout in the bar. All over, his body is still trembling. While he was at the sheriff's department, waiting for Tom with Malani, the deputy behind the counter asked him if he needed a blanket or a hot drink. Lorne declined both. He tried to hold himself still. He failed.

Now, he stands on his trailer steps and watches as Tom and Malani drive away in her blue BMW. He sighs, watching them go.

He hates that he's not going with them.

Lorne turns and presses his forehead to the door. His legs are weak. There's a pain in the left that feels like when he first broke it and he was lying in the hospital bed with his leg in a cast and the bones were knitting themselves back together. It's a pain he hasn't felt in almost ten years. He unlocks the door and goes inside, angrily tearing off his clothes and throwing them to the side as he makes his way to bed. He's tired, and he's shaken, and he's scared. And he's angry. He's so angry at himself. He lies in the bed and balls his fists and grinds his jaw. He stares at the ceiling and breathes deep through his nose.

In his mind, he replays the attack in the bar. Remembers how he instantly froze up, and Colin had to drag him down into cover behind the counter.

Lorne feels like a stranger in his own body. He feels like he has no control over it. A car could backfire and he'd be rendered a frozen, snivelling mess on the cold ground. He can't defend himself. Can't defend his friends. Can't protect anyone he cares about.

He can't help himself. He couldn't help Adam. He doesn't even have the strength to help avenge Adam. All he can do is get in the way. All he can do is slow Tom down. He's a liability. He causes more issues than solutions. He has nothing to offer.

Lorne is shaking again. His eyes are hot. He smothers his face with a pillow and he screams into it. When he takes it from his face, he's crying. The tears roll down his cheeks. He rolls onto his side and he closes his eyes, and he wishes he was better.

46

Halfway to Boulder, Tom took over driving. He power napped for the first half. For the second half, it has been Malani's turn. Both of them have been up all night. They're not feeling at their best. Before they left Samson, they stopped off at an all-night diner on the outskirts of town for something light to eat, and to purchase a few bottles of water to take with them.

Tom wakes Malani as they near Gabe Elcoat's office. They're only a couple of blocks away.

Malani stretches as much as she's able in the seat. She rubs her eyes. "What's the plan?" she says. "Are we going to go in and talk to him again?"

"I want to get a look at his office first," Tom says. "It's still early and it's unlikely that he's there yet. We'll get in, take a look around, see if there's anything worth looking at. We'll be there waiting and catch him when he arrives."

Tom reaches the street where Gabe's office is, but something catches his eye and he doesn't stop the car. He keeps going to the end of the block and rounds the corner.

"What's up?" Malani says. "Did you see something?"

"Three men in a car," Tom says. "Black Chevy. Parked down the road on our left. They had a clear view of the office."

Malani nods. "Sounds like we spooked him the other day."

Tom nods. They sit by the kerb, the engine idling. There was no one else on Gabe's street. It hasn't come alive yet.

"What do we do instead?" Malani says.

Tom looks back over his shoulder. He can see the office. He can see the car. Can see the backs of the heads of the three men inside. "We've got a clear view from here," Tom says. "For now, we'll watch. As the day goes on, we'll have a better idea of where we stand. Our main priority until we figure out what to do is to make sure no one sees us. I assume you've been on stakeouts before?"

"I've done plenty in my time," Malani says. "I don't miss them."

"Let's get some more rest. We'll sleep in shifts. You go first. I'll wake you if anything happens."

Malani makes a pillow of her jacket and reclines her seat. She presses her jacket pillow against the door and rests her head against it. She closes her eyes. It doesn't take her long to get back to sleep. Tom watches her for a moment as she drifts off, her breathing growing shallow and thick. He turns back toward the car and the office. Watches. He sees the man sitting in the back of the car occasionally turn and survey the street. He looks back, down toward the end of the block. Tom is parked out of view. He's not concerned about the man's roving eyes.

An hour passes. The neighbourhood starts to come alive. The road and sidewalk traffic both grow. The businesses nearby are opening. Tom can smell coffee and baked goods.

Gabe arrives at his office. His car, a white Mercedes, rolls to a stop in front of the Chevy. He gets out and looks toward the car already parked there. He smiles nervously. He stands on the sidewalk, watching the car and waiting.

The man from the back of the Chevy gets out and goes to Gabe. The two men in the front stay where they are. Gabe offers his hand to the man who approaches him, but the man doesn't shake it. He ignores it. Gabe awkwardly lowers his hand. He goes to his office door, fumbling his keys out of his pocket. He drops them. He picks them up and unlocks the door and they go inside.

The two men in the front of the Chevy don't go anywhere. They continue to watch the block.

Tom waits. The man who went inside with Gabe does not return. Tom checks the time. They've been in there for almost an hour. He doesn't know how long meetings with accountants usually run for, if this is what is happening. From the look of the men, and the way two of them have remained outside seemingly on watch, he has his doubts. He glances at Malani. She's fast asleep, breathing softly. Tom feels wide awake now. Wired. He waits another hour. The man does not emerge. No one else goes in.

Tom gets out of the car. He leaves Malani sleeping. No reason to disturb her. He's not planning on being gone long.

He walks away from the car and the block, going in the opposite direction. He takes a right turn down the back of the building opposite to Gabe's office. He becomes more cautious when he reaches the corner leading to the alleyway between two buildings. He can see Gabe's office directly opposite, but the glare on the window stops him from seeing inside. The black Chevy is parked a little way back, obscured by the front corner of the building. There's a dumpster a little further down the alley. Tom goes to it. Stays concealed. He ducks down and peers out. He manages to see past the glare, into Gabe's office.

Gabe is behind his desk, working. He looks how he did the first time Tom and Malani saw him. He's typing on his computer, his phone tucked between his ear and shoulder. The man from the Chevy is standing behind him, watching over his shoulder. His arms are folded. He looks bored. After a moment, he strolls out from behind the desk and walks up to the window. He looks to the Chevy. Flashes them a thumbs-up. Then he takes a seat.

Tom leaves the alleyway and returns to Malani. She's awake. She watches him return. "You been up long?" Tom says.

"I woke up as soon as you got out of the car," she says. "Where'd you go?"

Tom tells her what he has seen.

"It sounds like he's being guarded," Malani says. "This changes things."

"It changes things, sure," Tom says. "But we're still going to talk to him."

"What are you thinking?"

"I'm thinking we're going to have to wait until he leaves," Tom says. "We'll see where he goes – presumably home – and we'll see if his new guards go with him. We'll improvise from there."

47

Gabe stays late at the office. The businesses nearby are closing. The traffic is thinning. There aren't as many people around as there have been during the day.

Tom napped for a few hours earlier while Malani took over watch. She woke him at lunch time to tell him the two men from the Chevy had gotten out of the car. They were standing around, stretching out their legs. One of them poked his head into the office and then he walked away from the car, in the direction of Malani's BMW. Tom worried they were performing a sweep, something he would have expected them to have done much sooner. He and Malani slipped from the car and concealed themselves down an alleyway. They watched and waited. The man was not on a sweep. He was getting lunch. The other man stayed outside the Chevy, looking up and down the road, but not looking far enough. He leaned with one foot up on a tyre, and Tom caught sight of his shoulder holster. The man watched a young lady make her way down the block. He was distracted.

Distracted easily. He wasn't focussing on the things he should have been.

After lunch, the men guarding Gabe didn't get back out of the car. Tom and Malani were able to remain in the BMW. They were both done with sleep. As rested as they needed to be. They watched together. Waiting for something to happen. Waiting for Gabe to leave.

The streetlights are coming on when Gabe finally sets off, accompanied by the man who has sat inside with him all day. This man accompanies Gabe to his Mercedes. They turn the car around in the middle of the road and the black Chevy follows them.

Malani is behind the wheel. She follows. She knows what she's doing. She's had training. Knows to keep her distance. Knows to let a couple of other vehicles get between them.

They leave Boulder, heading south-east. They're on Route 36. The three lanes allow them plenty of space to hold back. The traffic here is busier. Tom and Malani keep the Chevy and the Mercedes in view. The Mercedes leads the way. The Chevy follows close behind, not leaving a big enough gap between the two vehicles for anyone else to slip in. They head eight miles down the road, then turn off. They're the only three cars to turn off. Malani keeps her distance.

"There's a Whole Foods up ahead," Tom says, pointing. "And there's a car behind us. Pull into there and let the car get past. Let them fill the gap."

"Keep your eye on them," Malani says, signalling.

Tom does. The car behind takes their place and Malani drives straight through the parking lot to the other side and pulls back out onto the road.

The Mercedes and the Chevy lead them to the town of Superior. Tom wonders if this is where Gabe lives. It looks like a nice place. They haven't had to drive far from Boulder. Just over fifteen minutes.

The cars up ahead turn down a neighbourhood. They're going slow. Tom thinks they're going to stop soon. "Hold back," he says.

Malani does. She stops on the corner and they both look down the road. The Mercedes and the Chevy both stop in front of a house on the right side of the street. All four men get out of the two vehicles. They stand briefly and converse. Gabe looks out of place with the three other men. They're taller than him, for a start, but they're better built, too. Young and muscular and healthy. They talk as if he's not even there. Gabe stands silently, looking at them each in turn as they speak. Finally, they separate. The two men who have been sat in the Chevy all day go inside the house with Gabe. The man who was in Gabe's office with him stays outside. He lights a cigarette and paces the sidewalk for a moment, looking the neighbourhood over. Eventually, he gets into the Chevy. He doesn't drive. He stays right where he is. He's on watch duty.

"This must be Gabe's," Malani says. "All right, so now we know what we're dealing with. Now we can plan."

Tom is watching the street. "I already have a plan," he says.

"That was fast."

"I work fast."

"Are you gonna share it?"

"Of course. But first, circle the block a couple of times, avoiding this street in particular. We don't want the guy in the Chevy to see us, but I need to get a better idea of the area's layout. After that, I'll tell you the plan."

"How long do I have to memorise it?" Malani says. "It's already dark. I figure we'll be going in soon."

"Not too soon," Tom says. "Couple of hours. Let them get settled first."

48

Tom and Malani make their way along the sidewalk on foot, walking close together, huddling as if they're in deep conversation. Tom is on the right, where he can better see, and Malani is on his left. They keep their faces obscured from the man in the Chevy, in case he should know what they look like. They're on the opposite side of the road to where he's parked. He's sitting in the front, behind the steering wheel. The side closest to them. He's smoking, with the window down. His arm holding the cigarette is dangling over the side. Idly, he glances at them. Tom sees him out the corner of his eye. The man is uninterested in them. He turns away, looking straight ahead, taking another draw on his cigarette.

Beyond the car, beyond the sidewalk and the lawn, Tom can see the house. Gabe's home. It's a big house. Wooden. The downstairs has a large bay window, but the curtains are drawn and no one is peering out. All of the curtains are closed at the front of the house.

Tom and Malani come parallel with the Chevy. They're

right next to the man and his open window. Less than nine feet between them. They take another couple of steps, make sure the area is clear, and then Tom spins left and runs back to the car. The man inside hears Tom coming, but too late, and Tom is too fast. There's not enough time for him to react. Tom grabs his arm dangling from the car and pins it to the door. He throws a punch in through the open window, catching the guard high on his cheekbone, dazing him. Tom hits him again, across the jaw this time, and he knocks him unconscious.

Tom has wondered who these three men are with. Has wondered if they're with the two who came into the bar, guns blazing. If so, they should be open game, but Tom doesn't know that for sure. For all he knows, they could be a private security firm whom Gabe has hired for his personal protection. They could have nothing to do with what has happened in Samson, or what happened to Adam. Until he knows better, Tom will do his best to keep hurting them to a minimum. He won't kill them, not unless his own or Malani's life is in immediate threat and there is no other recourse.

Tom reaches into the car and pats the man down. He's carrying a gun in a shoulder holster, same as on the guy Tom spotted earlier outside Gabe's office. It's a Glock. Tom hands it to Malani. She slides it down the back of the waistband of her jeans and covers it with her jacket. The man doesn't have any other weapons. Tom props him up, so it looks like he's still sitting and watching the area.

When he's done, Tom glances back at Malani. She nods. She's ready. They both are. Tom takes off at a run, moving down the side of Gabe's house. Malani is going to go to the front door. She'll take her time. Give Tom a chance to get into position. When he reaches the back of the house, Tom peers into the back yard. There's a lawn, and nothing else. No sign that it is used for any kind of recreation during the summer months. No sign of him having a family, either. There are no bikes or toys, or patches where children have trod down the grass.

Peering out, Tom checks the windows at the back of the house. The curtains are drawn here, too. He can see some shafts of light poking out from the sides of the blinds in what he assumes to be the kitchen. Peering in, he can't see anything.

He pulls out his Beretta, then he waits. Listens. He hears Malani knocking. She knocks hard. Loud enough for him to hear. It's a distraction. She's going to tell the men inside that her car has broken down. That she needs assistance. Tom thought on how the man on the street at Gabe's office was distracted by a young lady walking by. He clearly had a roving eye. Tom hopes that he is the one to answer the door to Malani. He'll be distracted enough by her beauty. Her story will barely matter. If on the off-chance there's any trouble, Malani has the Glock. She's more than capable of taking care of herself. Of course, if the door was answered by Gabe – who would recognise her – the plan would change. She would instantly stick the gun into his face and call for Tom. He hears someone answer the front door. Malani doesn't call, and so Tom knows that it is not Gabe who has answered the door. If the man in the car outside hadn't been armed – which was unlikely – Malani would have taken Tom's Beretta. In a way, if Gabe had been the one to answer the door this would all have been a lot easier for them.

Tom moves from window to window, peering through the gaps where he can. The curtains are too tightly closed.

He can't see inside the house. This makes things risky. He doesn't know the layout, and he doesn't know where anyone is. He can't hear any voices, but he doesn't hear the door close again, either. Malani said she can keep whoever answers distracted as long as he'd need.

Tom goes to the back door. It's locked. He isn't surprised. The door does, however, have a window. It's not concealed by a curtain. There is sheer netting on the other side that makes it harder to see in, but not impossible. Tom can see straight through the house, to the open front door, to the man leaning against the jamb there talking to Malani. She has the front of the house covered. Tom has the rear. Now he just needs to work out how to get inside.

He sees movement. A head emerges from a room off the hallway, looking toward the front door. It isn't Gabe. Too tall, and too much hair. The man sees his partner at the door, talking to a woman he can't see. He shakes his head and comes into the kitchen. He goes to the refrigerator. He searches for a while and then comes out with a soda can. Tom sees his opportunity. The man in the kitchen opens the can and takes a drink. Tom steps back and raises his Beretta. He shoots out the lock and then kicks the door wide.

The man in the kitchen chokes on his soda and it spurts past his lips. He turns to Tom, reaching for his gun in its holster. Tom points the Beretta at him as he strides forward, but the man continues to reach. Tom sees his eyebrows raise and his head tilt. He understands the look. Recognition. He recognises Tom. Tom, however, has never seen this man before in his life.

Tom reaches him before he can reach his Glock. He kicks him in the chest, which knocks him back into the open refrigerator door, snapping it off its hinges. He's on the ground, on top of the broken door, and winded, but he continues to reach for the gun. Tom swings down, slams his fist and the handle of his Beretta across his jaw, knocking out a couple of his teeth and subduing him. He groans, but he's not unconscious. Tom takes the Glock from him and keeps hold of it.

Looking up, he sees at the front door that the man there has his hands raised. Malani holds the Glock two-handed, and it's pointed right at his face. The man's head turns a little to better hear what is happening behind him, but he doesn't dare turn all the way around.

Gabe is in the living room. He stands, his back pressed up against the wall next to the fireplace. He's terrified. His eyes bulge out of his skull.

"Stay there," Tom says. He continues down the hall to the man Malani is covering. Tom cracks him in the back of the head with his partner's Glock. He drops to his knees. Tom puts his Beretta away, and with the Glock handle he slams it down into the side of the man's head until he's unconscious. There's some blood, and the man will wake up with a splitting headache, but he'll live.

Tom takes out the magazine and discards the rest of the gun. He hands the magazine to Malani. "Make sure you get his gun," he says, motioning to the man he's just put down. He returns to Gabe, who has not moved. Tom pulls his Beretta back out. He doesn't point it at Gabe. He doesn't need too. He's unarmed, and he's far from dangerous. "Come here," he says, and Gabe is quick to oblige.

With a hand clamped on his shoulder and the Beretta jammed into his lower back, Tom forces Gabe from the house. They throw the front door closed behind them. They head for Malani's car, parked at the end of the street. Malani runs ahead, pulling out her car keys.

"Please," Gabe says, "what do you want?"

"You know what we want," Tom says, shoving the barrel of the Beretta in deeper, drilling it hard enough to leave a bruise above Gabe's right kidney. "You should have spoken when we first came to see you."

49

Gunnar and eleven of his men land in America. They've flown in a C-37A private jet. It lands at an airstrip outside Denver. They were in the air for sixteen hours. After the jet drops them off, it taxis back around to refuel, and then takes back off into the sky. Gunnar doesn't know where it's going next. He never asked, and he doesn't care. Florian sorted out the flight. He sorted out the vehicles that are parked at the airstrip waiting for them, too. He'll deal with the return flights to Sudan when the time comes.

Gunnar slept most of the flight. He wanted to be rested for America. For Rollins. He shoulders his kit. His men do the same. They make their way to the vehicles Florian has procured. Three vans. All black.

Florian was on his laptop on the flight. Monitoring what they were heading into. There was bad news from Gabe. Well, not Gabe precisely. Gabe is gone. The bad news came from the three men who were supposed to be guarding him.

Rollins got the drop on them. Put a hurting on all three of them. Took Gabe away with him.

Florian woke Gunnar toward the end of the flight to inform him of this. Gunnar said nothing. Processed the information.

They get into the van. Gunnar rides shotgun. One of his men drives. Florian sits in the back, behind Gunnar. "What's the plan?" he says. He has his radio ready to convey Gunnar's orders to the other vans.

Gunnar snorts. He spits out the window. "First of all, get in touch with the three who were supposed to be guarding Gabe," he says. "Tell them to meet up with us."

"What about Gabe?" Florian says.

"Gabe is a lost cause. They already have him. He's going to talk. He's going to tell them everything they want to know. What we need to do is get ahead of their discoveries."

"Samson?" Florian says.

Gunnar nods. "We're going to Samson. And we're putting an end to all of this bullshit."

50

Tom and Malani drive Gabe out to the middle of nowhere. He's stuffed in the trunk of Malani's car. Tom is driving. When he stops, there is no sign of light anywhere around. The darkness here is absolute. Tom leaves the headlights on. He and Malani get out of the car and go to the back. Malani opens the trunk and Tom grabs Gabe by the collar. He pulls him out of the car and dumps him on the ground. Gabe coughs. Tom kicks him up the ass until he stumbles to the front of the car and the headlights.

Gabe lands flat on his back. He's breathing hard, like he's just run a sprint. It's not exertion that has worn him out. It's fear. He looks up at Tom, and he's terrified. Tom pulls out the Beretta. He doesn't point it at Gabe. He just wants him to be able to see it.

"I don't want or need to hurt you," Tom says, "but I have no problem with doing so if you don't tell me what I want to know."

Gabe holds up his hands. He looks close to tears. "You don't need to hurt me," he says.

"Then tell me what I want to know," Tom says.

Malani stands beside the car, watching.

"Anything," Gabe says, breathless. "Anything you want, I swear."

"Sit up," Tom says.

Gabe does.

"Tell me about Adam Lineker," Tom says.

"What do you want to know?"

"Everything. How did you know him? What was he involved in? Don't leave anything out."

Gabe wipes his mouth with the back of his hand. His tongue flickers out, moistening his lips.

"Don't keep me waiting," Tom says.

Gabe nods. "Uh – where to start? I'm just trying to figure out where to start."

Tom fires a bullet between Gabe's legs. Gabe squeals and shuffles back. He's panting. "Figure it out fast," Tom says.

Gabe is desperate to talk now. "Have you heard of the Aries Group? Mercenary group. They operate anywhere that will pay them, but they're most active in Africa."

"I've heard of them," Tom says. "But only vaguely. I don't know much about them."

"They were founded – and they're still led – by a man named Gunnar Slaughter. He used to be in the US Army, but–"

"I can do my own research on the Aries Group," Tom says. "I don't need to know about their founding and their activities. I don't give a shit about their history. Bring me up to date. What did they have to do with Adam?"

Gabe sighs, like he's about to say something he knows Tom won't like. "Adam was a member."

Tom absorbs this. "He was a mercenary?"

Gabe nods.

It makes sense, Tom thinks. Adam worked overseas, and he never gave anyone much information on where he was at any given time, or what he was doing. He looks back at Malani. The edge of the glow from the headlights shows her features. She's shocked. She looks back at Tom.

"He never gave any indication that he was in any kind of danger like that," she says. "I would never have guessed that he was a *mercenary*." She stares out into the darkness, looking as if she's having doubts about anything that Adam may have ever told her.

"It's not the kind of thing he'd be likely to share," Tom says. "He didn't even tell Lorne."

"You're sure of that?" Malani says.

"I'm certain," Tom says. "Lorne would have told us. This is going to be just as much of a shock to him." Tom turns his focus back upon Gabe. "Did the Aries Group kill Adam?"

"I don't know," Gabe says. "I... Listen, Adam wanted out. You don't want me to give you a full rundown of the Aries Group – fine, I won't, but you need to know this: They are *brutal*. You don't fuck with the Aries Group. And some of the things they were doing, what they were getting into, it wasn't sitting right with Adam. This isn't anything he was telling me himself, but I was told to keep an eye on him. To see how he was acting. They said he'd gone soft. He wanted out of the Aries Group, and they were aware of that. But did they kill him? I don't think so. If they did, they've kept it secret from me, and they wouldn't do that – they wouldn't keep it secret from anyone. They'd want everyone to know. I read that he killed himself, but if the Aries Group had done it, I don't think they would've made it look like a suicide. They would've made a show of it. Made an example of him. You understand?"

Tom nods.

"They wouldn't be bothered about trying to cover up what they'd done. Any given member of the group is barely in this country anyway. There'd be no trail. It would run cold. There'd be no tracking them down. They could be anywhere in the world. So I don't think that they killed him."

"You don't look like the rest of them, Gabe," Tom says, "so I'm guessing you're not a part of the Aries Group, are you?"

"I'm not a *member,* no, but I'm an integral part of its operating procedures."

"How so? What do you do for them?" Tom already has an idea, but he wants to hear Gabe verify it.

"They launder money all over the world," Gabe says. "Including here in the States. I'm one of their accountants, though no one would ever find any record of me working for them."

"That's how you knew Adam," Malani says. "He was bringing money to you."

Gabe nods. "That's right. Because of our proximity, Adam was tasked with bringing me a rucksack of money every few months, and then I got it nice and clean for the Aries Group. That's why they told me to keep an eye on him and see how he was acting. They knew he wanted out, and they didn't want him to do anything stupid like try to disappear with their money."

"Adam had an important job," Tom says.

"It was. It wouldn't have just been a case of convenience that he was sent my way. They must have really trusted him, too – at first, anyway. Before he started wanting out. Setting him loose off a jet with that kind of money? You can't entrust that to anyone you have even the *mildest* of doubts about."

"How much was he bringing you?"

"It varied. But to give you an idea, his last trip to me, he was due to bring five million dollars."

"Due to?" Tom says. "He never turned up?"

"He died," Gabe says. "And the money is missing, and Gunnar does not like any of his money to be unaccounted for."

Tom and Malani exchange glances. Tom considers this, and he can see that Malani is doing the same. Whatever Adam had involved himself in, this is verification that the Aries Group did not kill him. If they had, they wouldn't be looking for their money. They'd have it already. They would have taken it right after making his death look like a suicide.

Whoever *did* kill him is still out there. But now, just like with the militia, Tom is stuck with a new problem.

"The men at your house," Tom says, "guarding you, they're Aries Group?"

"Yes."

"What do you know about the shooting at a bar in Samson?"

Gabe hesitates.

"Well?" Tom says.

"They were Aries Group, too. They were sent to find the money. They weren't having any luck. They were starting to get desperate. I can understand that – Gunnar Slaughter is not a man you want to be on the bad side of. From what I could tell of what the three guys today were talking about, their buddies were planning on shooting up the bar to kill *you*, Rollins, and then they were gonna take away some guy called Lorne to get him to talk. To tell them what he might know about the money. They figured he was the guy most likely to know anything about it, and you were too much of a liability to leave living. They narrowed it down to either Lorne, or Adam's ex-wife."

"Olivia?"

"I don't know her name. Me and Adam never made small talk. But apparently the two of them stayed close, so either she or Lorne could have been by the house and found the money after Adam killed himself. Or else he entrusted it to them, for whatever reason. Look, I don't know, but that's who the Aries Group are planning on going after."

"There's more of them close by?" Tom says.

"Gunnar himself has come over," Gabe says, and there is genuine fear on his face. "And he'll have brought his best men. Stone-cold killers, all of them."

"He's already here?"

"He's probably nearly at Samson by now."

Tom can feel Malani looking to him, but Tom doesn't look back. He already knows what she's thinking. They need to get back to Samson. They need to warn the town of what is coming. "Call Lorne," Tom says without turning. "If you have a number for Olivia, call her too. And call the sheriff. Tell him something bad is coming."

"The sheriff?" Malani says. "Are you sure?"

Tom nods. "Call him. I think he's ready to make up for his mistakes."

Malani pulls her phone out and moves away to place her calls.

"What will Gunnar do?" Tom says.

"From what I hear about you, Rollins," Gabe says, "I'm sure you can guess."

"And what if they don't know where his money is?"

"Then he'll kill them. Simple as that. Gunnar doesn't waste his time or mince his words. He wants his money back, Rollins, and he's determined to get it one way or another. He'll wipe Samson off the face of the Earth – believe me, he's done worse in Africa." Gabe swallows.

"He's willing to destroy a town and kill everyone in it for five million dollars?"

"He's done worse for less. And as far as he's concerned, that money is *his*, so this is personal."

Malani comes back. "I can't get through," she says.

"No signal?"

"I've got a couple of bars," Malani says. "I should be able to place a call."

"It sounds like he could already be there," Gabe says.

Tom stares at him. He turns to Malani. "Get in the car – I'll drive. Look up the Aries Group. Tell me anything you can find on them. A picture of Gunnar will be a big help." They hurry into the BMW.

"Hey," Gabe says, still on the ground. He starts to push himself up. "Hey! What about me? You can't leave me here!"

Tom slams his foot down on the accelerator and spins the car around, kicking up dirt that sprays over Gabe. Tom doesn't care about him. Leaving him here is exactly what Tom intends to do. He can make his own way home in the dark. Malani does not protest. They need to get back to Samson.

51

Gunnar stands on the outskirts of Samson and looks across the town. He doesn't give much thought to where his men go when they're on leave. Doesn't give any kind of consideration to where they might live. It feels strange to know that this is the place that Adam Lineker called home.

He grunts, looking at the twinkling lights. Florian stands near him. "Very pretty," Gunnar says. "But it looks so goddamned boring."

"These mountains remind me of home," Florian says. "More than half of Austria is mountainous, did you know that?"

Gunnar ignores him. He doesn't care. "Is everyone in position?"

There are three men flanking Gunnar and Florian. Everyone is armed and ready to move in. Dressed in black. Woolen hats jammed down upon their heads. Camo upon their faces. AR15s strapped across their chests, Glocks in their holsters. They're itching to move in. Gunnar can sense it. It comes off them in waves, and it makes him eager to go, too. He scrapes his teeth across his bottom lip.

Florian gets on the radio and checks everyone's progress.

Jason and Harry provided details on their people of interest. Pictures of their faces. Their addresses. Gunnar wants to get in, find where his money has gone, and get out. If possible, he wants to kill Tom Rollins, too. Rollins has killed two of his own, and caused a very long headache. Things should not have been this difficult. They should not have taken this long. Gunnar will make him pay for this. The money, however, is his priority. Rollins is a dessert. If they can't find him here, Gunnar is sure they'll find him somewhere down the line.

"Everyone is in place," Florian says, "ready to move in on your say."

"Cut the power," Gunnar says, "and then we go in."

They're at the town's generator. Gunnar hears its electrical hum fill the air. Florian and a couple others head inside. The overnight engineer and the security guard are already dead. Gunnar killed them himself. Slit their throats from ear to ear, cut through the sinew all the way through to the bone. Gunnar's blood was hot, and killing these two men helped to calm him. He could think more clearly once he had some blood on his hands.

Gunnar watches the town. Within five minutes, the lights go out. Gunnar grins. Samson is cut off. It's in darkness. The only lights left are the ones on vehicles.

Samson is cut off from more than its electricity and its internet. The Aries Group have placed jammers at all four corners of the town. No one can call in or out. Gunnar and his men stay in touch via radio. The sheriff's department will have radios, too, but at max they have a range of ten to twenty-five miles in perfect conditions. The closest town to Samson is Fraser, fifteen miles away. The station could also have a radio capable of reaching a further frequency. An isolated place like this, Gunnar would be surprised if they didn't. He's not concerned, though. They won't have a chance to contact anyone, whether in Fraser or further afield.

He gets on the radio and contacts the four men at the station. "Move in," he says. "Light it up. I wanna be able to see it from here."

"Roger that."

Gunnar looks toward where he knows the station to be. On the way over, on the flight, after he'd slept and after Florian had woken him to share news of what had happened with Gabe, they studied the layout of the town. When they reached Samson in the vans, before they took up their positions and planted the jammers, they made a couple of circuits to get an up-close idea of its layout. They're not rushing into anything. They're prepared.

It should not take the four men at the sheriff's department long to take and destroy the building. The men out there have been watching it for a while. There's only one deputy present.

Gunnar checks the time. Two minutes have passed since he gave the order for them to move in. Florian rejoins him. He looks in the same direction as Gunnar. All of them do.

Another minute passes, and then the night lights up over there as the sheriff's department explodes. The flame mushrooms into the night sky. Gunnar turns to the men closest to him and circles a finger in the air. "In the van," he says, and then he gets back on the radio. "Everyone, move in. Kill any motherfucker that gets in your way."

52

Lorne has not managed to sleep through the day, but his shaking has finally stopped. When he glances at himself in the mirror, however, he still sees a ghost looking back. A frail, sunken-eyed thing that he long ago had to accept as himself. This is him. This is how he looks now. He's a stranger.

There's no work today. No shift at the bar. It's closed, after what happened. Colin says he's not sure when he'll reopen. He'll have to clean up the blood first, and deal with all the bullet holes. He said he'd like to get it back open sooner rather than later – it's his business, his livelihood, after all – but also to hold a memorial for the four men who were killed there. Four regular customers. A show of respect. Colin has said he'll call Lorne when he gets everything dealt with. Lorne wonders what it's like for Colin out there, in his small house directly behind the bar. He wonders what it's like for him, to live so close to where the gunfight occurred, and where the bodies lay.

Lorne doesn't mind no work today, or tonight. He

couldn't have faced it anyway. The automatic gunfire, and the single shots of Tom's Beretta, still ring out in his ears. He's sat in front of the television since he gave up on trying to get to sleep, but he's barely heard a thing. Every loud sound from outside has caused him to flinch – the slamming of a door, or a shouting passerby who was too close to his window. Lorne has spent the day sitting still, in front of the television, and concentrated on his breathing. Long and deep in through the nose, and slow and controlled out through the mouth. Gradually, his hearing has returned, if not the colour to his skin.

It's late, now. It's dark. Lorne wishes he could sleep. He's too scared to try, because he's too scared of failing again. Instead he'll wait, and hope that sleep will creep up and take him without his realising.

He hasn't eaten anything today. He's barely drank. He's not hungry. He has no appetite. If he tried to eat anything, he thinks he'd likely just throw it straight back up. It's happened before when he's felt deep in the throes like this. Of course, it's never been caused by anything as extreme as the bar getting shot up and four men killed right in front of him.

The television plays a football game. Lorne can't tell if it's new or old. He doesn't keep up. He's not paying much attention. It's background noise, and it's light. As darkness has fallen, Lorne has not bothered to turn on the lights. Other than the television, he sits in darkness. The noise, the commentary, offer some form of comfort. They make him feel like he isn't so alone.

Outside, the streetlights are shining. If Lorne turns his head, he can see lights on in the trailers around him. He feels a pang of jealousy, not for the first time, directed toward the people inside them. Going about their lives. Their normal, everyday, unafflicted lives. He sighs and turns back to the television, and abruptly the television goes off.

Everything goes dark. A deep darkness, though. Lorne frowns. He looks outside. It's not just him, not just his trailer. The streetlights are off. The lights in the surrounding trailers have gone out. It's an inky black darkness to his unfocussed eyes. Lorne blinks against it. The only true light comes from the stars, peering out from behind the mountains.

Lorne gets to his feet. He feels uncomfortable in the sudden, unexpected darkness. He can hear people calling to each other outside. Asking each other if they're having the same problems. Asking if anyone knows what has happened. Lorne feels his right leg beginning to bounce beneath him. His left aches. His anxiety levels are rising. He grits his teeth. Gradually, his vision adjusts. He continues to blink against it. In the distance, he hears a faint rumble, like thunder. It sounds familiar. He's heard sounds like it before. They plague his dreams. It sounded like an explosion.

He steps outside the trailer and looks around, wondering how far the power cut has reached. There's no illumination so far as he can see. Only errant headlights in the distance cutting through the dark. The only time Lorne has seen darkness like this before is out in the wild, where there is no electricity. He saw it out in Afghanistan, in the desert, with no civilisation for miles around. Nothing but the stars. It's the same right now. The stars provide the only light.

Although, that's not true. There is something, coming from far across the town. He steps down from his trailer and rounds it, looking off into the distance. Others, standing on their steps and their porches, have noticed it too. It's a fire. It belches dark fumes into the sky, blotting out the moon. The explosion he heard.

"What is that?" someone says. "What's burning? What's out there?"

"It ain't the sheriff's department, is it? That's over that way."

Lorne hears what they say, and he thinks they're right. That *is* the direction of the sheriff's department. His blood runs cold.

"What do you think's happening out there?" someone says.

"I dunno, but a burning sheriff's department shouldn't have killed all our power."

This feels wrong to Lorne. He doesn't like it. There's a raging fire, and yet he can't hear any sirens, whether fire service or cops. He can't discern if this feeling is something he can sense, or if it's his paranoia. Either way, he doesn't want to hang around here. Trying to keep his hands still, he pulls out his phone and tries to call Tom. The call won't go out. It won't even ring. He types out a text to tell Tom about the power cut, but the message won't send.

Behind him, Lorne hears a vehicle approaching. He turns toward the sound, hoping that it is Tom returning, but it doesn't sound like Malani's BMW. What he sees instead, is a dark shape crawling up the road, its headlights off. Lorne makes out the faint shape of a jeep. It parks a couple of trailers away from his own. It doesn't come any closer, but dark figures dismount. Lorne sees weapons. Automatic rifles. It's too dark to see what kind.

He counts six shapes. They're coming towards him. They're coming toward his trailer.

Lorne drops to the ground, flat on his belly, hoping they

haven't seen him. It doesn't seem like they have. No one calls out. They don't run. They spread out and make their way over, their steps cautious. They're getting closer. Lorne knows he can't remain where he lies. One of them is likely to trip over him. He shuffles forward, crawling on his elbows and knees until he gets under the trailer. When he reaches the middle he stops and lies flat and tries to catch his breath, looking left and right, seeing their legs approach from the front and the back. Lorne wonders why the others nearby haven't noticed them yet. They could still be distracted by the distant fire. Or else they *have* seen them, same as Lorne did, and they saw their weapons. So instead of standing and gawping, they've gone inside and they've ducked down low. They're not calling to each other anymore. No one is speaking. Lorne doesn't know the answer. He has no way of knowing.

But what he thinks he *does* know is who these people are. He thinks they're from the militia. The ones Tom mentioned as having escaped. He thinks of their jeep, and he thinks of the outlines of their heads – of how they had wild hair and beards. And one of them was tall. Bear's second. Skinny Long, Tom said he was called. They've come back to Samson. They've come looking for Tom, for what he did to them.

Lorne watches two pairs of legs reach the door to his trailer. They find the door unlocked and they go in. Four others remain outside, at each point of the trailer, covering it. Lorne hears footsteps above him. He swallows. Keeps his breathing as quiet as he's able. Tries to ignore the gnawing feeling that courses through him, wanting him to break down and tremble all over, or to panic and paralyse.

The two men inside the trailer are louder as they make

their way out. Lorne hears them kicking their way through. They're annoyed. They can't find him. They kick the door open. The men outside can hear their frustration. They all converge around the front.

"They ain't in there," someone says. Skinny Long?

"Shit," someone else says. "What now?"

Lorne notices movement out the corner of his eye. Off to his left. He turns to it. He sees dark shapes coming through the darkness, melting out of it, coming toward his trailer, same as the militia did. More men. Armed. They don't look like the militia, though. From what Lorne can see of them, they're clad all in black. They don't have wild hair and beards. They run forward at a slight crouch, knees bent, automatic rifles held in front of them and pointing. These men look trained. They look like soldiers. They remind Lorne of his time in the Army.

Lorne thinks he counts five of them, one less than the militia, but he can't be sure. The pitch darkness makes it so difficult to tell.

These new arrivals get closer to the trailer. It seems like they've noticed the militia, although the militia don't seem to be aware of them. Not yet.

Lorne doesn't want to be here when the two sides come face to face. Whoever these new arrivals are, he doubts they've come with good intentions. Between them and the militia, he assumes one of the groups is responsible for the power being off.

Lorne needs to get out of here. They might not look under the trailer, but they also might. He doesn't want to run that risk. As quietly and carefully as he can, he pushes himself up on his elbows and knees once again and starts crawling forward, heading to the rear of the trailer.

The militia spots the other group. Lorne hears it. "What the hell's this?" someone says.

Someone, Lorne doesn't know from which side, opens fire. The other side fires back. He falls flat on the ground and covers his head with his hands, forcing his palms into his ears. He closes his eyes tight, his teeth bared. The shooting is loud. It's deafening. He hears it thud into the side of his home, and into the trailers nearby. Even through his hands, he can hear people crying out. Can hear them screaming.

Lorne can't stay here. He knows he can't. If he stays here, they'll find him. If they find him, he's dead. He forces his hands from his head and his ears. He slaps himself and shakes his head. Looking around, he sees running legs. He sees people diving. Someone is lying on the ground not far from him, off to his right, and firing their rifle. If they were to turn their head, they'd see Lorne.

Lorne pushes on. He reaches the end of the trailer and gets out, pushing himself up onto a knee and looking around to make sure it's clear enough for him to run. His body screams at him not to go. It wants him to lie back down. It wants him to lie down forever.

Rising to his feet, biting his bottom lip, Lorne runs. He runs toward the trailer opposite him, down the side of it, around the back of it and to the far corner where he can peer out. While he rests briefly, his left leg throbs. He sees the gunfight still going on. He can't tell who's winning. He doesn't care. The two sides are preoccupied with each other. He starts running again. Makes his way through the darkness, his arms and legs pumping. Heads to the edge of the trailer park. He's making for the bar. He can't think where else to go.

Behind him, the night continues to erupt with sustained

bursts of fire. Lorne flees from it, and ignores the feelings that try to bring him down, and the voices that tell him to stop. Ignores everything in his mind and his body that has held him back for the last decade. Ignores it all, and concentrates solely on saving his own life.

53

Tom drives fast.

Malani looks ahead, leaning closer to the windshield. "We're close enough," she says. "We should be able to see Samson from here. Where is it? It's like it's disappeared."

The mountains reach up into the sky, and beneath them is a sea of darkness.

"They've killed the power," Tom says. "It's not surprising. They've planted jammers. It makes sense that they'd cut the electric."

As they get closer, a light appears amidst the sea. Stars disappear above it. A fire.

Malani gasps. "Oh, no," she says.

"What is it?"

"That's the sheriff's department," she says. "It's burning."

"You're sure?"

"I used to work there. I know exactly where it is."

Tom glances across. He can see the fire. Can see how it is

fading, but it still burns fiercely. He wonders if anyone was inside. Wonders if any of the sheriff's deputies remain alive.

That doesn't matter right now. He can't think about the sheriff or his people. He needs to get closer – to get back into town. There's nothing he can do for them out here. If any of them are still out there, they need to take care of themselves for now. They've been trained. Now is the time for them to put that training to use.

As Tom turns to look forward, he notices a car at the side of the road. If he hadn't looked toward the fire he wouldn't have seen it. He slows the car. He kills the lights.

"What's happening?" Malani says. "What are you doing?"

"I wanna check something out." Tom stops the car. He turns off the engine. He peers into the darkness.

"We can't stop – we need to keep going."

"Not if we're heading straight into a trap."

Malani looks around. "What did you see?"

Tom peers into the darkness. "There was a car back there. It looked like someone had tried to hide it. Before we go any further, I need to take a closer look." Tom starts to get out of the car. He pulls out his Beretta.

"I'm coming," Malani says, pulling out the Glock.

Tom approaches the car behind the bush. Malani covers his back. It's a Toyota. Tom peers through the branches. There are two people inside, both sitting up front. Neither of them is moving. They look like they could be sleeping. The head of the man in the driver's seat is turned to the side, his chin almost resting on his shoulder. The woman in the passenger side has her chin lowered to her chest. Tom does not think they are sleeping.

Remaining cautious, he rounds the bush. Gets closer.

The window on the driver's side is open. Tom motions to Malani to stay where she is and cover the area. She acknowledges him. Tom goes up to the window. He's not surprised to find that the two people inside are dead. Both of them have been shot a couple of times through the chest. Up close, Tom can see their blood. Judging by the open window, Tom assumes someone waved them down. Someone who maybe looked official enough to get them to stop – or someone who was heavily armed. Beneath the door, he sees where dirt has been scraped away from the paint by someone leaning against it.

Tom goes to the back of the Toyota. There are handprints in the trunk's dirt. The car has been pushed offroad. Tom returns to Malani, and tells her what he suspects.

"If they're still out here, they must have seen us coming," Malani says. "And they're probably wondering why we suddenly pulled over and killed the lights."

Tom nods. He looks around, scanning the sides of the road. "They're probably coming toward us right now. They could be worried we've seen the Toyota."

Tom can't see or hear anyone approaching, but he's not surprised at this. He doesn't think they've reached him and Malani yet, or seen them. If they had, they'd have likely opened fire. He tells Malani to remain where she is. To duck down behind the Toyota and stay put while he goes in search of the shooters. Malani does, Glock raised and ready.

Tom heads out into the dark. He keeps his Beretta in hand, but he also pulls out his KA-BAR. He has no idea how many killers there could be. At least two, he thinks, judging by the markings on the car from when they've pushed it offroad. If he comes across one, he's going to want to find out where the other is. The knife will help punctuate his questions. If they're too dangerous to talk to, his Beretta will put them swiftly in the dirt.

He moves forward a few paces and then pauses, listening, and looking toward the other side of the road, too. He continues on, repeating the process. Finally, he hears someone approach. They move similar to how he does. They're still coming, though. They haven't heard Tom. He steps to the side, hides himself behind a tree, and waits. He leans back slightly and peers around the back of the tree when he hears them getting closer.

There are two men. They leave six feet of space between themselves. They're armed with AR15s. They pause and look toward the road. They communicate in hand signals that Tom can't make out. They continue. Tom conceals himself fully behind the tree again. He lets them get closer. They're almost upon him now.

The first man passes. Tom shoots him in the back of the head and then swings the Beretta into the face of the second man. He freezes, caught by surprise. He doesn't raise his hands. Doesn't drop his rifle. He and Tom stare at each other, neither of them flinching.

"Aries Group?" Tom says.

The man grins, flashing vicious teeth. He tries to swing his rifle up, but he's not fast enough. Tom shoots him between the eyes. He pauses, waiting, keeping the Beretta raised and looking into the darkness. He can't hear anything else. No one else comes. The noise does not draw them out.

Tom searches the two dead men. As well as the AR15s, they have Glocks. The Glocks were what they killed the people in the Toyota with. He takes the AR15s from their bodies, strips them of their ammo, and returns to Malani. He remains cautious on the way, ever wary of an ambush. He hands one of the rifles to Malani.

"Aries Group," Tom says. "Two of them, dead now. I don't think there's anyone else out here. These two were to stop anyone else from getting into town. Didn't get a chance to question them. The one I left alive would rather eat a bullet than speak."

"There was no struggle with those two in the Toyota," Malani says. "No bullet holes in the vehicle. They were executed, and they didn't even see it coming. If they're killing people this cold-blooded out here, what are they doing in Samson?"

"Whatever it is, we're gonna have to stop them," Tom says. "Get in the car. Let's go."

54

From across town, Gunnar can hear the gunfire even before his men radio in. "The hell's happening out there?" he says.

"Hard to explain, sir," the man at the other end says. His accent is English. "We were advancing upon Lorne and Rollins's trailer, and there were already armed men outside. We assumed this to be the militia that Jason and Harry relayed to us. Doubted they'd be up for a conversation so we advanced upon them while we had the element of surprise, rather than waste it and find ourselves in a firefight." Gunnar can hear gunshots through the radio. They're getting fewer and further between now. It sounds like things are calming over there.

"Sounds like you've found yourselves in a firefight regardless."

"Yes, sir, but we expected this. We didn't think they'd go down without one. We wiped most of them out in our first advance, though. There were six of them altogether, and we got three of them dead straight off the bat."

"Losses on our side?"

"Just one, sir. The militia are fleeing now, sir. Only two of them left. They're in a jeep. Heading your way, by the looks of it. You could be able to see them soon."

"If we see them, we'll deal with them. Lorne and Rollins?"

"Trailer is empty, but one of the men saw someone run off toward the bar. We're going in pursuit now."

"Keep me posted."

Gunnar rides in a van. Florian is driving. He relays what he's been told. "If we see that jeep, we shoot on sight. This town has given me enough fucking problems."

"Yes, sir," Florian says.

Gunnar looks down the road, waiting for the vehicle to come into view. He gets back on the radio. Calls the two men out at the sheriff's department. "How are things out there?"

"We had a few people approach – drawn by the flames, seemed like. More curiosity than anything else. We chased them off."

"Any sign of the sheriff? The other deputies?"

"Not yet, but we see some promising headlights on the horizon."

Gunnar smiles. "Good. When you're done out there, join up with the rest of us."

Florian points ahead. "Jeep," he says.

The jeep tears around a corner, almost toppling. The driver is frantic.

"Stop the van," Gunnar says. "Everyone out! Kill that goddamn jeep."

Florian remains behind the wheel, but the three men in back jump out of the side door and spread across the road. Gunnar joins them, his arms folded. "Fire at will," he says.

The three men in front of him open up. The jeep swerves as the bullets hit both it and the driver. He loses control. The jeep flips. It crosses the road end over end and doesn't stop until it hits the nearest building. It looks like a florist. The jeep smashes through its window. The jeep is on fire. The flowers inside quickly catch the flames, and it begins to spread. An alarm – battery powered, most likely – begins to sound.

Gunnar approaches, taking his Glock from its holster. He sees the two men lying on the road, thrown from the vehicle. The passenger is dead, his neck broken. The driver is still alive, but he's bleeding badly where bullets have caught him in the left shoulder. His arm is almost hanging off. He's a tall man. Long and thin. He looks up at Gunnar, coughing blood.

Gunnar grunts, shaking his head. "Waste of our fucking time," he says, then shoots the man through the head.

55

Tom and Malani pass close to the sheriff's
department. There's a couple of cruisers parked
near to it, their headlights on and their sirens
flashing. There's a gunfight. The deputies are pinned down
behind their cruisers, fired upon with AR15s. There are four
of them. They fire back at their attackers when they're able,
but without much luck. It's too far and too dark for Tom to
see which of the deputies they are. He can't see if the sheriff's
present, either.

"How many deputies are in town?" Tom says.

"Six altogether," Malani says. She's biting her lip, staring
at the shootout and at the flaming building that illuminates
them. Tom knows what she's thinking. He doesn't need to
say anything and neither does she. She's worrying who
might have been on duty tonight. Who might be inside that
building. Who might be dead.

Tom can see the Aries Group who fire upon the deputies.
There are two of them. They're behind cover, moving
between cars and low walls. "We're gonna get behind them,"

he says. He turns off the BMW's lights and heads around the back of the burning building. He does a wide loop so the shooters don't see or hear them. He parks the car far back and he and Malani head up on foot. They take the AR15s, though they're not wielding them. They're strapped to their backs. They carry the handguns, pointing them low as they traverse the dark ground, careful not to trip. They run toward the shooting.

They come up behind the shooters. The cruisers are practically destroyed now. Their headlights are shot out and their sirens are smashed, too. The windshields are shattered. The tyres are burst. There's very little left for the deputies to shelter behind. The only light cast now is from the fire. Tom can feel the heat coming off the burning building. It's dying down, but the way it burns, it seems like a gas fire. Like they hijacked the gas mains inside, put a torch to them. Or else planted a bomb directly beneath them.

There's a shooter on the right, and the other is way over on the left. Tom motions to Malani that he will take the one on the right. She understands. She veers to the left. They both stay low and creep up, cautious of the shots that come from the other direction, whizzing by overhead. Tom drops down and crawls. Malani does the same. They need to get close, and as fast as they can. The shooters won't remain where they are for long. Soon, they'll start moving again. If they turn, Tom and Malani need to be sure to land a kill shot. Their handguns can't match up against the AR15s, especially so close. They'll be torn apart.

Off to the left, there's movement. The shooter is starting to turn. Malani can't waste her opportunity. She fires into his back, three shots, aiming for where he is broadest. All of the bullets find their home. The shooter twists, falling to the ground. His finger is still on the trigger. His AR15 fires wildly into the air. Malani dives upon him, pushing the rifle skyward to avoid it turning upon her or Tom.

The shooter in front of Tom turns as his partner is gunned down and his shots twist and go skyward. The second shooter starts to turn his rifle toward Malani. Tom fires upon him. The bullet embeds in his side. He doubles over but doesn't go down. He starts to turn to Tom. Tom shoots him through the mouth. He goes down.

Malani calls to the deputies. "Don't shoot! Don't shoot! The shooters are dead!"

There's a pause, and then the sheriff calls over. "Malani?" he says. "That you?"

"Me and Rollins! We're coming out!"

The sheriff and his deputies rise carefully from behind their cover as Tom and Malani approach. "Well, shit," Rooker says as they get close. "Look at the pair of you. Glad you turned up when you did."

"Glad we passed when we did," Tom says.

Tom recognises the deputies with him. Anderson, Norton, and Lowell. The only three whose names he knows. They're all cut up and bloody from the gunfight, mostly from shards of glass that have rained upon them as their vehicles were destroyed.

"Who was inside?" Malani says, tilting her head back toward the burning building.

Rooker sets his jaw, his face solemn. "O'Neal," he says. "Haven't seen any sign of her out here – can only assume she's dead in there."

Malani shakes her head. "Damn it."

Rooker nods. "Anderson and I were out on patrol when the lights went out. Then we saw the fire. Saw where it was coming from. Saw how it wasn't just any old fire – it had been an *explosion*. Couple that with the sudden power cut – we feared the worst. We got here around the same time Norton and Lowell did. Soon after that, those bastards sprung a trap on us. We've been able to keep in touch between ourselves by radio, but we can't get hold of anyone else. Ain't been able to call anyone, either."

"There's a jammer," Tom says. "Got to be. And if they took out your building, that was probably to destroy your long-range radio, as well as your armoury. Those radios you're carrying, they might not be able to reach far enough."

"You don't need to tell me," Rooker says. "Already tried."

"It was probably to get you here, too," Tom says. "Lure you in, then eliminate you. If they get rid of the small police presence in town, they don't have anything else to worry about." Tom looks at Malani. "Gabe warned of this. He said they'd wipe this whole place out."

"Who's *they*?" Rooker says.

Tom gives him and the deputies the condensed version. Tells him what he and Malani were able to learn on their drive back about Gunnar Slaughter and the Aries Group. He tells them about Adam being a member, too, and about the money. These are important details. He can't leave anything out. The money is the whole reason Gunnar and his men are here.

"Holy shit," Rooker says when he's finished. He and his deputies exchange looks. They've never had to deal with anything like this before, and their heavier weaponry is lost inside the burning building. "How many are we dealing with?"

"Four less than they came with," Tom says. "That's all we can know for sure right now. The two we killed back there –

make sure you strip them of their arms. You're gonna need them."

"Wait a minute, wait a minute," Anderson says, holding up her hands. "He's going to kill everyone in Samson just for some *money*?"

"That's right," Tom says.

"Where *is* the money?"

"We don't know," Tom says. "And right now, finding it shouldn't be our priority."

"We have to stop them," Malani says. "Innocent people are going to get killed if we don't. Innocent people *have* been killed. We need to forget about the money. That doesn't matter right now. We might never know where it is. It's unimportant. But come morning, if we don't stop the Aries Group, this whole town could be burned to the ground. No one is coming to help us. We're the only ones who can stop what is happening."

"We need to split up," Tom says. "Sheriff, you and your people need to get out into the town and do what you can."

"What are you doing?" Rooker says.

"I'm going after Lorne," Tom says, "and Olivia. I need to make sure they're both safe."

"I'm coming with you," Malani says.

"I wouldn't have it any other way."

In the distance, they can hear gunfire. It seems to come from all over the town. People could be fighting back against the invaders. If they are, they're likely to get themselves killed.

"All right," Rooker says, turning to his deputies. "We're outgunned and we're potentially outnumbered, but you heard what Malani said. There's nobody else here but us. We're all this town has. Anderson, you're with me. Norton and Lowell, you're together. We're gonna have to use our own cars. Go wherever you hear trouble."

They all respond that they understand, that they've got it. They all call him sir. When they say it, it's almost like they feel a sort of pride in him they'd forgotten they might have ever possessed.

Tom and Malani don't hang around. They race back to the BMW. Tom dives behind the steering wheel.

"Who first?" Malani says.

"Lorne."

56

L orne doesn't go into the bar. He goes around the back, to where Colin lives, and pounds on his door. Colin doesn't answer straight away. Lorne steps back and looks the way he has come to see if anyone is following. He squints into the darkness, but can't see anyone approaching. The gunfire has stopped. He doesn't like that. At least when they were shooting at each other he knew where they were.

He can feel his heart hammering. His eyelids flutter. His head feels light. Too light. Like he's about to pass out. He slams the flat of his hand against Colin's door.

"Who's out there?" Colin calls through.

"Colin, it's me," Lorne says, and he manages to make himself heard but he notices that his throat is tight and his words are strained.

Colin opens the door. "Lorne," he says, "the hell are you doing pounding on my door like that in a power cut? I was thinking you were a damned looter or something!"

Lorne gasps, trying to catch his breath. He notices that

Colin is holding a Remington 870 shotgun. The barrel is pointed at the ground. "Did you hear the shooting?" Lorne says.

"Jesus, is that what it was?" Colin says. "What was–"

"They were coming after me," Lorne says, and his throat closes and he can barely breathe. He presses his back up against the wall and claws at his throat. He closes his eyes tight and tries to calm himself. Tries to breathe through his nose, to fill his burning lungs.

"Lorne, are you okay?" Colin says. "Did they get you? You hurt?"

Lorne manages to get some air into his body. He opens his eyes. He turns to Colin in time to see his head burst. His blood sprays over Lorne, into his face, into his eyes and mouth.

Lorne falls to the ground along with Colin's corpse. He looks back. He sees the men from the trailer, clad all in black and wielding AR15s. There are four of them. Two hold back, watching, almost amused. Two advance upon him. They have him covered with their rifles. Lorne pushes himself back along the ground, grabbing at his throat again. He presses up against Colin's body. He feels something cold beneath his hand. It's the shotgun's stock. Lorne freezes. He swallows. He can taste Colin's blood.

"Lorne Henkel," one of the men says. He has an accent that Lorne doesn't recognise. He's not American, though. "On your feet. Come with us."

One of the two holding back gets on a radio. "We have Lorne," he says. He's English. "We'll be with you soon."

The man that spoke directly to Lorne is nearly at him. He reaches out. Lorne squeezes the shotgun beneath him. Between him and Colin's dead body. Lorne's breathing is fast and sharp, in and out, in and out. Hyperventilating. His vision swims.

He brings up the shotgun and pumps it. The man closest pauses, surprised. Lorne blasts him in the chest.

He's thrown across the ground. Lorne turns, scrambles to his feet, and he stumbles and runs through Colin's house as automatic fire opens up behind him. It tears through the sofa and the chair as he passes them by. Windows and cups and bottles shatter. Lorne throws himself to the ground. He has been in Colin's home before. It's not a big place. He knows his way around it. He stays low and crawls, keeping the shotgun close. He doesn't think about how he feels. Like back at the trailer, he ignores the part of him that wants to stop and to lie down and to hold still. The part of him that stiffens and seizes his limbs. The part that squeezes his lungs and his heart. The throbbing in his leg where his bones were broken so long ago, and upon a different continent. Instead, he thinks of the Army. Remembers his training. He keeps pushing. Keeps going forward. There is no alternative.

He gets to the kitchen at the rear of the small house and pushes himself up. His arms strain in protest. Again, he ignores them. Ignores everything that isn't interested in keeping him alive. He looks around. Next to the back door, there is a hanger on the wall holding keys. Lorne grabs the one for the back door into the bar.

The shooting has stopped at the front of the house. He thinks about what they could be doing. Checking their fallen comrade, no doubt. Seeing if they're still living. Lorne doubts it. They took the shot full in the chest. If they're somehow still alive, it won't be for much longer. Their chest cavity must be wide open.

After checking him, they'll inspect the way into the

house. Assess how safe it is for them to enter. Then, when they gauge whether it's clear or not, they'll come in after him. At least one of them could already be making their way around the back of the house to cut him off. Lorne peers out of the kitchen, back down the hall. He sees two of the men coming through the living room, stepping lightly, AR15s raised. They're silent. He never heard them enter the house. He fires the shotgun at them, spooking them, sending them diving into cover. The round tears a chunk out of the wall, but doesn't do much worse.

Lorne hurries to the back door in the kitchen. It's locked, but the key is already in the door. He turns it and steps out. Behind him, in the house, the two men have fired back, but Lorne is nowhere near where they're aiming.

He steps outside. His ears are ringing. He steps blindly backward to the rear of the bar, shotgun pointing out ahead of him. The magazine carries four rounds. He's used two. Two remain. Three men are after him. He didn't have time to look for more ammo.

Lorne reaches back with the key, jabbing it at the lock. He looks between the rear corner of the house and the kitchen door. He manages to get the key into the lock, finally having to glance back to see where it is. As he turns his attention back, he sees someone appear at the corner of the house. The man he assumed would attempt to come around the back. He peers around the brickwork. He sees Lorne and begins to raise his rifle. Lorne already has the shotgun raised. He squeezes the trigger. The side of the man's skull evaporates in a cloud of blood. He drops to the ground. At the kitchen, the two remaining appear. Lorne throws himself backward into the bar as they fire upon him. From the ground, he scrambles to the door, pushing it shut and locking it again.

There is one round remaining in the shotgun.

The two men attempt to get the door open. They fire upon it but Lorne is already clear. It's dark in the bar, but his eyes have already adjusted to the darkness outside, and it doesn't take long for him to be able to look around this familiar room.

It's still in chaos from the shooting. The tables and chairs are upended. The blood is still pooled on the floor at various spots where the six men were killed.

The two outside have blasted out the lock on the door. Lorne scrambles over the top of the bar and drops behind it. He remembers the last time he was here. He was frozen. He couldn't breathe. He'd given in to his weakness at the first sight of trouble. If he gives in again, he's dead. He holds the shotgun tight, hearing the two men step cautiously inside. They look around. Lorne stays where he is, as still and quiet as he can be. They have night vision. They weren't wearing it outside, but he remembers seeing it at the trailer.

Lorne lies still on his back, the shotgun resting on his chest. He turns to the right. There are a couple of bullet holes in the counter's panelling close to where he is. He shuffles closer and peers out. He sees the two men. They're spreading out. One of them heads away from where Lorne is. The other is coming directly toward him. He's stepping lightly, one foot tentatively in front of the other. Sweeping the area.

Lorne waits. There's nothing else he can do.

The man closest to him is going to look behind the counter. It's the focal point of the room. The most obvious place to search. Lorne tries to think what he can do. There's only one round left in the shotgun, but two men he needs to shoot. One of them is far away. Lorne isn't sure he could get him from across the room. He looks toward him, and wonders if his aim could be good enough. So far, he's been lucky. More than that, he's been *close* to his targets.

When he was in the Army, Lorne had been a good shot. He'd never had any problems at the target range. Bullseyes, every time. But that was a long time ago. A long, *long* time. Lorne is out of practice. Lorne's hands aren't as steady as they used to be. They tremble.

He squeezes the shotgun. His hands aren't trembling right now. They can't. He can't let them. Lorne looks through the hole between both men. He formulates a plan. He has to be confident in it. There can be no room for doubts. Doubts will lead to his death. His hands will tremble. His chest and throat will tighten. His limbs will paralyse.

The man closest to him is nearly at the counter. He's getting ready to peer over the top. To find Lorne a sitting duck. Lorne moves fast. Faster than he has in a very long time. He pushes himself upright and grabs the man as he begins to lean. He pulls him over the counter, and dumps him down behind it. He kicks him in the face and hopes this is enough to momentarily subdue him. The other man across the room hears. He wheels on the sound. Lorne raises the shotgun and sights along it. He squeezes the trigger.

As he does so, the man on the ground grabs his leg and trips him. The shotgun blast goes wild, hitting the ceiling, causing wood chips and plaster to come raining down. Lorne falls. The shotgun is empty. Empty, but not useless. He uses it to club at the man who has dragged him down, slamming its barrel into his face, cutting up his lips and busting his nose.

The other man fires a short burst. He fires at where Lorne stood just a moment before. Bottles above shatter and shards of glass rain down around them. "Come on out, Lorne!" the man says. "You don't have any chance, and you know it! Get off my buddy and give yourself up!"

Lorne doesn't listen. He continues the struggle. The man on the ground fights back. He's bigger than Lorne, and stronger, but Lorne was able to catch him by surprise earlier, and now he's on his back. This gives Lorne at least a little advantage. The man grabs at the barrel of the shotgun and pushes it out of his face. He spits blood into Lorne's eyes, and then manages to strike him across the jaw with a short punch.

The impact is heavy, despite the limited reach, and Lorne falls to the side. He spies the jagged neck of a broken beer bottle. The man is grabbing at his throat. Lorne reaches for the broken bottle. He manages to clasp it around the neck, and he drives the glass into the man's face. Into his eyes. He opens his mouth as if to scream, but Lorne clamps his spare hand over his mouth to silence him. He doesn't want the other man to hear. If it sounds like his friend is dying or dead, he'll open up on the counter without hesitation. The wood panelling is no match for an AR15.

Lorne drives the jagged bottle into the side of the man's neck, and presses down with all of his weight as he convulses, bleeding out. When he's sure that he's too weak to cry out, Lorne grabs for his dropped rifle. He begins to rise, pressing the stock into his shoulder and sighting through his right eye. He keeps his left open to find where the other man is across the room. He exhales as he rises. He thinks he'll get a split second before the other man realises that it's not his friend standing. That it's Lorne, and he's armed.

Lorne puts this split second to use. Stretches it for all it's worth. He finds the other man. He hasn't moved. He's on a knee, waiting, his rifle already raised. The man hesitates while he waits to see who is standing. Lorne squeezes the trigger before he has the chance to do the same. The AR15 cuts him down.

Lorne stands, breathing hard, and waiting. He makes sure the man across the bar doesn't get back up. He makes sure the man at his feet, whose blood he's standing in, that he's dead, too. He looks toward the front and back doors into the bar. They're clear. No one is trying to get in. Right now, no one else is coming for him.

Lorne puts the AR15 down on the counter top and presses his forehead against the cool wood. Already, the shakes are returning. His chest is getting tight. He stumbles out from behind the counter, away from the dead man there, away from his spreading blood. The blood, the death, it makes him think of Colin. Reminds him of his face evaporating right in front of him. It reminds him of Adam, too. Of finding him there in his house, dangling by that rope.

The front door to the bar is kicked open, and a dark shape falls through, dropping to a knee to make itself a harder target. It holds an AR15, raised, sweeping the room. Lorne scrambles for the rifle atop the bar, wishing he hadn't put it down.

"Lorne!"

The voice is familiar. Lorne stop and turns. He blinks, trying to make out the face. The man stands. Behind him, someone else enters the room. A woman now. "Tom?" Lorne says. "Malani?"

Tom hurries to him, Malani following. They both hold him, making sure he's all right.

"We heard the gunfire," Malani says. "We thought...we thought the worst, to be honest."

Tom looks around the bar. He sees the two dead men. He squeezes Lorne's shoulder. "You did good," he says. "Jesus Christ, you did good. How do you feel?"

"Like I'm going to throw up and pass out," Lorne says. He looks at his hands. They're shaking. He can't stop them now. Even the sense of relief that floods his system at the sight of Tom and Malani cannot calm him completely.

"Hold it together," Tom says. "You've come this far, but you need to go a little further. We're not leaving you here alone."

Lorne swallows, though he's glad he's no longer by himself. "Where we going?"

57

Gunnar hasn't heard anything from his men. They're not checking in. Gunnar doesn't radio them. Doesn't try to find out where they are or what they're doing. If they're not checking in, they've failed. If they've failed, they're dead.

He turns to Florian. Florian watches the road ahead, navigating the route they plotted out before they began their assault upon the town. "The militia caused us problems," he says. "And Rollins too, no doubt. But Lorne is supposed to be some kind of invalid. They should have got hold of him long ago."

Florian nods.

Gunnar sighs. "It looks like we're going to have to do everything ourselves." He looks out of his window. In the dark, he can't see much of the buildings they pass. He looks toward the outline of the distant mountains growing up into the sky. "A small nothing town like this should not be causing us this much fucking grief. In and out, that's all. If Jason and Harry had done their goddamn jobs in the first place–"

Florian cuts him off. "Up ahead," he says. "That's the house – and there's movement."

Gunnar looks. He sees the movement. Sees people rushing in and out of the house with torches.

"Kill the headlights and pull over," Gunnar says.

Florian does as he's told.

"Switch to night vision," Gunnar says, addressing the whole van. He pulls his own down over his face.

"It looked like they were loading a car," Florian says.

When the glow of the night vision kicks in, Gunnar sees that this is exactly what they're doing. Two of them. A man and a woman. They wear thick jackets against the cold of the night. The woman is Olivia. Gunnar recognises her. Jason and Harry sent images. They sent images of the man, too, but Gunnar can't remember his name. He doesn't care. The man could prove useful, though. They could make Olivia talk through him. Break his arms and his legs, bloody up his handsome face, see how long Olivia can hold out before she tells them what they want to know. Gunnar doesn't think it'll take long at all. Of course, at the same time, he's been looking forward to questioning Olivia up close and personal. She's an attractive woman, and Gunnar knows there is much he could do to make her speak. He won't want her to, not straight away. He likes it when they play tough first. Play a little hard to get. It's more fun to break them that way.

They throw a final bag into the back of their Ford, a holdall, and then jump inside the vehicle. They don't bother to close and lock the door of their house.

"What are they doing?" Florian says.

"Looks like they're fleeing," Gunnar says. "Must be scared of the dark."

Florian chuckles. "Orders?"

"Run them off the fucking road," Gunnar says.

Florian has not turned off the van's engine. He leaves the headlights off. Olivia and her boyfriend are pulling away from the house, now. The man is driving. It's hard to tell which way they're going to turn.

Florian doesn't wait long enough to find out. He's already accelerating, speeding down the road toward them, his foot flat on the pedal.

"Brace yourself," Gunnar calls into the back. He holds onto the hanger above his head and steadies himself with his free hand against the dashboard. His body tenses.

They make impact. Florian drives the van into the rear of the Ford, striking it in the rear driver's side door as it pulls back from the driveway. He hits hard. Gunnar hears the crumpling of plastic and metal. The shattering of glass. The roaring of two engines coming up against each other, neither of them willing to give.

The van has the height and weight advantage. The wheels of the Ford begin to rise. The car begins to roll. Florian continues his advance, holding the steering wheel tight in both hands, his arms juddering. He stops only when the Ford is rolling.

Gunnar watches it go. It makes two revolutions, and then stops on its roof. The van waits. Gunnar sees the people inside struggling to unbuckle themselves and get free. It doesn't look like they're too badly hurt.

"Cut them loose," Gunnar says. "We want the woman alive. The man is expendable. If he behaves himself, bring him along – he might be useful later. If he plays up, don't hesitate to put him down. This is the end of our objective, but it's not the end of our night. Plans have changed. Looks like we're going to have to get hold of Lorne and take care of Rollins ourselves. Keep that in mind."

In the back of the van, the three men open the side door, preparing to get out.

"Adam's ex-wife is an attractive woman, as I recall from the pictures," Florian says, looking at Gunnar.

Gunnar smiles.

Florian knows what the smile means. "I hope the crash didn't bang her up too badly."

"Bruises fade," Gunnar says. "But I don't mind too much. You know I don't have any problem with a woman looking a little beat-up."

"Just a little?" Florian says.

Gunnar laughs. "Sometimes even a lot. Depends on who's done the beating."

The three men from the back are out of the van. They haven't come into view yet. Gunnar and Florian sit tight. They look to the crashed car.

Another vehicle speeds in front of it, cutting off their view. A man and a woman jump out. They're in uniform. A sheriff and his deputy, though it's a civilian vehicle. They take cover behind the car and hold out their weapons. The sheriff has a Glock. The woman has an AR15. Gunnar wonders if it's been taken from one of his men. He wonders if that man is dead. For his own sake, he'd better be. Gunnar will not stand any man of his being disarmed by some small-town cop, and especially not a female one.

"Stay right where you are!" the sheriff says. "Not another step!"

Gunnar and Florian look at each other. They both start to laugh.

58

Tom rounds a corner. Olivia's house is up ahead.

"There's something going down," Malani says.

"Looks like a standoff."

Tom stops the car, slamming his foot down on the brake. He turns off the lights and hopes no one saw them coming. "Lorne, if you're not feeling up to it, stay here."

"I'm coming," Lorne says, his expression grimly resolute. "I've got this far tonight."

The three of them get out of the car, all of them armed with taken AR15s. "On me," Tom says, and then makes his way forward through the dark, staying low.

He can see more clearly what is happening up ahead. Sheriff Rooker and Deputy Anderson are in a standoff with the Aries Group. Behind them, it looks like there's a car on its roof. Tom recognises the car. It's Olivia and Stan's Ford. He can't see any sign of Olivia and Stan. He sees Rooker and Anderson steadfast, and three members of the Aries Group opposite them.

The van's headlights come on, illuminating the scene

before it. Its front doors open. Two more men get out. They join the three others. Tom can only see the backs of their heads, but he thinks one of them must be Gunnar. Malani was able to find a picture of him online. It gave them an idea of whom to look for, and what they're going up against.

Tom, Malani, and Lorne reach the back of the van. Tom can hear who he assumes to be Gunnar call to Rooker and Anderson. "If you know what's good for you, Sheriff, you should turn yourselves around and leave right now. This doesn't concern you."

"This is my town," Rooker says. "Everything in it concerns me."

"It's your funeral, Sheriff. You're outnumbered and outmatched. This isn't going to take long. Can't say you weren't warned." Gunnar motions to his men. "Kill them," he says.

"Hold up!" Tom says, stepping out from behind the van, AR15 raised. Malani and Lorne follow him. They cover the Aries Group, who turn toward them at the sound of his voice.

Gunnar's eyes narrow at the sight that greets him. He grunts, then turns his head and spits. "Rollins," he says. "I've heard a lot about you."

"And I've heard very little about you," Tom says.

Gunnar laughs. "Is that an attempt to insult me?"

"Just the truth."

"Uh-huh. I assume you heard what I told the sheriff and his deputy here. I'm gonna give the three of you the same offer. Walk away right now."

"Don't attempt to insult *us*," Tom says. "That's a lie, and we all know it."

"And why would I lie to you?" Gunnar says, but he's smirking.

"You've already sent your men after us. You're not going to let us just walk away. And besides, we're not letting you take Olivia."

Gunnar stares at Tom. He's smiling a little. Tom can read his expression. Gunnar is sizing him up. Gunnar has heard about Tom, and he wants to test his mettle. Tom would like nothing more than to give him the opportunity, but it's more likely that Gunnar is about to die in a crossfire.

"Looks like our numbers have evened up," Rooker says. "I'm gonna give *you* a warning – if you wanna live, put down your weapons and give yourselves up right now."

"We're not gonna tell you again," Tom says.

Gunnar sucks his teeth. He looks toward the sheriff, and then back toward Tom and the others. The other man who got out of the van with Gunnar stands close to him. He has a sour look on his face. Gunnar taps him on the chest with the back of his hand. Tom braces. Something is about to happen.

"Kill them all!" Gunnar says, and then dives to the side with the man beside him.

Of the three Aries Group in the standoff with the sheriff and Deputy Anderson, one of them remains facing in that direction and the other two spin on Tom, Malani, and Lorne.

Everyone opens fire. The Aries Group don't stand a chance. Their bodies shake and convulse as they're peppered with bullets from both sides. They barely get any shots off. The ones they do go harmlessly wide.

Tom notices that the van is moving. Gunnar and the other man have managed to get back inside. They're trying to get away. The passenger side door slams shut. The van begins to speed forward. It rams into the back of the sheriff's car. The sheriff fires upon it, but it doesn't stop. Gunnar is going to get away.

The side door of the van is still open, though it slides back and forth on its rollers. Tom spots it. He dives inside. The van lurches forward as he lands. The side door slides shut.

"Rollins!" Gunnar says, looking back. "So good to see you!"

59

Gunnar dives into the back of the van, tackling Tom to the ground. He's a big guy, but he's fast, and more spry than Tom would have expected. Gunnar wrenches the AR15 out of Tom's hands and throws it toward the back of the van. Gunnar is heavier than Tom. He takes advantage of this. He presses down. He headbutts Tom in the centre of the face. The scab on the bridge of his nose cracks easily. From the force of the blow, Tom thinks Gunnar may have opened up a new cut, too.

The van rocks as it drives. "Florian!" Gunnar says to the driver. "Hold it steady while I kill this prick."

Florian doesn't concern himself with holding the van steady. He's more preoccupied with getting them clear.

Gunnar pins Tom to the van floor. "What was the plan, Rollins? Jump on board and think we wouldn't notice?"

"The plan was to stop you," Tom says. "We're not through yet."

Gunnar laughs. Tom's legs are free. He brings up his right knee, slams it into Gunnar's spine. Gunnar isn't expecting it. It knocks him off balance, but not off Tom. It gives Tom enough space to get his arms free. Gunnar punches him. Tom feels more scabs break open. More blood pours. The back of his head bounces off the metal floor. Gunnar pulls out his Glock. He points it at Tom's face. Tom grabs his wrists and forces the gun out of his face. It fires three times. The bullets go through the back door. One of them ricochets off and bounces around the inside of the van. Wherever it eventually settles, it doesn't do any of the three men any harm.

Gunnar fights against him. He won't let go of the Glock. Tom strikes through his arms. Punches him twice in the face. Gunnar laughs it off, but Tom can see that this is for show. The blows are rocking him. Tom hits hard. It doesn't matter how much bigger than him Gunnar is, the punches hurt.

Tom grabs his arms and drags them down, keeping the gun out of his face. Tom sinks his teeth into the inside of Gunnar's right wrist. He feels the thin skin there split. Blood squirts into his mouth.

"Mother*fucker*!" Gunnar roars.

Gunnar drops the gun. Tom spits blood and gouges at his eyes. Gunnar can't hide how he's hurting now. He stumbles back. Tom pulls out his Beretta. From where he sits, Gunnar lashes out with a boot. He kicks the gun out of Tom's hand. Gunnar launches himself off the ground and charges him. Blood drips from his wrist. Blood drips from Tom's face. Gunnar wraps his arms around Tom's waist and slams his body into the side wall of the van.

"Cool it back there!" Florian says, the van swerving.

On the ground beneath them, the two handguns slide by. The Glock and the Beretta. Tom tries to catch one with his foot. It scrapes past. Gunnar punches him in the stomach.

Tom coughs. Gunnar is reaching for a gun. Tom pretends to go limp. Lets him get a gun. Gunnar catches his Glock as it passes. He brings it up. Tom is ready. Florian is off to his right. With his left forearm, he slams it across Gunnar's bloodied wrist, knocking his aim off and loosening his grip. Tom wraps his own hand around Gunnar's fist and pushes up the gun. He points it at the back of Florian's head. Tom squeezes Gunnar's fist. His finger depresses the trigger.

Blood sprays out the front of Florian's head, covering the inside of the windshield. His hands drop from the steering wheel. His body slumps forward. His foot, however, does not leave the accelerator. The van spins. It's out of control. It falls onto its side. Onto the driver's side. They scrape across the ground. Tom and Gunnar cannot keep their balance. They're thrown down. Carried along by the van's momentum. Tom feels his limbs pinned down by the force. He tries to fight against it, reaching for his KA-BAR.

Gunnar sees what he's doing. He braces himself. As the van's momentum slows and they can move more freely again, Gunnar jumps for him.

Tom pulls his knife out. He raises it. Gunnar lands on it. Tom feels his blood run down through his hands. Gunnar groans and rolls to the side. Tom pulls the knife out. It was in his stomach. Gunnar coughs. He breathes deep, clamping a hand down over the wound.

"Ah, *fuck*," he says. "You stuck me good, you son of a bitch." He starts to laugh. "Tougher than your old friend, ain't you? Adam, I mean. He was getting soft. Didn't have the stomach for it anymore. I'll bet you don't have that problem, though, do you? We could've done some glorious things together, you and I."

Tom pushes himself up and presses the blade to

Gunnar's throat. He feels blood drip from the tip of his nose. "You should've stayed in Africa."

"My men know I'm here," Gunnar says. He talks fast, his eyes flickering down toward the knife at his neck. "And they know all about *you*. The Aries Group is five thousand strong, worldwide. You won't be able to escape us. Not even your government friend will be able to keep you safe from us."

Tom frowns at this. He doesn't know whom he's talking about.

"*Unless*," Gunnar says.

"Unless what?"

"You let me go. Take that knife away from my neck and walk away. Let me go, and I forget about you. The Aries Group forgets about you. Just drop the knife and walk away."

Tom takes the knife away from Gunnar's neck, and drives it through his heart. He leans in close while Gunnar is still living, while he can still hear. "Let them come."

60

Tom pushes his way out of the back of the van. He's retrieved his Beretta, and has put both it and the KA-BAR away.

A car pulls up, its headlights blinding him. It pulls to a stop. It's Malani. Lorne is with her. They come to him, help steady him. "How are you?" Malani says. "Are you okay?"

"Better than them in here," Tom says, tilting his head back toward the upended van. "How far did we get?" He looks around. It's hard to tell where they are when the only light comes from Malani's car.

"Just a few blocks," says Malani. "They only had you for about five minutes."

"I'll bet it was a long five minutes in there," Lorne says, peering inside.

"Let's get back," Tom says.

"Do you need to rest?" Malani says. "It's okay to slow down. It looks like it's over, Tom. There isn't any more sign of the Aries Group. Lowell and Norton are circling, but they haven't seen anything."

"How are Olivia and Stan?" Tom says.

"Rooker and Anderson are cutting them out."

Tom wipes blood from the corner of his mouth. He looks at Malani's car, and then back at the van lying on its side. He thinks back on when they first pulled up on the standoff. How Olivia and Stan's car was on its roof, but it was in the middle of the road. Tom dwells on this momentarily. He thinks about the positioning. The placement. He frowns. Olivia and Stan were *inside* the car. He wonders how they came to be there. Did they spot the Aries Group coming and they were trying to escape when Gunnar and Florian rammed them? How could they know who was coming? Inside their house, so far as they should have been aware, there was a power cut. They might have heard distant gunshots, they might have even spotted the sheriff's department burning, but it would have been far safer for them to stay indoors.

"Tom?" Malani says. "Are you there? Can you hear us?"

He doesn't respond.

"You all right, buddy?" Lorne says. "Shit, does he have a head injury? I can't see any sign of a head injury."

"Why were they in the car?" Tom says.

"What was that?" Malani says.

"Come on," he says. "We need to go back. I need to check something."

Malani and Lorne exchange glances, but they follow him into the car. Malani drives. Tom tells her to go fast.

"It feels like you're in emergency mode, Tom," she says. "But the emergency is over. What gives?"

"It's not over," Tom says. "Not yet."

"What's going on here?" Lorne says. "What are you thinking?"

"Why were they in the car?" Tom says. "Where were they going? They couldn't have been trying to escape Gunnar – they didn't get far enough. You saw the positioning of where they'd landed, right? They must have only just reversed off their driveway."

"Why is that a big deal?" Malani says.

"It might not be," Tom says. "But it's bugging me, and I need to know why."

When they get back to the sheriff and the others, they find that Stan has been cut free, but Rooker is reaching into the car and still working at Olivia. Rooker and Anderson pull her out together. While Anderson checks her over for injuries, Rooker turns and sees that Tom has returned.

"That was a hell of a move you pulled," he says. He leans closer, inspecting Tom's bloodied face. "I'm assuming you came out on top?"

"Wouldn't be here if I didn't," Tom says.

Tom looks past the sheriff. Olivia and Stan regroup. They hold each other. Stan presses his lips to Olivia's ear to whisper something. She nods.

"Let me check on Olivia," Tom says, stepping around the sheriff and going to the couple. Malani does not join him, and neither does Lorne. Lorne stays by the BMW. Malani holds back and talks with Rooker. Tom reaches Olivia and Stan. "How are the two of you doing? Looks like a nasty crash."

Olivia has a trickle of blood running down the side of her face from her temple. They both look bruised and roughed up, though not as badly as Tom. "I thought we were dead," she says. "When they crashed into us like that – I didn't understand what was happening."

Stan grunts.

"We're lucky you all turned up when you did," Olivia says.

Tom looks at the car on its roof. He looks at it for a long time. He turns back to Olivia and Stan with deliberate slowness. "Where were you going?"

Olivia appears unsure how to answer. Stan is silent. Tom acts like he hasn't noticed. He turns his attention to the car and goes over to it. He kneels down to look into the backseat.

"What are you looking at?" Stan says, stepping forward.

"You've got bags in there," Tom says, straightening. "Were you going somewhere?"

"Vacation," Stan says. "We're not gonna miss it just because there's a power cut. Power cut doesn't affect the car."

"It's a bad start to your vacation. Where were you planning on going?"

"Road trip."

"Sounds like that's out the window."

"Maybe we'll book ourselves onto a flight."

"Uh-huh. Why don't we get you and Olivia inside? It was a bad crash. The two of you need to rest."

Stan hesitates. He looks back at Olivia.

"Listen, is everyone all right here?" Rooker says. "We need to get going and check in on the rest of the town. I'll check back in here once we know everyone's all right."

"We appreciate it, sheriff," Stan says. As Rooker and Anderson hurry back into their car and set off, Stan turns his attention back to Tom. "The rest of you can be on your way, too. We're fine now. We can take care of ourselves."

"We'll help you in," Tom says.

"You don't need to."

"I insist."

Stan doesn't move. He stares at Tom. His fists are balled.

"What's the matter, Stan?" Tom says. "You seem awfully aggressive. I'm just offering to help. The crash got you all shook up?"

Stan looks Tom over. Like he's appraising him. Sizing him up. The same way Gunnar did. He sees the blood on Tom's face. The still-oozing cuts.

"Stan," Olivia says. "It's okay, Stan. They just want to make sure we're all right." To Tom she says, "It's just like you said – the crash has got him all shook up. Let's just go inside and try to settle. Come on, Stan. We can come back for the bags later."

Stan shoots her a look.

"It's okay," she says. "They're not going anywhere. We can get them later, after everyone's gone." She stares at Stan, until eventually he nods.

Tom thinks about pushing them on the bags. Offering to carry them in. He doesn't. He wants to get them inside. Get them where it's enclosed. Tom motions for Malani and Lorne to follow. They go to the front door. Olivia pushes it open. She doesn't have to unlock it.

"I thought you were going on vacation," Tom says.

Olivia stiffens.

"Leaving the door unlocked, especially during a black-out, is pretty careless."

"Uh," Olivia says. "That – that's my mistake. I don't know how I missed that."

Except, Tom thinks, she didn't attempt to unlock the door. She didn't pull out her keys. She wasn't instantly surprised to find it unlocked. She knew it was unlocked. She just wasn't expecting anyone else to notice.

Tom picks up on a nervous, jittery energy coming from both Olivia and Stan. Stan tries to hide it behind bravado and macho posturing. Olivia has a more difficult time disguising it. It could be from the crash, Tom knows, but he doubts it.

Neither Olivia nor Stan step inside. They block the doorway and look at the others like they expect them to leave.

"Maybe we should step in a moment," Tom says. "Make sure you're both okay. No concussions, nothing serious like that."

"We're fine," Stan says.

"It's dark in here," Olivia says. "Maybe if you come back in the morning–"

"I would," Tom says, cutting her off, ready to get to the point, "but I have a feeling that come the morning, the two of you won't be here anymore."

"What – what do you mean?" Olivia says.

Tom doesn't try to get them inside now. He has them blocked at the doorway. This will have to be enough. He comes right out and voices his suspicions. Their reactions will tell him all he needs to know. "Did you kill Adam?"

Olivia is shocked – shocked at the accusation, or shocked at the realisation?

"Tom?" Malani says.

"What are you talking about?" Lorne says, stepping closer.

Tom ignores them. His focus is on Olivia and Stan. "If I go and start pulling the bags from your car, what am I going to find?"

But then Stan does something stupid. He answers Tom's question. He answers whether they killed Adam or not. He answers in the affirmative as soon as he lunges for Tom's Beretta.

Tom twists away from him and brings a knee up, catching him in the chest. To his left, Olivia darts into the house, throwing the door shut behind her. Malani gives chase, throwing her shoulder into the door and forcing her way in.

Stan catches Tom by surprise with a backfist, striking him across his bloodied cheek and knocking him dizzy. Tom is weary from the fight in the van. Not as sharp as he would otherwise be. Stan is quick to follow up with a left jab. Tom manages to bring up his forearm to protect his head. He blocks most of the punch, which turns into a glancing blow to the side of his head.

Lorne charges at Stan. He tackles him to the ground, rolling across the lawn with him. Lorne is screaming. Tom picks up only some of what he says – "You motherfucker! You son of a bitch!" are among the choice phrases. He punches at Stan, trying to get at his face, but Stan has covered up. He blocks Lorne's shots, and then twists his hips to throw him off, and throws a swing which catches him in the jaw and knocks him flat onto his front.

As Stan pushes himself up to a knee, Tom points the Beretta at him. Stan spits, "You gonna shoot me?"

"No," Tom says, and he drops the gun to the grass. "I'm not gonna waste a bullet on you. And I don't need to."

Stan grins. He gets to his feet. He motions toward the KA-BAR. "You gonna stick me with that?"

Tom takes the knife out and drops it tip first into the grass. It buries itself there. "Don't need that, either," he says.

On the ground behind Stan, Lorne rolls over and tries to push himself up. He's still conscious, but he's dazed and hurting.

Stan comes forward, fast, and Tom thinks he might be

trying to grab at the weapons Tom has dropped. Tom cuts him off easily enough, meeting him halfway across the lawn. Stan throws a punch. Tom catches his right arm and throws his own arm up beneath it in an uppercutting motion. Stan's arm bends the wrong way. His bone snaps. It breaks through his skin. Blood sprays. Stan screams. Tom spins out from under his now-broken arm and swings back with his left elbow, catching Stan under the ear at the corner of his jaw. The jaw dislocates, and Stan is unconscious. He collapses to the ground, in brief respite from the pain in his arm. Tom goes to Lorne and helps him up.

Malani reemerges from the house, dragging Olivia along with her. Olivia is crying and struggling. She sees Stan on the lawn and her knees go weak. She knows it's over for them. She knows they've been caught.

61

Tom sets Stan's broken arm, and they keep him and Olivia bound separately in the living room. They light the area with a lamp Malani found in the cupboard under the stairs.

Lorne catches Tom in the kitchen. "What did you mean out there? About searching their bags. What's in their bags?"

"Money," Tom says. He gives him a quick rundown of everything Gabe Elcoat told them.

Lorne looks lost. He looks like a rug has been pulled out from under him. "Adam was a mercenary? All these years? You're *sure*?"

Tom nods. "He was trying to get out, though. And the Aries Group knew it. It sounds like if those two through there hadn't killed him, the Aries Group would have."

Lorne's eyes narrow. "Why are we keeping them alive?" he says. "They killed Adam – they *killed him*. And all this time they've been right here in town, right under my nose, like they never did a damn thing wrong."

"I'm not going to kill them, Lorne," Tom says. "And neither are you."

"Why not? Why the fuck not?" This is the angriest Tom has ever seen Lorne.

Tom waits a moment for him to calm down before he speaks again. "Because look at them, Lorne. Look at this house they live in. They're going to admit what they did, and then they're going to go to prison. Do you know what prison is going to be like for people like them? It's going to be hell. They're going to suffer. Every day of their lives, they'll suffer. They might still be alive in there, but not all of them will survive."

Lorne steps back. He's shaking his head. "I'm not sure," he says. "I don't know if that's enough."

Tom places a hand on his shoulder. "Look at me, Lorne." Lorne does. Tom looks back at him for a long time, silence between them. "The rest of their lives, they have to live with what they've done. They'll be behind bars. It's not a world they'll recognise. It will tear them apart. That's worse than anything we could ever do to them right now."

Lorne still looks unsure, but he nods. "I trust you," he says, and leaves it at that. He might not like it, but he trusts Tom, and he won't protest any further.

Malani is in the living room with Olivia and Stan. They're gagged for now, though Stan is still unconscious. Olivia stares around with wide, frightened rabbit eyes. Malani watches them both with her Glock in hand. She watches them, but simultaneously she appears lost in thought. Tom reckons she's probably thinking of Adam. Of how she didn't fail him. Of how he was failed, and betrayed, by others. Soon, they'll know what happened. For now, they'll give Olivia a little longer to stew.

"I'm going out to the car," Tom says, snapping Malani out of her thoughts. "Lorne is just in the kitchen. He's fine, but he needs a minute. I'll be right back."

Malani nods.

Tom goes to the car. He gets down onto his knees and checks the bags in the backseat first. They hold clothes. Nothing important. He manages to get the trunk open and a couple of holdalls fall out. There are clothes in these, too, but not many, and in the bottom of both holdalls, concealed under the garments, is the money. Tom stares at it and takes a deep breath. Despite the fight with Stan and Olivia's attempted escape, seeing the money makes it all seem real. They killed Adam for this money – money that wasn't even his.

He takes some of the money and puts it into Malani's trunk. He leaves the clothes on the road and transfers the money into one holdall. He carries it inside. He drops it on the living room floor in front of Olivia. Her already wide eyes are bulging now. Lorne comes through to rejoin them. Tom pulls the gag from Olivia's mouth.

"Tell us what happened," he says.

Olivia glances at Stan, sees that he is still unconscious, and he can already tell that she is going to attempt to blame it all on him. "It wasn't my idea," she says, proving him right. "It was all Stan. He–"

"Cut the bullshit," Tom says. "I don't want to hear a story. I want to know what happened. The truth."

Olivia swallows. There is a bruise high on her right cheek that she did not have immediately after the crash. Malani has not said what happened after she caught up to Olivia, but Tom can see how she subdued her. Olivia does not speak.

Tom prompts her. "The two of you kept in touch, right? So tell us what happened that day. Did you go to see him? Did you see the bag of money?"

Olivia closes her eyes. She nods. "He was in the kitchen," she says, breathing out as she speaks and sounding almost relieved. "We would keep in touch, just message every now and then, and he mentioned that he was coming home. I was passing by, so I called in to see him. I didn't bother to knock. I didn't need to. He always just told me to come straight in anyway. So I went straight in – the door wasn't locked – and I found him in the kitchen."

Tom glances at Lorne out the corner of his eye. He's sitting on the edge of the sofa, and he's staring at Olivia. Unblinking. His hands are on his thighs, and he scrunches up his jeans, squeezing them tight.

"I think I caught him by surprise," Olivia says. "He was at the kitchen table. I couldn't tell what he was doing. He might've been counting the money or something, I don't know. But he scrambled to hide it. And that was when I spotted the bag under the table, full of cash. And I saw how much it was – well, I couldn't tell exactly, but I could see that it was a *lot*. More than I'd ever seen in my life. Adam zipped the bag up and put it in a cupboard and I acted like I hadn't seen it. He stayed casual too. I don't know how long I was there with him for. We made small talk, but I couldn't tell you a single thing we talked about. All I could think about was that money. I left and I came here, I came home, and I...I told Stan about it."

"Are you going to blame him while he can't defend himself?" Malani says. It's the first thing Tom has heard her say in a while.

Olivia shakes her head. "No. I'm not going to blame it all

on him. We talked it through. We...we agreed on what we were going to do together."

"You agreed to kill him?" Lorne says, his mouth twisting.

"It wasn't like that," Olivia says. "We weren't going there to kill him. We were just going to speak to him. We were going to...to *persuade* him to cut us in on whatever it was. To share it. If he needed to, Stan was going to intimidate him. But when we got there—"

"Didn't we already tell you to cut the shit?" Malani says.

Olivia blinks.

"I used to be a deputy," Malani says, "and now I'm a therapist. I *know* when people are lying to me, Olivia. You were good, I'll give you that. You've had me fooled up until now, with your crocodile tears and your red eyes, but I see you now. It's all been an act. It's always been an act between the two of you, hasn't it? Adam used to tell me that he hoped you were happy, and I think he meant it, because if you were happy that meant you would leave him alone."

Olivia's face transforms. Suddenly, she looks like a different person. Harder. Colder. Her eyes are dry. She smirks, and there is no humour in it. "For years, I put up with his shit. And you know what, Doc? No one paid *me* to do it. No, you talked to him and he gave you money for the privilege. Where the fuck was *my* money? All of his shit, for all of those years – hell, he even forced this useless son of a bitch into my home." She looks at Lorne.

Lorne doesn't shrivel. He doesn't back down from her. He stares straight back.

"I wanted what was owed to me," Olivia says. "He'd been holding out on me. The alimony he paid, he claimed it was all he could afford. But then I walk in, and he's got bags of loose cash in the house? Bull*shit*. I lost years of my life to that motherfucker. I lost the *best* years of my life to him, waiting for him to come home from war, only for him to run off over and over and over again. I waited for him to care about me and he never did! He never cared about me the way he cared about *Lorne*. So if he wouldn't care for me, he'd pay me for my time."

"I'm glad that you're finally being honest with us," Malani says, "and that you've finally shown us your true face."

Olivia sneers.

"What happened?" Tom says. "How did you kill him?"

Olivia has nothing else to lose. "We went over there and we confronted him about the money. I told him he'd been holding out on me and I wouldn't stand for it. He started babbling, started saying things that, at the time, didn't make any sense. Like how we had no idea what we were getting involved in, and that it wasn't his money. He said he hated where it came from and he wanted out of that life. It didn't make any sense to me, not then. I thought he was talking about oil. I thought he was having some kind of an ecological existential crisis.

"We drowned him out. Me and Stan. We told him not to be so stupid and selfish. I was up in his face. I told him we were taking the money. Adam grabbed me by the shoulders. He looked so scared. He was going to try and plead with me, I think. Reason with me. But he'd grabbed me, and Stan didn't like that. He got behind him and wrapped an arm around his neck. He was choking him. He had his forearm across his windpipe. They fell back onto the ground. Stan was choking him out. Adam had gone limp. Stan started to let go."

She pauses. She looks at them each in turn. Her eyes

linger on Lorne the longest. "I told him not to stop," she says. "I pressed down on his arm, and I pressed down until Adam was dead. And good fucking riddance."

"You made it look like a suicide," Tom says. "Did you go there *with* the rope? Did you find it at his place?"

"We had some at home. We hadn't taken it with us. We had to come back here and get it. Then we took the money. Stan wanted to split right then and there." She snorts. "He never really thought things through. I told him we had to wait a little while so we didn't look suspicious. When the power died tonight, we got worried it was whoever Adam was involved with. He never said who they were. We were thinking gangsters or something. We weren't expecting a goddamn army to come after us. Even if it wasn't them, we figured the dark was a good cover for us to get out. So we tried to run..."

She trails off. They're up to date.

They sit in silence for a while. Olivia stares back at them, defiant.

"I should kill you," Tom says. There's no emotion in his voice. Lorne sits up at this, looking toward him. "Both of you. But I won't. You're going to go to prison, and you're going to rot there. But I want you to understand this – I don't know how long you'll go away for. I don't know how many years or decades it's going to be. Maybe it'll be for the rest of your life, I have no idea. But I want you to hear this, to understand it, and to remember it. And make sure that Stan knows this, too. If and when you eventually get out, start running. Start running and don't stop. Hide yourself away. Because if I find you, I *will* kill you. The rest of your life, behind bars or out, you're going to be looking over your shoulders."

Olivia's defiance wavers as the reality of what he's said sets in, at the promise he has made.

Tom motions to Lorne to come with him. He turns to Malani. "Are you okay to watch them?"

"Yeah," Malani says. "Where are you going?"

"We're going to find the sheriff."

ome the morning, the sun rises and light returns to the town. There is a subdued hush over Samson. The people that live here move tentatively, inspecting the damage that has been done to their home. During the night, the sheriff's deputies, with Tom's help, managed to find the jammers around the town. Able to radio out, they've called for outside help. Ambulances are in town now, and the fire service. State police. The centre of town is busier than the outskirts.

The state police have taken Olivia and Stan away. They had to stay in their home, bound in their living room, until the morning. Malani stepped temporarily back into her former role as a deputy to keep them guarded. The sheriff didn't have anywhere else to keep them. They passed the money on to the sheriff. Four million dollars. Olivia looked up when she heard the amount and she frowned, but she didn't say anything.

Tom, Malani, and Lorne stand close to Olivia and Stan's overturned car in the morning light.

"It's going to be a while before they get the power back on," Malani says. "Sheriff Rooker said probably another night at least."

"Rooker stepped up last night," Lorne says.

"He really did," Malani says. "Whatever you said to him, Tom, it must have gotten through."

Tom looks around. "I know this is abrupt," he says, "but it's time for me to go."

"What?" Lorne says. "So soon?"

"There's going to be a lot of questions from all the new arrivals in town," Tom says. "I don't want to have to answer them."

"So you're just going to leave?" Lorne says.

Tom takes Lorne to one side. "I wasn't going to be here forever," Tom says. "I didn't intend to leave so soon, but the time has come. I'll leave you a number, Lorne. If you ever need me, call it and I'll come running."

Lorne doesn't say anything. He looks pained. He's lost Adam, he's lost Colin, and now he's losing Tom.

Tom embraces him. After a moment, Lorne hugs him back. Tom slips a note into his jacket pocket. Lorne doesn't notice.

"Malani," Tom says. "Can you give me a ride out of town?"

"How far do you want to go?" Malani says.

"Just take me to the outskirts. I can make my own way from there."

"On foot? Without a vehicle?"

"I can catch a bus," Tom says. "And I'm not in any kind of rush. I've got time on my side. I don't have anywhere else I need to be."

"Okay," Malani says. "No problem. Lorne? Do you want to come with us?"

Lorne looks at them both. He's silent for a while, his jaw set. Finally, he shakes his head. "I'm going to walk. I could do with the air."

Lorne stays where he is and watches them as they drive away.

"It's a shame you're going so soon," Malani says.

"I would have hung around a few more days, but it looks like I don't have much choice," Tom says.

They ride in silence until they reach the edge of town. Tom's bag is in the back of the car. He puts his Beretta and KA-BAR inside. "This will do," Tom says. "You don't have to take me any more out of your way than you already have."

Malani pulls over. "Are you sure?"

"This will do," Tom says. "I've got something I need to do before I move on. It's not far from here."

Malani looks curious at this, but she doesn't question him. He doesn't get straight out of the car. They look at each other.

"It's been good knowing you, Tom," Malani says.

"Likewise," Tom says. "Good luck with the future. I hope Samson gets its power back soon."

"We all do."

Tom starts to get out of the car, but Malani places her hand on his arm and pulls him closer to him. She kisses him. It's a long kiss.

"All right," she says, releasing him. "You can go now."

63

L orne gets back to the trailer park. The bar is covered in police tape, and cops swarm the area. He knows that they'll want to talk to him soon. He doesn't offer himself up. If they want him, they can come and find him.

He heads for his trailer, but he can't get to it. The area is cordoned off. The dead bodies there are concealed under blankets. More cops and forensics move around here. Lorne sighs and walks away. He puts his hands in his jacket pockets. A piece of paper brushes his fingers. Lorne pulls it out. It's a note. It's from Tom.

By the time you read this, I'll be gone. Go to yours and Adam's spot.

It doesn't say anything more. Lorne reads the note over, and then checks the back for more. There is no more. Lorne looks around, as if suspicious that someone could be watching him, like they could know what it says on the note. He turns and continues walking. He heads out of town, and goes to his and Adam's spot. He's curious why Tom has directed him there. He half-expects to find him there.

As he eventually gets closer, he sees that Tom is not present. No one is. It looks like it always does. Isolated. Alone. Peaceful.

Lorne goes to the tree, wondering why he's here and what he's supposed to be looking for. When he reaches the tree, it doesn't take him long to see that something is different. At the base of the tree, the ground has been dug up. Lorne goes to it, lowering himself to his knees and digging the dirt back up with his hands.

In the dirt, he finds a plastic bag. He pulls it out. There's another note from Tom inside. It's longer this time.

Adam would want you to have this money, Lorne. One million dollars. Be careful with it. No sudden expensive purchases. Treat it like money you've just robbed from a bank. Use it for yourself, Lorne. Use some of it to see Malani. She can help you. Maybe you can fix up the bar, take it over? I'm not going to tell you how to live your life. This money is yours now. Do with it what you will.

Take care of yourself, Lorne. It was good to see you again.

Tom.

Lorne looks into the bag. It's full of money. Lorne doesn't smile. He doesn't laugh or cry. He doesn't feel anything. He leaves the money where it is and sits next to it with his back against the tree. He looks toward the town. He looks up at the sky. His eyes are hot. He closes them, and feels a light breeze blow across his face. He takes a deep breath.

"I miss you, Adam."

EPILOGUE

Antoine Fournier remains in Sudan. The Aries Group is almost finished here. Their mission is coming to its end. Abdul Mohamed is dead. Antoine himself put the bullet through his skull.

They've kept up to date with what has happened in America. In Colorado. In Samson. They know that Gunnar Slaughter is dead. They know that Florian is dead. They know that so many other of their brothers in arms are dead.

Antoine is in charge now. Suddenly, he finds himself at the head of the Aries Group. Sitting in a tent on the outskirts of another conquered village, he talks with his new second in command. With the death of Gunnar and so many others, many within the Aries Group have found themselves promoted.

"What do we know about Gunnar's death?" Antoine says.

Members in America have placed bribes to find out exactly what happened in Samson. "Stabbed," Antoine's second says. He's American. "Looked like he was in a fight in the back of a van. Stabbed to death, but the weapon was never found. Florian was in the same van. Took a bullet shot to the back of the head."

"The killer?"

"They don't know."

"But we can guess," Antoine says. "Tom Rollins."

"He disappeared soon after the siege. No sign of where he's gone since."

Antoine leans back in his chair and strokes his chin. "You have his information?"

The man nods.

"His picture?"

He nods again.

"Good," Antoine says. He stares at the tent wall. He thinks of Gunnar, and the last time he saw him. He thinks of Tom Rollins – a stranger, a man he has never met, and yet someone for whom he holds almost unyielding hatred. He wonders where he could be. Where he's hiding. It doesn't matter. Wherever he is, wherever he might go, they will find him. It could take years. It doesn't matter. They *will* find him.

"Put out the word," Antoine says. "Put out his information. His picture. Every member of the Aries Group, notify them of Tom Rollins. Tell them what he has done. Tell them what he has taken from us."

The second nods. "I'll get right on it. When we find him, what do you want to happen? Kill on sight? Raise the alarm?"

Antoine looks at his second. "Tell them it's open season."

ABOUT THE AUTHOR

Did you enjoy *Ghost Team*? Please consider leaving a review on Amazon to help other readers discover the book.

Paul Heatley left school at sixteen, and since then has held a variety of jobs including mechanic, carpet fitter, and book-shop assistant, but his passion has always been for writing. He writes mostly in the genres of crime fiction and thriller, and links to his other titles can be found on his website. He lives in the north east of England.

Want to connect with Paul? Visit him at his website.

www.PaulHeatley.com

ALSO BY PAUL HEATLEY

The Tom Rollins Thriller Series

Blood Line (Book 1)

Wrong Turn (Book 2)

Hard to Kill (Book 3)

Snow Burn (Book 4)

Road Kill (Book 5)

No Quarter (Book 6)

Hard Target (Book 7)

Last Stand (Book 8)

Blood Feud (Book 9)

Search and Destroy (Book 10)

Ghost Team (Book 11)

The Tom Rollins Box Set (Books 1 - 4)